# THE STAR AND THE SHAMROCK

## JEAN GRAINGER

*This book is dedicated to all the brave parents who entrusted their precious children to the Kindertransport.*
*And to my own darling girls Éadaoin and Siobhán who I held a little higher as I researched this book.*

# PROLOGUE

*Belfast, 1938*

The gloomy interior of the bar, with its dark wood booths and frosted glass, suited the meeting perfectly. Though there were a handful of other customers, it was impossible to see them clearly. Outside on Donegal Square, people went about their business, oblivious to the tall man who entered the pub just after lunchtime. Luckily, the barman was distracted with a drunk female customer and served him absentmindedly. He got a drink, sat at the back in a booth as arranged and waited. His contact was late. He checked his watch once more, deciding to give the person ten more minutes. After that, he'd have to assume something had gone wrong.

He had no idea who he was meeting; it was safer that way, everything on a need-to-know basis. He felt a frisson of excitement – it felt good to actually be doing something, and he was ideally placed to make this work. The idea was his and he was proud of it. That should make those in control sit up and take notice.

War was surely now inevitable, no matter what bit of paper old Chamberlain brought back from Munich. If the Brits believed the peace in our time that he promised was on the cards, they'd believe anything. He smiled.

He tried to focus on the newspaper he'd carried in with him, but his mind wandered into the realm of conjecture once more, as it had ever since he'd had the call. If Germany could be given whatever assistance they needed to subjugate Great Britain – and his position meant they could offer that and more – then the Germans would have to make good on their promise. A United Ireland at last. It was all he wanted.

He checked his watch again. Five minutes more, that was all he would stay. It was too dangerous otherwise.

His eyes scanned the racing pages, unseeing. Then a ping as the pub door opened. Someone entered, got a drink and approached his seat. He didn't look up until he heard the agreed-upon code phrase. He raised his eyes, and their gazes met.

He did a double take. Whatever or whomever he was expecting, it wasn't this.

# CHAPTER 1

*Liverpool, England, 1939*

Elizabeth put the envelope down and took off her glasses. The thin paper and the Irish stamps irritated her. Probably that estate agent wanting to sell her mother's house again. She'd told him twice she wasn't selling, though she had no idea why. It wasn't as if she were ever going back to Ireland, her father long dead, her mother gone last year – she was probably up in heaven tormenting the poor saints with her extensive religious knowledge. The letter drew her back to the little Northern Irish village she'd called home... that big old lonely house...her mother.

Margaret Bannon was a pillar of the community back in Ballycreggan, County Down, a devout Catholic in a deeply divided place, but she had a heart of stone.

Elizabeth sighed. She tried not to think about her mother, as it only upset her. Not a word had passed between them in twenty-one years, and then Margaret died alone. She popped the letter behind the clock; she needed to get to school. She'd open it later, or next week... or never.

Rudi's face, in its brown leather frame smiled down at her from the dresser. 'Don't get bitter, don't be like her.' She imagined she heard her late husband admonish her, his boyish face frozen in an old sepia photograph, in his King's Regiment uniform, so proud, so full of excitement, so bloody young. What did he know of the horrors that awaited him out there in Flanders? What did any of them know?

She mentally shook herself. This line of thought wasn't helping. Rudi was dead, and she wasn't her mother. She was her own person. Hadn't she proved that by defying her mother and marrying Rudi? It all seemed so long ago now, but the intensity of the emotions lingered. She'd met, loved and married young Rudi Klein as a girl of eighteen. Margaret Bannon was horrified at the thought of her Catholic daughter marrying a Jew, but Elizabeth could still remember that heady feeling of being young and in love. Rudi could have been a Martian for all she cared. He was young and handsome and funny, and he made her feel loved.

She wondered, if he were to somehow come back from the dead and just walk up the street and into the kitchen of their little terraced house, would he recognise the woman who stood there? Her chestnut hair that used to fall over her shoulders was always now pulled back in a bun, and the girl who loved dresses was now a woman whose clothes were functional and modest. She was thirty-nine, but she knew she could pass for older. She had been pretty once, or at least not too horrifically ugly anyway. Rudi had said he loved her; he'd told her she was beautiful.

She snapped on the wireless, but the talk was of the goings-on in Europe again. She unplugged it; it was too hard to hear first thing in the morning. Surely they wouldn't let it all happen again, not after the last time?

All anyone talked about was the threat of war, what Hitler was going to do. Would there really be peace as Mr Chamberlain promised? It was going to get worse before it got better if the papers were to be believed.

Though she was almost late, she took the photo from the shelf. A smudge of soot obscured his smooth forehead, and she wiped it with the sleeve of her cardigan. She looked into his eyes.

4

'Goodbye, Rudi darling. See you later.' She kissed the glass, as she did every day.

How different her life could have been...a husband, a family. Instead, she had received a generic telegram just like so many others in that war that was supposed to end all wars. She carried in her heart for twenty years that feeling of despair. She'd taken the telegram from the boy who refused to meet her eyes. He was only a few years younger than she. She opened it there, on the doorstep of that very house, the words expressing regret swimming before her eyes. She remembered the lurch in her abdomen, the baby's reaction mirroring her own. 'My daddy is dead.'

She must have been led inside, comforted – the neighbours were good that way. They knew when the telegram lad turned his bike down their street that someone would need holding up. That day it was her...tomorrow, someone else. She remembered the blood, the sense of dragging downwards, that ended up in a miscarriage at five months. All these years later, the pain had dulled to an ever-present ache.

She placed the photo lovingly on the shelf once more. It was the only one she had. In lots of ways, it wasn't really representative of Rudi; he was not that sleek and well presented. 'The British Army smartened me up,' he used to say. But out of uniform is how she remembered him. Her most powerful memory was of them sitting in that very kitchen the day they got the key. His Uncle Saul had lent them the money to buy the house, and they were going to pay him back.

They'd been married in the registry office in the summer of 1918, when he was home on brief leave because of a broken arm. She could almost hear her mother's wails all the way across the Irish Sea, but she didn't care. It didn't matter that her mother was horrified at her marrying a *Jewman*, as she insisted on calling him, or that she was cut off from all she ever knew – none of it mattered. She loved Rudi and he loved her. That was all there was to it.

She'd worn her only good dress and cardigan – the miniscule pay of a teaching assistant didn't allow for new clothes, but she didn't care. Rudi had picked a bunch of flowers on the way to the registry office, and his cousin Benjamin and Benjamin's wife, Nina, were the witnesses. Ben was killed at the Somme, and Nina went to London, back to her family. They'd lost touch.

Elizabeth swallowed. The lump of grief never left her throat. It was a part of her now. A lump of loss and pain and anger. The grief had given way to fury, if she were honest. Rudi was killed early on the morning of the 11th of November, 1918, in Belgium. The armistice had been signed at five forty five a.m. but the order to end hostilities would not come into effect until eleven a.m. The eleventh hour of the eleventh month. She imagined the generals saw some glorious symmetry in that. But there wasn't. Just more people left in mourning than there had to be. She lost him, her Rudi, because someone wanted the culmination of four long years of slaughter to look nice on a piece of paper.

She shivered. It was cold these mornings, though spring was supposed to be in the air. The children in her class were constantly sniffling and coughing. She remembered the big old fireplace in the national school in Ballycreggan, where each child was expected to bring a sod of turf or a block of timber as fuel for the fire. Master O'Reilly's wife would put the big jug of milk beside the hearth in the mornings so the children could have a warm drink by lunchtime. Elizabeth would have loved to have a fire in her classroom, but the British education system would never countenance such luxuries.

She glanced at the clock. Seven thirty. She should go. Fetching her coat and hat, and her heavy bag of exercise books that she'd marked last night, she let herself out.

The street was quiet. Apart from the postman, doing deliveries on the other side of the street, she was the only person out. She liked it, the sense of solitude, the calm before the storm.

The mile-long walk to Bridge End Primary was her exercise and thinking time. Usually, she mulled over what she would teach that day or how to deal with a problem child – or more frequently, a problem parent. She had been a primary schoolteacher for so long, there was little she had not seen. Coming over to England as a bright sixteen-year-old to a position as a teacher's assistant in a Catholic school was the beginning of a trajectory that had taken her far from Ballycreggan, from her mother, from everything she knew.

She had very little recollection of the studies that transformed her from a lowly teaching assistant to a fully qualified teacher. After Rudi was killed and she'd lost the baby, a kind nun at her school suggested she do the exams to become a teacher, not just an assistant, and because it gave her something to do with her troubled mind, she agreed. She got top marks, so she must have thrown herself into her studies, but she couldn't remember much about those years. They were shrouded in a fog of grief and pain.

# CHAPTER 2

*erlin, Germany, 1939*

Ariella Bannon waited behind the door, her heart thumping. She'd covered her hair with a headscarf and wore her only remaining coat, a grey one that had been smart once. Though she didn't look at all Jewish with her curly red hair – and being married to Peter Bannon, a Catholic, meant she was in a slightly more privileged position than other Jews – people knew what she was. She took her children to the synagogue, kept a kosher house. She never in her wildest nightmares imagined that the quiet following of her faith would have led to this.

One of the postmen, Herr Krupp, had joined the Brownshirts. She didn't trust him to deliver the post properly, so she had to hope it was Frau Braun that day. She wasn't friendly exactly, but at least she gave you your letters. She was surprised at Krupp; he'd been nice before, but since Kristallnacht, it seemed that everyone was different. She even remembered Peter talking to him a few times about the weather or fishing or something. It was hard to believe that underneath all that, there was such hatred. Neighbours, people on the street, children even, seemed to have turned against all Jews. Liesl and Erich were scared all the time. Liesl tried to put a brave face on it – she was such a wonderful child – but she was only ten. Erich looked up to her so much. At seven, he thought his big sister could fix everything.

It was her daughter's birthday next month but there was no way to celebrate. Ariella thought back to birthdays of the past, cakes and friends and presents, but that was all gone. Everything was gone.

She tried to swallow the by-now-familiar lump of panic. Peter had been picked up because he and his colleague, a Christian, tried to defend an old Jewish lady the Nazi thugs were abusing in the street. Ariella had been told that the uniformed guards beat up the two men and threw them in a truck. That was five months ago. She hoped every day her husband would turn up, but so far, nothing. She considered going to visit his colleague's wife to see if she had heard anything, but nowadays, it was not a good idea for a Jew to approach an Aryan for any reason.

At least she'd spoken to the children in English since they were born. At least that. She did it because she could; she'd had an English governess as a child, a terrifying woman called Mrs Beech who insisted Ariella speak not only German but English, French and Italian as well. Peter smiled to hear his children jabbering away in other languages, and he always said they got that flair for languages from her. He spoke German only, even though his father was Irish. She remembered fondly her father-in-law, Paddy. He'd died when Erich was a baby. Though he spoke fluent German, it was always with a lovely lilting accent. He would tell her tales of growing up in Ireland. He came to Germany to study when he was a young man, and saw and fell instantly in love with Christiana Berger, a beauty from Bavaria. And so in Germany he remained. Peter was their only child because Christiana was killed in a horse-riding accident when Peter was only five years old. How simple those days were, seven short years ago, when she had her daughter toddling about, her newborn son in her arms, a loving husband and a doting father-in-law. Now, she felt so alone.

Relief. It was Frau Braun. But she walked past the building.

Ariella fought the wave of despair. Elizabeth should have received the letter Ariella had posted by now, surely. It was sent three weeks ago. Ariella tried not to dwell on the many possibilities. What if she wasn't at the address? Maybe the family had moved on. Peter had no contact with his only first cousin as far as she knew.

Nathaniel, Peter's best friend, told her he might be able to get Liesl and Erich on the Kindertransport out of Berlin – he had some connections apparently – but she couldn't bear the idea of them going to strangers. If only Elizabeth would say yes. It was the only way she could put her babies on that train. And even then... She dismissed that thought and refused to let her mind go there. She had to get them away until all this madness died down.

She'd tried everything to get them all out. But there was no way. She'd contacted every single embassy – the United States, Venezuela, Paraguay, places she'd barely heard of – but there was no hope. The lines outside the embassies grew longer every day, and without someone to vouch for you, it was impossible. Ireland was her only chance. Peter's father, the children's grandfather, was an Irish citizen. If she could only get Elizabeth Bannon to agree to take the children, then at least they would be safe.

Sometimes she woke in the night, thinking this must all be a nightmare. Surely this wasn't happening in Germany, a country known for learning and literature, music and art? And yet it was.

Peter and Ariella would have said they were German, their children were German, just the same as everyone else, but not so. Her darling children were considered *Untermensch*, subhuman, because of her Jewish blood in their veins.

# CHAPTER 3

$\mathcal{E}$lizabeth let herself in the front door. It had been a long day. The children in her class were fascinated and terrified by the prospect of war and Hitler and all of it. So many of them had lost grandparents, uncles and cousins the last time out, but she could see the gleam of excitement in the little boys' eyes all the same. She'd tried to get off the subject, but they kept wanting to return to it.

Hitler and the Nazis were absurd. He really was a most odious little man, and if the news was to be believed, his treatment of his own people was truly terrible.

She'd heard it discussed at the school, in the teacher's lounge, on the bus, in the corner shop. It was all anyone could talk about: Hitler and the Nazis and how he would have to be stopped.

She dropped her hessian bag full of exercise books and filled the kettle. She'd have a cup of tea before starting her corrections.

As she stood waiting for the kettle to boil, she saw the letter once more. Absentmindedly, she opened it, preparing to throw the entire contents in the bin. Nothing from Ballycreggan was of even the vaguest interest to her.

To her surprise, however, the envelope did not contain a letter from an estate agent. Instead, there was another smaller envelope inside, addressed to her, but at her mother's home in Ballycreggan. The post office must have redirected it. She pulled out the flimsy envelope with its foreign stamps. Intrigued, she opened it and extracted a single sheet.

*Dear Elizabeth,*

*Please forgive my audacity at writing to you like this. We have never met, but I am Ariella Bannon. My husband, Peter, was, I believe, a cousin of yours. His father, Paddy, was your father's brother. I am a Jew.*

*Peter and I have two children. Liesl is ten and Erich is seven, and I am desperate to get them out of Germany. My husband is missing – I assume he is dead – and I fear for the safety of my children if I do not manage to get them away until all of this is over.*

*A family friend can arrange for them to leave on the Kindertransport, but I cannot bear to put them on not knowing where or to whom they would be going. I know it is a lot to ask, but I am begging you – please, please take my children. I will see that you are paid back every penny of the expense incurred by having them as soon as I can, but for now, there is nothing to do but throw myself on your mercy and pray.*

*I have tried to get a visa to leave with them, but I have been unsuccessful.*

*They are very good children, I promise you, and would do everything you say, and Liesl is very helpful around the house. They are fluent in English and can also speak French and Italian. If you can find it in your heart to help me, you will have my eternal gratitude.*

*Yours faithfully,*

*Ariella*

*PS. Please write back by return, and if you can agree, I will make the arrangements as soon as possible. Every day, things get worse here.*

The kettle whistled, but Elizabeth switched off the gas beneath it. She sat down, forgetting all about her tea. She reread the letter.

A million thoughts crashed over her, wave after wave. The primary feeling was sympathy – poor Ariella, what a choice to be faced with; the poor woman must be out of her mind. She never knew her cousin was called Peter; in fact, she had to rack her brain to even recall a mention of either her uncle or her cousin. Somewhere in the deep recesses of her memory, she thought that her mother may have said something, but it was a vague recollection at best.

This woman wanted Elizabeth to take over the care of her children. They would be her sole responsibility for a time as yet to be determined. Could she do it? She was a teacher, but she'd never been a mother, and she knew nothing of raising children. Who would take care of them when she was at work? Where would they sleep? Her house only had two bedrooms. What if they hated her, hated life in England? What if they cried to go back? Elizabeth liked her own company and her small silent home – it was an oasis of calm after a day in school – and the idea that she would soon have to share it with two little strangers filled her with trepidation. But Ariella would not have asked if she were not desperate. Elizabeth would have to do it.

She sat at her kitchen table, trying to visualise this German family, her cousins. She thought she may have remembered a few Christmas cards as a child – they were a different shape to Irish ones, square rather than rectangular, and they were more like postcards. Pictures of snowy mountains. When her father died, even the Christmas cards stopped. Her mother was certainly not going to have anything to do with foreigners.

She had enough money to pay whatever costs would be incurred in taking care of two children. Her mother's legacy remained untouched in the bank, and her teaching salary was building up year after year. She'd paid Saul for the house, though after Rudi's death, he tried to write it off, and apart from a few groceries, she had hardly any outlay.

The irony that she was going to get a chance to be a mother, after all these years, was not lost on her.

She had hoped that she would become pregnant right away after she and Rudi got married in June of 1918, and she did. The joy of that memory was chased immediately by the horror of that child's loss. She'd never had another relationship, though there had been a few overtures from men over the years. It was like she was frozen inside. She couldn't allow herself to feel that deeply again. They say that grief is the price of love, but it was a price she could never pay again.

It took years to come to terms with the fact that not only had she lost Rudi but that she was never going to be a mother. And now here she was offering to be just that to two total strangers.

Sighing, she pulled out a notepad and pen and took note of the address in Berlin.

'Dear Ariella...' she began.

# CHAPTER 4

'Why are you crying, Mama?' Erich's little face was pinched as he came into the bedroom. Hastily, she stuffed the photos under the pillow and turned to him. Ariella longed to see his open smile once more, but it had been a long time since anyone in their house had smiled.

'I'm not, my darling. I just had something in my eye.' She smoothed his dark hair, and his big brown eyes looked up at her with absolute trust. He'd stopped asking where his papa was, but at night, he insisted on sleeping in her bed and would whisper, 'You won't leave, *Mutti*, will you?'

She hated lying, and technically, she didn't lie. She would not be the one doing the leaving, but she would put her darling children on that train if it were the last thing she ever did. She and the rest of the Jewish community watched with horror as each day it seemed the Nazis got stronger. The thugs in the brown uniforms operated entirely without check, and non-Jews just stood by and did nothing. Well, most did. People who tried to stop it ended up missing, like Peter.

She'd sold everything she could sell, and now there was no money left. There was hardly anything to eat, and she gave Liesl and Erich what little she could scavenge. She knew she was weakening due to the lack of food, but she had no choice.

Elizabeth's letter had come just in time. Frau Braun had handed the post over wordlessly but with a hardness in her eyes. Ariella was used to that look now.

Elizabeth would take them. She sounded nice and kind and explained that she no longer lived in Ireland but in the English city of Liverpool. If Ariella were happy with the children going there, she would be glad to offer them a home for as long as was necessary. They would leave Thursday night from the *Lehrter Bahnhof*. It was Tuesday, and she would have to tell the children that night. Try as she might, she could not find the words. Every explanation she came up with died on her lips as she rehearsed over and over in her head.

She had their suitcases packed. The organisers were very specific – one small sealed suitcase each and no more than ten *Reichsmarks*. That particular rule didn't apply to her, as she had no money to give them. She embroidered their names into each garment at night as they slept, laundering and preparing quietly. She put in photographs of herself and Peter, and of the four of them at her cousin's child's bar mitzvah. She added one of Peter and his father, and on the back she wrote, 'Paddy and Peter Bannon from Ballycreggan, Ireland'. It might help them, who knew? They would be given tags with their names and a number to place around their necks, and a corresponding number would be placed on the suitcase. The children would be accompanied all the way to England, and she was assured they would be placed into the care of her husband's cousin once on British soil. The woman who organised the Kindertransport was kind, if harassed looking. Ariella knew what a wrench it was, but she also knew that Liesl and Erich were the lucky ones. They only got on because their father was gone, and because Nathaniel had pulled some strings.

Liesl appeared at the door. She was so like Peter it took her breath away sometimes. Dark hair, dark eyes and a slight build. She was so clever, and so creative. She had been top of her class before all of this horror. Neither child had been to school for a long time. Their school was closed to Jews. Some feeble attempts were made at providing a

Jewish school, but it was far away and it wasn't safe for them to be out on the street, so Ariella kept them at home. She spent her days improving their English, and when they asked why they didn't do their French or Italian exercises as they always did, she said English was the best of all the languages. They read books, wrote stories and played make-believe to build their already extensive vocabulary.

Ariella had tried at the beginning to maintain their schoolwork, but in the face of everything that was happening, it all seemed so pointless. So instead, she read them stories, and they drew pictures and played imaginary games. She tried to keep things somewhat normal, though in reality, it was nothing of the sort.

'*Mutti?*' Liesl asked. She was a perceptive child; she knew something was wrong.

Ariella took a breath. She would have to do it. She led them to the bed and sat them down. How often had they crept in to that very bed on weekend mornings for a cuddle with her and Peter? He would tickle and play with them, telling them funny stories about talking dogs and tap-dancing parrots. She would get up and run down to the bakery for bread, and they would breakfast together on their little terrace in the spring and summer, and in the sunny kitchen on winter mornings. Peter's job with the bank was a good one, and they had a very nice apartment. She'd heard of lots of Jews being evicted from their homes and the Nazis moving their people in, but that hadn't happened to her yet. It was only a matter of time, though.

'My darlings, I have something to tell you, and you are going to have to be very brave, as brave as the knights we were reading about in the story last night.' She forced some brightness into her voice. Her children eyed her warily; there were no nice surprises these days.

'You two are going on a very exciting adventure to England, and you'll be going first by train and then by boat. And when you get there, Papa's cousin, a lovely lady called Elizabeth, is going to take you to her house. There are other children to play with and lots of food, and it is going to be wonderful.' She refused to allow the tears that stung the back of her eyes to fall.

'But you're coming too, *Mutti?*' Liesl asked uncertainly.

'No, my love, not at the moment – this is a train just for children. I will follow later, once I get the papers I need together.' She tried to make it sound like a minor bureaucratic hiccup, not the almost complete impossibility it really was.

'No, *Mutti*, we'll wait and go when you are going.' Liesl was adamant.

'I'd love that, Liesl, I really would, but you and Erich have to go ahead and I'll follow you. It will be easier for me to get a permit and all of that if I am alone. And Cousin Elizabeth is going to take very good care of you...' She knew she needed to convince Liesl. Erich would go where she told him, and if Liesl was with him, he would be all right. But her daughter had her father's stubborn streak. Peter was a wonderful man but obstinate sometimes, and Liesl was just like him.

'No!' Liesl shouted. 'I won't go without you! I can't!'

Erich was starting to get upset now as well.

Ariella caught her daughter's eye, willing her to understand, silently pleading with her to go along with it for Erich's sake. 'You can, darling, I promise you. You can do it. You'll be taken care of all the way, and all you and Erich need to do is stay together, look after each other, until I can join you.'

'We can't stay here.' The words dropped like heavy rocks.

There was something about her daughter's voice... She often wondered about it afterwards. Something changed in Liesl.

Ariella gazed deeply into her daughter's eyes. All her life, she had made things better for her – bandaged her knee when she fell, cut the crusts off her toast, stitched the eye back on her teddy bear – but there was no fixing this, and her look communicated that in a way no words ever could. 'No darling, we can't. This is not a country for us any longer. We must go.'

A long pause until eventually Liesl spoke. 'And you promise you will follow us? You swear you will?' The girl's eyes burned into her mother's.

'I will. While I have breath in my body, my beautiful children, I will do everything I can to get to you. But now you will have to be brave and strong, everything Papa and I know you are, and take that train. Will you do that for me? For Papa?'

Erich looked up at Liesl and put his hand in hers. Solemnly, she answered for both of them. 'We'll go, *Mutti*. We'll stay together, and we'll wait for you in England.'

Ariella opened her arms, and they moved into her embrace. The three of them stood there for a long time.

# CHAPTER 5

*E*lizabeth stood at the barrier along with all the other Londoners awaiting people getting off trains at Liverpool Street station. At the appointed time, a group of children led by several adults issuing instructions in a foreign language that she assumed was German appeared at the platform and walked into the main concourse.

Elizabeth went up to a woman she judged to be in her sixties, who was carrying a clipboard and had a whistle around her neck.

'Hello. My name is Elizabeth Klein, and I am here to collect two children, Liesl and Erich Bannon?' It felt odd to be saying her maiden name to identify two little strangers. She had not been Elizabeth Bannon for so many years.

The woman looked at her as though she was slightly confused.

'You are involved with the transfer of German refugee children, are you not?' Elizabeth asked. Perhaps she'd asked the wrong person.

'Yes, yes...of course, yes. Let me get the list. I'm sorry, it's been a long journey and I...I'm sorry. Now what did you say your name was?' The woman was European, her English heavily accented.

Around them, other people were approaching other adults in the group, all with the same purpose. The children stood together, huddled and terrified. Elizabeth was shocked to see so many really young children, even a few toddlers in the arms of older ones. They made a pathetic sight.

'Klein, Elizabeth Klein, and I am to collect Liesl and Erich Bannon.' Elizabeth spoke clearly and slowly.

The other woman ran her finger down a list until she came to an entry for Bannon. 'Yes, we have them here. You're their father's cousin it says here?' The woman checked her list again, removing and replacing her half-moon spectacles several times.

'Yes, that's right,' Elizabeth confirmed.

'And your address?' the woman asked, eyeing Elizabeth for the first time.

'Fourteen Barrington Close, Liverpool.' Elizabeth waited until the woman confirmed it, then glanced once more at the huddled group of children. Which two were they, she wondered.

'Right. Well, if you just wait, I'll get them for you.'

The woman walked towards the group and called, 'Erich und Liesl Bannon, *deine Cousine ist hier.*'

Two children stepped forward from the centre of the group and followed the woman back to where Elizabeth stood.

'Have you met before?' she asked.

'No, no, we haven't.' Elizabeth smiled at the children and put out her hand. '*Willkommen, freut mich dich kennenzulernen.*' She used the only German phrase she knew.

Liesl accepted her hand. 'Nice to meet you,' she replied shyly in English.

'Hello, Liesl,' Elizabeth said, relieved. Ariella said they spoke English fluently, but she did wonder if their mother had just said that to convince her to take them.

'And this must be Erich?' She turned to the little boy, hiding behind his sister.

'Yes. This is my brother.' Liesl gently nudged him out, and he moved a few inches so she could at least see his face.

Elizabeth got down on her hunkers to be eye level with him and spoke very slowly. 'I am Elizabeth, and I am going to take care of you.'

She didn't know if he understood or not, but his sad little eyes locked with hers, and she hoped he felt reassured.

She filled out the necessary forms, took their suitcases from the pile on a large trolley, and together they walked out into the July sunshine.

Over tea and a sticky bun, she discovered they could both speak English as fluently as their mother had promised.

'*Mutti* can too,' Erich said proudly. 'My papa works for a bank, so he doesn't need it, but my *mutti* learned it when she was young, and then she taught us.'

'Well, that's wonderful. I'm so relieved because I can't speak German at all. I was worried how I would communicate with you.' She smiled and was happy to note some of the tension leaving them.

'Do you have a dog?' Erich asked.

'No. I don't have a dog, but there is a little cat that comes for a saucer of milk every day – I leave it in the backyard for her. Perhaps you would like to take over feeding her, Erich?'

The little boy seemed enthusiastic about the prospect, and Elizabeth turned her attention to Liesl. 'So, Liesl, how are you feeling? You must be tired, I imagine?'

Elizabeth talked to children all day long, and she knew – behind her back at least – that many of the parents and staff thought she did better talking to the children than the adults. But there was something different about this. She was nervous.

'Yes,' Liesl confirmed, but contributed nothing more. She never let go of Erich's hand, even as she sipped her tea.

'Well, we have to stay in a hotel tonight because it would take too long to get back to where I live this evening. So I thought we could stay here in London and take the train to Liverpool tomorrow.'

She felt foolish. When she'd booked the Devonshire Arms Hotel off Finsbury Park, she thought it might be a treat for them. But now that she'd met them, she realised they were lost and sad and so far from their home – where they slept was the least of their problems.

'It's going to be all right,' she said, though she had no idea whether or not that was true.

'Our *mutti* is coming really soon,' Erich said with such conviction that Elizabeth wondered if he was trying to convince her or himself.

'When she can get a visa.' Liesl was gentle, but the remark showed a maturity that should not have been there in a child so young.

Elizabeth put her teacup down and took a chance – she put both hands on the table, palms upward, inviting the children to take them.

Liesl looked at the hand and then at Elizabeth's face. Erich never took his eyes off his sister. Slowly, the girl slid her hand into Elizabeth's. Erich followed her lead, doing the same. She closed her fingers over theirs and gave their hands a squeeze.

Years of teaching had given her a respect for children that other adults often lacked. They were just small people. They were not stupid or oblivious; in fact, the opposite was often true. Children often knew more about what was going on than adults did.

She found that truth, or as close to it as possible, was always the best approach.

'Liesl, Erich, I know this must seem so strange and difficult. I can't imagine how sad you must be, and how hard it was to leave your *mutti*. We will hope and pray for her and for your papa every night. She asked me to care for you, and I will do my best. I don't have any children of my own because my husband, Rudi, died in the last war, so I might not be very good at it.' She gave a small smile, but both children remained impassive.

'But I promise you, I will try my best. I know you wish you were with your parents, of course you do, but for now, it isn't safe for you to be in Germany...' She didn't know how far Ariella had gone in explaining the rising anti-Semitism.

'Because we are Jews, and Hitler hates us,' Liesl said darkly.

'Yes, he does. But he is a terrible man, and all the other countries of the world, the good countries, will not stand for him much longer. He is a bully, and you know what happens to bullies, don't you?' She smiled again, and this time, she got a ghost of a smile back.

'They get their comeuppance in the end?' Erich asked, and Elizabeth chuckled at his uniquely British turn of phrase.

'Exactly, Erich. And nasty little Hitler will get what's coming to him, don't you worry about that.'

He smiled, a proper smile this time. She was winning.

'So how about once we've finished our tea and buns, we'll walk to the hotel and check in. We can buy a postcard to send to your *mutti* on the way, just to let her know you got here safely. Then you can write properly once we are back home – I'll give you paper and stamps. There's a playground in the park opposite, so once we've posted the card, perhaps we could go for a walk? Then we'll have dinner and a good night's sleep, and we'll take the train home tomorrow. How does that sound?' She also knew that making children feel like they were part of the decision-making process was liberating and reassuring.

'We'd like that,' Liesl answered.

They walked out of the café and straight into the hustle and bustle of the city. The children followed Elizabeth, who was carrying both of their suitcases. A policeman was directing traffic, and he gestured that they should cross the road. She felt Erich move closer to her. When she looked down at him to see what the problem was, she saw the terror in his eyes.

Before she had time to say anything, Liesl spoke. 'It's all right, Erich. He's a nice British policeman. He won't hurt us.'

The little boy looked to Elizabeth for confirmation. She made a split-second decision. She took Erich's hand and led him to the uniformed bobby.

'Excuse me, Officer. I just wanted to introduce you to Erich and Liesl Bannon from Berlin, and I was just about to explain that you can always trust a British policeman.'

He met her eye and understood, and immediately, he bent down to be eye level with them. 'Well, young man and young lady, you are both very welcome in England. And so long as you don't try to rob any banks or blow up Buckingham Palace, you won't get any trouble from us. You don't have any plans like that, do you?' he asked with pretended sternness, and Liesl giggled.

'No, sir,' Erich replied, awestruck.

'Well, in that case, you will get on very well. Now, one thing I must tell you is the cars go the other way here, so be very careful crossing the road, do you hear me? You must remember to look both ways.' His tone was gruff but his eyes were kind.

'Our mother told us that,' Liesl confirmed. 'Thank you, Officer.'

The policeman stood up and walked out into the traffic once more, halting it specially for the little trio as they crossed the road.

# CHAPTER 6

*A*riella waited inside the apartment block door. Uniformed men passed by outside. It was becoming too frightening to go out on the street these days, but she needed to eat something. The apartment was totally bare. She'd been instructed to register her home as Jewish property, and it was only a matter of time before it was taken from her. Most Jews had been evicted from their homes last year. Theirs was in Peter's name, so she had been safe for a while, but someone had reported that Peter was gone. A local Party member – she remembered he owned a cobbler shop two streets away; he'd repaired their winter boots a few years ago – called and instructed her to report and register the property. She did as he told her. Last year, she'd complied with the decree that she add 'Sara' to her given name. Her identity card now read 'Ariella Sara Bannon' and displayed a large 'J'. If one was found to be without the card in public, it resulted in immediate arrest, but carrying it made her feel marked. She preferred to stay indoors, but she was so hungry. She had neither a ration card nor any money, so she had no idea how she was going to eat.

Frau Braun passed by on her bicycle as Ariella stepped out onto the pavement. She would forever remember the day the postwoman handed her a postcard eight days after she put Liesl and Erich on the train. It had a picture of the Tower of London on it, and on the back, it said in German, 'We arrived safely, *Mutti*. England is nice, and Elizabeth is very kind. Come soon. We love you. Liesl and Erich xxx.'

Each night she slept fitfully, that card under her pillow. Her children were safe.

Ariella walked down the street, keeping by the wall, when Frau Braun stopped her bicycle and walked it back to her.

Ariella looked at her warily. Hubert Braun was in the Party, and his wife wore a triangular National Socialist Women's League pin on her lapel. Her only child, Willi, was in the Wehrmacht, and she was every inch the perfect German hausfrau. Hitler would love her. She had a girlish figure, despite being at least in her late forties and had hard features. Her steely gaze landed on Ariella accusingly.

'What are you doing?' the other woman demanded.

Ariella felt her mouth go dry. She couldn't speak. On the road beside them, several military vehicles passed, followed by a large black car with swastika flags on the bonnet.

Frau Braun went on. 'Your children are safe. Your husband is dead. You will soon no longer enjoy your nice apartment.'

Ariella was frozen. Fear, hunger and grief were knotted together in the pit of her stomach, preventing her from responding. Peter probably was dead, but did Frau Braun know for sure?

The other woman moved close, almost hissing. 'Don't you understand? You are a Jewess, and alone, you should not be on the street like this.'

A single tear slid down Ariella's cheek.

'Get off the street,' Frau Braun said as she got back on her bicycle.

# CHAPTER 7

*iverpool, August, 1940*

Elizabeth tried to make the spam sandwiches look more appetising by adding some parsley she had growing on the windowsill. They were going on a picnic before school began again after the holidays to see the barrage balloons down by the docks.

Liverpool was the largest port on the west coast of Britain and the main link to America. Naval ships and merchant vessels filled the Mersey between Liverpool and Birkenhead, and the river was a hive of maritime activity.

She had worried that all the talk of the war and seeing the military vessels would upset the youngsters further, but if anything, seeing the might of the British fleet was reassuring.

The children were generally cheerful during the day, but as night fell, their anxiety rose. The worry about their parents was always there.

Over and over, Erich asked what had happened to his mother and Liesl tried to reassure him, though Elizabeth could tell she was just as anxious as he was. The previous night after dinner, he'd started again. 'What if they've hurt her?' he asked repeatedly, his brown eyes filling.

'Erich, I've told you, they won't hurt women and children. They just want us to leave, and we have. They might have taken *Mutti* to work in one of their factories – remember we heard that on the news? They have factories in Germany just like here, making things for soldiers, so she's probably there. And they won't let them write letters because they might be giving away secrets about German guns or whatever.'

Erich's complete trust in his older sister broke Elizabeth's heart, but she backed Liesl. 'I think Liesl is right. Remember all the slogans we see, "loose lips sink ships" and "keep mum, she's not so dumb"? Well, the Germans want to keep their secrets too, so they wouldn't allow anyone to write letters.'

He seemed convinced...until the next time. Elizabeth and Liesl shared a glance.

Liesl was a tall eleven year old now, and Erich was eight, and in so many ways, it felt like they were her children. She loved them dearly, and any doubts she might have had about her ability to care for them were gone.

Elizabeth gathered the gas masks and the picnic from the kitchen table, knowing Liesl and Erich would be in the hallway, inside the front door, waiting for the post as they had every single day since they arrived.

There had been one letter from Ariella two weeks after they arrived, but nothing since.

Elizabeth tried to shield them from the worst of the news coming out of Europe, but the war was all pervasive. Hitler had defied everyone and marched into Poland last September – a year ago now – and the countries of Europe seemed to be falling like dominos – Denmark, Norway, Holland, Belgium. She'd cried when she saw the heroism at Dunkirk, the flotillas of fishing boats that rescued the men. The promise she made to Erich on the first day – that Hitler would get what was coming to him very soon – rang hollow now. It looked like he was unstoppable. That puffed-up buffoon Mussolini joining him was a blow, but the fall of France felt sickening. Nothing now stood between Hitler and Britain but a narrow stretch of channel.

Two nights ago, Erich had come into her bed, crying because he was convinced Hitler was coming and there was nowhere left to run. She tried to soothe him, but what the child said was right.

Children from the Liverpool area had been evacuated to Wales when war broke out, but since no German bombs had fallen on the city despite the Battle of Britain raging since mid-July, many of the little ones had returned. Elizabeth had seen her class of inner-city pupils almost disappear, but slowly but surely, they were coming back with tales of milking cows and hunting for eggs and all manner of country pursuits.

Liesl and Erich were just like Liverpudlians now and had even begun to speak in a Liverpool accent, which she found endearing. They'd made friends, and apart from the obvious heartache of being separated from their parents, they were happy.

'Righto!' She tried to sound bright. These were the last few days of the summer holiday and school would be back in session next week, so she wanted to make the most of their freedom. 'Shall we go?'

She didn't need to ask if there was anything in the post from Ariella.

'Elizabeth,' said Liesl as they strolled down the street in the bright August sunshine, Erich running ahead, playing with the yo-yo Elizabeth had bought him. 'Do you think the British should move all the ships they have here to the other coast to stop Hitler?'

She sighed inwardly. Liesl's thoughts should be on dolls or dresses, not troop movements and megalomaniac Germans. 'Well, I suppose that's a point, but do you know what I think?'

Liesl looked at her; they were almost the same height.

'I think that Mr Chamberlain did his best to try to avoid this war, but that didn't work, so now we are being led by Churchill, and he is ready for the fight. And I trust him. Remember what he said, victory at all costs? And it was going to be blood, sweat, toil and tears, but we would prevail? I believe him, so all we have to do is support our government and do our bit, and we will win – we have to.'

Liesl nodded slowly. 'I hope so,' she said quietly.

She was a thoughtful child and very sensitive. She took her vow to care for her little brother very seriously and was initially a little reluctant to relinquish that to Elizabeth, but now she trusted her. She was well able for school, and her English was impeccable. But she was a bit of an oddity in her classroom, and because she was German, she had received a few nasty remarks. Erich too had been bullied, and in lots of ways, Elizabeth couldn't blame the local children. Germany was the enemy, and the refugees were German; therefore, they must be the enemy.

She asked the principal's permission to address both Liesl's and Erich's classes, and she went in and explained why the children were there and how they were not the enemy, how they had much bigger reasons to hate Hitler than those British children did. And the nastiness did seem to stop after that. They'd both been invited to birthday parties and to their friends' houses for tea, so at least there was that. Thank God Ariella had the sense to teach them English; Elizabeth could not imagine how much more difficult the transition would have been if she hadn't.

'How do you feel about starting in Mr Crouch's class on Monday?' Elizabeth knew her somewhat odd colleague was feared by the younger children.

'Nervous. Everyone says he's very fierce,' Liesl admitted. 'But I'm hoping he will be all right. Melanie Colbert said he hated the Germans so much after the last war, he talked all the time about how bad Germany was, so I'm extra nervous.'

'He won't take that out on you, don't worry. It's true, he is deaf in one ear and blind in one eye because of a German bomb in the last war, but he's all right really.' Her colleague was a bit of a tartar, and she hoped he would be kind.

'I think you're right.' Liesl smiled. 'Remember at the start nobody liked us because they thought we were like Hitler? But you explained, and they are nice to us now since they know we are Jews and living with you, so hopefully Mr Crouch will be like that.'

'I'll let you in on a secret, but you mustn't tell anyone. Promise?'

The girl nodded.

'He has three cats called Twinkle, Fluffies and Snoodles. He has pink collars on Fluffies and Twinkle and a blue one on Snoodles, and he talks to them every evening like they are human.'

Liesl giggled. 'Is it true?'

'Would I lie to you?' Elizabeth winked.

It was good to hear the child laugh.

The day was a great success. The sun shone, and the barrage balloons drifted silently overhead, their long wires anchored to the ground.

'Dive-bombers would get stuck in those,' Erich said knowledgably. His friend Charlie's father was an ARP warden and a font of all wisdom according to Charlie and, vicariously, Erich.

'Really?' Elizabeth asked.

'Yes, and they force the enemy aircraft to go higher into the range of anti-aircraft guns, so we can get them that way,' Erich explained, delighted to inform.

Elizabeth smiled. The 'us' and 'them' were very evident in the conversation of this little German boy.

They were awed by the ships, and they even stopped on the way home for a small bag of barley sugars to crown off the day.

After tea and a bath in the regulation five inches of tepid water, the children sat on the couch and Elizabeth read to them. Though they were both more than capable of reading by themselves, they loved her to read a long story, a chapter a night. They were in the middle of *Gulliver's Travels*.

As soon as the children were in bed, Elizabeth sat down with a cup of tea and read the paper. She kept the newspapers out of sight during the day – the children didn't need to know the details of the latest atrocity – but now she read with growing despair of the progress of the war.

Rationing made food scarce and expensive, though of course there was always the black market. She had not had to resort to using it and hoped she wouldn't have to, but having Liesl and Erich to care for had changed everything. Rudi smiled down from his brown leather frame.

It struck her how little time she had for talking to him these days. Before the Bannons arrived, she used to talk to him every night as she made her dinner or darned her stockings, but since Liesl and Erich's arrival, she was so busy.

They asked about him, and she told them funny little stories, but she realised that she'd known Rudi for such a short time. She'd been sent to St Catherine's Primary School by the nuns in Ballycreggan. They knew going to university would not have been an option financially, and even if it was, her mother would never have paid for it. But she was bright, so they suggested she go to England to become a classroom assistant. It had all been going fine until she met Rudi. He worked in his uncle's fish-and-chip shop, and she and some other teaching assistants she was friendly with used to stop off there for chips after the odd trip to the cinema.

Rudi asked her out, and she remembered blushing to the roots of her chestnut hair. She was only sixteen, and if the nuns found out, there would be holy war, but something about him made her say yes. For a full year, they courted, and she realised that she'd not felt love since her daddy died. Rudi was fun and handsome and full of chat, and she loved him. He couldn't wait to join up, and on the day of his eighteenth birthday, in February of 1918, he did. The photo on her dresser was taken the day he got kitted out. He was so proud, and so was she. Her chap was going off to fight for king and country. The naivety of it stung her still.

She and Rudi had to keep their relationship under wraps. If the nuns thought she was seeing anyone, they would have had a fit. And a Jew? Impossible. So she and Rudi saw each other when they could. The night she was found out was printed indelibly on her brain.

She'd gone back to the residence after meeting Rudi for a walk and a cup of tea. She lived in an annex of the convent with teaching assistants and nurse's aides who worked at the adjacent St Catherine's Hospital. She was called to the Reverend Mother's office.

Mother Gertrude was terrifying in her white cornette headpiece and black tunic, scapular and cowl. Only her eyes, nose and mouth were uncovered. The Sisters of Charity ran a school, a hospital and an orphanage from the same campus, and they were feared and respected in equal measure. Elizabeth had never been in the office before.

The nun began without preamble. 'You have been keeping company with a young man, who I believe is of the Jewish faith.'

She might as well have said Elizabeth was cavorting with a mass murderer.

The nun went on in her monotonously ominous voice. Someone had told on her, reported that she was seeing Rudi and that he was a Jew. The nun had written to her mother, expressing her horror and disgust, and she had received word that Elizabeth was to pack her things and go home immediately. Her mother wanted to see her.

She was dismissed.

There was no opportunity to explain, and anyway, what the nun said was true. She was seeing Rudi, and he was a Jew.

Elizabeth dreaded going back to Ballycreggan, as she knew that her mother would be furious. But perhaps if she explained how nice and how respectful Rudi was? He didn't try to grope her in the back row of the pictures like other boys. They'd kissed a few times, and it was lovely, but he would never push her.

She ran to Rudi's house and told him everything. There and then, he got down on one knee and proposed. He even had a ring. He'd been planning it for weeks, but now that she was going back to Ireland, maybe if her mother knew he was serious about her, it would make her understand. He would have gone with her, but he had been called up to his regiment that weekend.

With a heavy heart, but with a tiny diamond on her left hand, she crossed the Irish Sea.

The last conversation she ever had with her mother still rang in her ears all these years later.

'If you go off with that Jewman, then let me tell you, my girl, you will be dead to me, do you hear me? Dead. I'd rather you were. So don't you come running back here to me when he gives you a couple of brats and turns out to be a conniving scoundrel. They all are, mark my words. They'd sell their own mother for a shilling, so don't say you weren't warned.'

Elizabeth had pressed hard on the small diamond ring Rudi had given her. How could her mother decide she hated him even though she'd never even clapped eyes on him? Elizabeth had come home to tell her she was engaged, and while she didn't expect the red carpet, the visceral hatred against Rudi because he was a Jew shocked her.

Her indignation and hurt on his behalf gave her the strength she needed. 'Well, Mother, I will marry Rudi, and if you don't want anything further to do with me, then that's fine. Goodbye, Mother.' She walked out the door.

She could still see the scene. She had been wearing a lilac coat and matching cloche she'd bought – she'd saved her salary for months to buy it – and carrying a small valise.

Margaret and Elizabeth never said another word to each other. She had thought her mother might soften. Elizabeth sent a Christmas card every year, signing it just 'Elizabeth', but she never got a response. She wrote to say Rudi had died, but again, nothing. Her mother was like granite, and now it would never be resolved.

It was funny – she had never really felt like she fit in anywhere. Back in Ireland, she was a Catholic in a largely Protestant community, so she was the outsider and not to be trusted. In Britain, she was seen as Irish, and if she were to go back to Ballycreggan now, they would surely see her as English. She was a widow of a Jew, but she wasn't a Jew herself, so she didn't fit there either.

She knew people found her a bit distant, and she supposed she was, but it was just easier than all the explanations. She found talking about Rudi and the child she lost hard even now. It was easier to keep a distance. A woman without a husband or a child was an oddity. Most of the war widows she knew had remarried, and many either had children before their husbands died or had them subsequently. She didn't fit in. She hadn't really at any time in her life. When she was small, maybe she had felt something like contentment. Her father was lovely, but he died, and that was the end of that.

She had never felt like that with Rudi. He was her home. And now with the children, she felt that familiar warmth of belonging as well. It frightened her to think how much she loved them. Any day, their mother could turn up and reclaim them, and of course, she hoped she did – it was what Liesl and Erich wanted so very much. But the

thought of letting them go now that she'd opened her heart to them...
Well, it was horrible. It struck her how, in such international chaos,
she had found something like peace for the first time since Rudi died.

She locked up and went to bed, nodding off into a peaceful sleep.

Either the siren or Liesl's scream woke her. She sat bolt upright in
bed and realised the bedroom was bright, though the bedside alarm
clock said three a.m. Before she had time to process this, the entire
street shook. She ran to the landing, colliding with her young charges.

'They're coming, Elizabeth, they're coming!' Liesl was terrified,
and Erich cried and clung to her.

'Don't worry, my darlings, don't worry. Get your dressing gowns
and slippers – we need to see what's happening.'

She tried to remain calm, but her hands were trembling as she tied
the knot on her own dressing gown and shoved her feet into her slippers under the bed.

She ran downstairs and opened the front door, the children
behind her. Her neighbours were out on the street, and the skies were
full of what seemed like hundreds of enemy planes. It was petrifying.
The air was filled with dust and acrid smoke that stung their eyes. She
didn't know whether she should go back inside or make a run for it to
the bomb shelter a street away.

Before she had time to make up her mind, she heard someone call
her name. It was Mrs Lewis from three doors down.

'Mrs Klein, bring those kiddies in here! My Stan built a shelter in
the garden, and it's the safest place. We've got plenty of room - come
on, come on!'

Elizabeth ushered the children through the Lewis house, shouting
over the noise to cover their mouths and noses with their hands. It
was hard to see where she was going, and she clung to Liesl and Erich
as she followed Mrs Lewis out the back door and into the shelter. The
structure was built of concrete blocks and corrugated iron and
covered in earth. Elizabeth and the children followed Mrs Lewis
inside.

It was large, as she had said, surprisingly so, with a bench running
around the inside walls. Elizabeth greeted the rest of the Lewis family,

three little girls between five and ten and a boy of around twelve. She'd taught the boy, James, last year.

'Stan's on air raid duty. I just pray he'll be all right. He made me promise we'd come down and bring whoever we could with us. I'm glad I saw you, Mrs Klein –' The rest of her sentence was drowned out by the horrific screech – like some horrible banshee – of a bomb falling, and as it hit, the entire shelter shook. Dust and splinters of wood fell on top of them, and Erich screamed.

'It's going to collapse on us, Elizabeth! We are going to be crushed!' He clung to her, terror in his eyes.

Elizabeth tried to hold him to her breast as tight as she could as bomb after bomb fell. Talking was impossible.

On the other side of the shelter, Mrs Lewis assumed the same position, clinging to her children as they alternately screamed or went rigid with fear.

Mrs Lewis was a chubby chain-smoker who wore a kerchief on her head and seemed to spend most of each day scrubbing her front step. Elizabeth, despite being neighbours with her since she moved into Barrington Street, had barely ever spoken to her.

'It will be over soon,' Elizabeth said, but her voice was drowned out by an ear-splitting boom that caused more shuddering and dislodged earth.

'What if this collapses on top of us?' Liesl shouted urgently.

'It won't, don't worry!' Elizabeth yelled back, trying to make herself heard over the cacophony. 'Mr Lewis is a builder. He knew what he was doing when he built this.' She snuggled closer to the girl, gripping her arm on one side, Erich on the other.

On and on the pounding went. Sirens screeched and shouts and whistles filled the air. It was the loudest night of Elizabeth's life. There was nothing to do but sit and huddle and hope for the best. It was too loud for conversation, so the two women sat with their arms around their children, trying to look confident.

After several hours, the pounding stopped, and a few moments later, the all clear was sounded. Elizabeth released the children, stiff and sore from holding them so tight, and she caught Mrs Lewis's eye.

What were they going out to? Could anything have survived that unmerciful pounding? All of the children looked to the two women, desperate for reassurance.

'Righto. Best get out there and see what's what.' Mrs Lewis tried to inject some authority into her voice, and Elizabeth took her lead.

'Thank you so much for sharing your shelter. Mr Lewis is certainly a fine builder, isn't he, children?' Elizabeth forced a smile, and Liesl and Erich nodded uncertainly.

Elizabeth removed her shawl from her shoulders and placed it in her lap. 'Now, there's going to be a lot of dust and smoke, so if we tear this up, we can each place it over our nose and mouth when we go out.'

She tore the garment into strips, handing a piece to each of the children, saving the last pieces for herself and Mrs Lewis. The women helped the children tie the fabric around their faces, and then James pushed at the shelter door. It wouldn't budge.

'Somethin's blockin' it outside,' he said, trying to keep the panic out of his voice.

Before either Elizabeth or Mrs Lewis could reassure him, they heard muffled voices and scraping and sounds of shovels. Someone was moving rubble and stones from the bomb shelter entrance. The door was pulled open from the outside within minutes, and Mrs Lewis expressed her relief. 'Stan, oh Stan, thank God you're all right!'

'I'm fine, Kit. How about the little ones? Everyone all right?'

Stan Lewis's face was black with dirt, and his ARP uniform was very much the worse for wear, but he looked relieved his family were safe. His daughters ran to him and he held them tight.

Elizabeth allowed the family their reunion and went past them, clinging tightly to Liesl and Erich. Stiff, sore and chilly from the damp air in the bunker, they emerged, blinking in the morning light. The air was hazy with dust, and the pungent smell of smouldering material assailed their nostrils.

They gazed around in horror. The whole street was flattened. Immediately, Elizabeth looked to where her house had once stood. The entire terrace was gone. Furniture, clothing, curtains...all smouldering amid bricks, glass and flames. It was a horrific sight. They could see all the way to the docks, as the buildings that had until the previous day obscured their view had been demolished.

'They broke our house, Elizabeth,' Erich said, tears pouring down his little face.

'They did, darling, they did. But we're still here.' She hugged them close and surveyed the scene. Everything was gone. Her home, all her memories, her only photograph of Rudi, the children's pictures of Ariella and Peter...everything they owned, gone.

# CHAPTER 8

*Ballycreggan, County Down, Ireland, September, 1940*

Talia cycled up the hill in the predawn light, the sweat causing her thin dress to stick to her back. She'd kept the bag of painting stuff as light as she could, just a few watercolours – she preferred oils, but they took too long to dry and smudged more easily – a little easel, a pencil and some brushes. There was no canvas anyway, but she'd managed to find some paper in the draper's shop in Ballycreggan, so that would have to do.

Finally, she rested, laying her bike on the grass and sitting down. She perched on a clifftop overlooking the Irish Sea, and it was almost possible to see the Scottish coast. It was breathtakingly lovely.

Vienna was beautiful, and the architecture never ceased to impress her, but this wild, rugged beauty was not like anything she'd ever seen before. Ballyhalbert Bay with its sandy beach stretched out before her, and she took out her pencil and began to sketch. The area was unusually busy, with lots of army vehicles and cars, but that didn't distract her. Using her pencil to determine scale and perspective, she quickly had the entire scene drawn.

There seemed to be some sort of construction going on just behind the beach – that would explain all the traffic. Land was being cleared and earth-moving equipment was in situ, ready for whatever it was they were doing.

Once she was happy with the scene, she placed the paper on her small easel that Daniel had made for her. He'd seen her trying to balance her paintings on stones and offered to build one, and it certainly made life easier. It was easily folded, and she could pop it in her bag with her paint and brushes.

He'd seen some of her work, all landscapes, and had been impressed. Her two years at the Vienna Academy of Fine Arts, interrupted by the war, had served her well. She had a lot more to learn, of course, but she had a natural flair. Daniel had been so complimentary, she'd blushed.

She really wanted him to like her, and he seemed to…but not like that. It was early days.

She mixed her paint on the little palette and got to work.

Cycling back, she realised it was coming close to nine a.m. and she needed to get back to the farm. She was in charge of the chickens, a job she detested because of the nauseating smell, but everyone had to take a turn because nobody liked it. She would have loved to have stayed up on the cliff painting all day, but that wasn't how things worked.

As she passed through the village of Ballycreggan, she saw Daniel coming towards her, a group of children beside him. They turned to go into Bridie's sweetshop. He gave her a wave, and she waved back enthusiastically and instantly decided to go in and join them.

ELIZABETH TRIED to hide her nervousness from the children as, for the first time since 1918, she put her key in the lock of the house she grew up in. They'd lost every single thing they owned; they had no clothes, no personal possessions. They had what they stood in. She was trying to make the move sound like an adventure, a new start. The children were worried. What if their mother came and couldn't find them? But she assured them that Ariella had written to her originally at this very address, so she would look here once she realised they were not in Liverpool.

The Bannon home was a handsome double-fronted house on the main street, with a large garden behind. It seemed smaller than she remembered – in her mind, it was enormous – but it was a substantial house nonetheless, and certainly far bigger than the little terraced house in Liverpool she had called home for so long. The grey cut-limestone façade hadn't changed at all, though the dark-brown front door needed a lick of paint. Perhaps she'd paint it red or blue or something more cheerful. Dark brown would be just the colour her mother would love.

The generously proportioned sitting room to the right of the large square entranceway smelled instantly familiar. What was it they said about smells? So much more evocative than the other senses? Nobody had been inside since her mother died, but there was that unmistakable aroma, and instantly, she was transported back decades. Baked soda bread, sunlight soap, lavender-water perfume. She closed her eyes; it was 1917 again, and she was standing in the doorway, leaving for England to work at St Catherine's. It was a lifetime ago.

As if in a trance, she walked into the sitting room. Liesl and Erich ran off to explore the house, but she just stood there, allowing the feelings to wash over her.

The ornate mahogany mantlepiece had the same photographs she remembered, now covered in a thin layer of dust. The faces of her parents on their wedding day – him smiling, her stern. Another of her father with a cup of some kind – she didn't know what it was for and her mother couldn't remember. Elizabeth's memories of her father were warm, and seeing his picture brought back the pain of loss she felt when she was only ten years old. The images of her mother elicited a different response; Margaret Bannon was a lighting demon by everybody's standards. She smiled at her recollection of the uniquely Irish phrase. She'd not called anyone a lighting demon for years.

Her mother was a woman who drew no pleasure whatsoever from life. Elizabeth regretted the relationship she never had with her; it had been a lonely life, an only child, a widowed mother, all culminating in an almighty fight that never got resolved.

She turned slowly, taking it all in, listening to the sound of footsteps upstairs as the children explored.

The brown fabric suite with the impossibly low seats was still there, yellowing antimacassars on the backs. Nobody could get up from the pieces with any degree of dignity. That was why, if they had visitors, her mother always sat on a hard kitchen chair. She said it was because of rheumatism, but the truth was it made her feel superior to see the parish priest or the neighbours or whoever called trying to drag themselves up from the sofa.

The curtains, also brown – *who on earth chose brown as a default colour for decorating for goodness' sake* – would need to be replaced.

Unusually in Ireland, and especially among Catholics, her mother too was an only child. Her father had a brother, Paddy, Liesl and Erich's grandfather, and she thought there might have been a sister as well but wasn't sure. Her father grew up in Cavan, but she was never taken there as far as she could remember, and Mother claimed she knew nothing further.

She wondered about her extended family as she wandered out of the sitting room, past the parlour and the dining room and into the bright kitchen that ran the width of the house at the back. The kitchen was immaculate, everything in its place, exactly as she remembered it. This was her home now.

The sunny kitchen had windows overlooking the garden, which was totally overgrown with weeds and tall grass. The cream AGA stove looked exactly the same. It was run on timber or turf, and she remembered the sensation of coming in from school on cold afternoons to the heat of the kitchen. The floorboards were dusty but nothing a good scrub wouldn't solve, and there were two wide dressers, one for crockery and cooking utensils and another for food. In the middle of the kitchen was the old pitch-pine table with six chairs.

How many meals had she eaten there; how often had she done her homework at that very table?

Memories came, unbidden, and Elizabeth felt a sting of regret. She remembered the day the Reverend Mother told Margaret that she was a very bright girl and would make a fine teaching assistant. She recalled the sheer exhilaration of someone recognising her hard work. Her mother took her excellent marks and achievements at school as if they were nothing less than she expected.

Elizabeth went upstairs, and as she reached the landing, it was once again so familiar. Erich and Liesl were in the main bedroom, her mother's old room, but Elizabeth went into hers. As she opened the door, her breath caught in her throat.

The cream eiderdown with the hand-embroidered butterflies covered the bed. She'd done the embroidery herself. The dressing table had her comb and brush and her china-faced doll called Mollie, which sat there, the frills of her pantaloons visible under her red velvet dress. Santa Claus had brought Mollie when Elizabeth was seven. There was a basket full of hairpins and, beside it, a bottle of lily of the valley talcum powder.

Slowly, she went to the wardrobe, and there, to her astonishment, were all her old clothes. She skimmed through dresses, cardigans and sweaters. In the drawers were underwear and stockings, and on a rack, the toes stuffed with newspaper, were all her old shoes.

There were other clothes too, those she'd worn as a child. She pulled some of them out; they would probably fit Liesl with a little alteration.

As she took it all in, Liesl appeared. 'This is such a lovely house, Elizabeth, and it's perfect. I don't know what I expected, but it wasn't this...' The child paused as she noticed the dark-green dress with the black velvet collar in Elizabeth's hand.

'I think this might fit you,' Elizabeth said, trying to keep her voice normal. She smiled. Poor Liesl had one dress, and it was getting too small. 'Here, try it on.'

Liesl pulled off her dress enthusiastically and stood there in her vest and knickers. Elizabeth helped the girl pull the dress over her head and closed the buttons at the back. Liesl looked in the mirror; it was perfect.

'It's lovely, but maybe whoever owns it...' the girl began.

'She doesn't mind,' Elizabeth said with a grin, delighted to see Liesl happy.

'How do you know?'

Elizabeth caught her eye in the mirror and put her arms around her waist. 'Because I own it, or at least I did when I was your age. There are lots of things, dresses, shoes – my mother must have kept everything.'

Liesl went to the wardrobe. 'There are adult clothes too. Were these yours as well?'

'Yes, but I was just a girl when I last wore them.' She smiled ruefully.

'I bet they still fit,' Liesl said, eyeing Elizabeth's trim figure. Rationing had seen to any extra weight the years had put on her hips and belly.

'Here, try this one.' Liesl extracted a beautiful red dress with a V-neck, fitted bodice and flared skirt.

'I don't know, Liesl. It's been twenty-one years...' Elizabeth looked at the tiny waist of the dress.

'Try it. I bet it fits, and even if it doesn't, you are so good at sewing, you can alter it. We have nothing, and we can't buy much because we don't have coupons. It's so wonderful your mother kept everything, isn't it?'

Despite her complicated feelings towards her mother and the confusion over why a woman who had turned her back on her only child had maintained her bedroom like a museum, Elizabeth had to agree. It was most fortuitous, and Elizabeth slipped off the skirt and blouse she had been given by a colleague in the days after the bomb attack. She stepped into the dress. To her surprised delight, the zip slid up effortlessly.

'See? I told you!' Liesl was smiling. They stood side by side, gazing into the mirror.

Erich appeared and said they both looked nice, but she could see his sadness. The children had been through so much. First losing their father, their school and their friends, then leaving their mother, then having the house in Liverpool flattened... It was too much for them to bear.

They had met a lady in the local solicitor's office when they went to collect the key, and though she spoke English, Erich and Liesl had no idea what she said because of her strong accent. They were worried about this new start, she knew.

'OK, I'll tell you what. Let's go up the street to Bridie's sweetshop. When I was a little girl, my daddy would take me in there for sherbet lemons.'

The children's eyes lit up at the thought of sweets. It was a rare treat these days.

They let themselves out, Liesl and Elizabeth in their dresses and Erich wearing the same grey pullover and flannel shorts he'd been wearing since they were donated to him by his friend Charlie's mother after the bombing.

'Will they hate us because we are German?' Erich asked quietly as they walked in the sunshine up the main street of Ballycreggan.

'Of course not. I'll explain everything and people will be kind,' Elizabeth reassured him, fervently hoping she was right.

'But at least in England, we were not the only ones. I think here we might be,' he said, looking doubtfully around at the small Irish village.

'Well, even if you are, people know what Hitler is like and what he's doing to the Jews. Once they know you're Jews, they will understand, I promise.' She kept her voice bright and willed her fellow countrymen and women to see them as the victims and not the perpetrators.

Together, they pushed open the bright-pink door of Bridie's sweetshop. It had been the same colour since she was a child.

To their astonishment, the shop was full, and not of Irish children. There was a tall, very good-looking man and a pretty young woman, and they were surrounded by children of all ages speaking in German.

Liesl and Erich looked to Elizabeth for an explanation, but she was as bewildered as they were.

'Now then.' Bridie Mac looked just the same. The shopkeeper must have been a young woman when Elizabeth was a child to say she was still there, but she looked exactly as Elizabeth remembered her – a sprightly, thin woman wearing a headscarf tied under her chin and a faded apron with what might have been balloons on it over a light-blue dress.

'One at a time, please.' The shopkeeper smiled.

Each of the children asked for something – some in halted English, while others could merely point. The man assisted them by speaking in German and then translating in accented English.

Liesl and Erich's eyes were like saucers.

Once each of the children had a few barley sugars or a lollipop, the man stood back and waved Elizabeth and her two to the counter.

'Excuse me,' Elizabeth said, unsure of how to proceed. Asking what they were doing there was too rude, but how could she phrase such a question politely?

'Yes?' The man turned to face her. He was tall, perhaps six feet, with olive skin, dark-brown hair and brown eyes. She judged him to be around her age. A light stubble covered his jaw, and he wore work-man's clothes – an open-necked shirt and dark-blue trousers. On his feet were heavy boots, and in his hand, he held a cap.

'I, um… I'm sorry, but I was just wondering… My children here' – she pointed at Erich and Liesl – 'well, my adopted children – I'm taking care of them until their mother can join them – are German, German Jews, and they were worried… Well, we were all worried…' She flushed, knowing she was being inarticulate, but the surprise of meeting a bunch of German children in a sweetshop in Ballycreggan, and having them escorted by this man, had thrown her completely. 'That they would be…' she finished lamely.

The man smiled and turned his attention to Liesl and Erich, addressing them in rapid German. Elizabeth was lost. The younger woman was helping the smaller children to unwrap their treats.

Liesl and Erich both smiled, then laughed. He handed over two coins to Bridie, who presented them with a lollipop each.

He then went around the group and introduced Liesl and Erich to each of the children. The group of German youngsters were a little shy initially, but within a moment or two, they were firing rapid questions at Elizabeth's two young charges and Liesl and Erich were answering animatedly. Bridie and Elizabeth exchanged a smile as Elizabeth moved to the edge of the counter.

'Welcome back,' Bridie said. 'And my sympathies on your mother's passin'.' Bridie's accent was as sharp as a knife.

'Thank you. It's nice to be back. The place looks lovely, just as I remembered it.'

'Och, sure, nothin' much changes around here, you know yourself.'

Once the introductions were over, the man turned to Elizabeth and stuck out his hand. 'Daniel Lieber, and this is Talia Zimmermann.'

Elizabeth took his hand. His fingers felt warm as he gently squeezed hers. She then shook the woman's hand. Talia's face was impassive; she neither smiled nor scowled. She held Elizabeth's gaze a fraction longer than usual for such a casual introduction, though. Elizabeth noticed the woman moved a little closer to the man; the slight gesture seemed proprietorial.

'Elizabeth Klein.'

'Nice to meet you, Elizabeth.' His smile was warm. 'These children are from the Kindertransport – Jews, we all are. We are staying at a property out of town.' He motioned his head out towards the coast. 'A farm, or at least it will be when we've finished working on it.'

She found herself mesmerised by the deep rumble of his voice. 'That's wonderful.' Elizabeth was happy. 'I don't mean it's wonderful that you had to come here, of course. I just meant for Liesl and Erich to have people to play with, and people who understand. My late husband was Jewish, but I'm not, and so I want to do right by their parents...' She was babbling again.

'And you live here in Ballycreggan?' Talia asked.

'Yes. Well, I'm from here originally, though I have not been back for many years. My house was destroyed in Liverpool during a bombing raid, and the school I taught in took a direct hit as well, so Erich and Liesl and I came here. My mother passed away a while back.'

'You're a teacher?' Daniel asked.

'Yes, for almost twenty years.'

He grinned. 'They need a teacher.' He jerked his head in the direction of the children happily jabbering away in German outside. 'I'm sure I will see you around, Elizabeth.' He held the door open for her as they walked out into the sunshine.

'Nice to meet you, Daniel and Talia. Goodbye, children, *auf Wiedersehen.*'

'*Auf Wiedersehen,*' they chorused in reply.

Liesl and Erich stood beside her, much happier than they were half an hour earlier. They waved goodbye to their new friends as they went one way up the street to buy some groceries and Daniel and Talia took the children the other way where an ancient-looking bus was parked. As they walked away, Elizabeth noticed what an incredibly beautiful couple Daniel and Talia were.

'ell, Mrs Klein, I think given the circumstances, if you could start on Monday, we would be delighted. The children from the refugee farm will arrive Monday morning, so if you feel that you could manage them in one class, my wife and I would continue to teach the local children, then we most certainly would be delighted to have you join our staff.'

Principal Morris of Ballycreggan Primary School beamed. He was a rotund man with a kind smile and a bald head. He'd told her he and his wife had been teaching there since 1928.

'While of course it is terrible what happened in Liverpool – and I offer you my deepest sympathy at the loss of your home and indeed your school – would it be terrible of me to say that you're the answer to my prayers?'

Elizabeth smiled. 'Of course not. And I'm just glad I had somewhere to go and could take my foster children with me. They've been through so much in their short lives. I just want some peace for them.'

'I understand. It is simply horrific what is going on over there, and we'll have to do our bit to make all of them feel welcome. I just know that you, with all your experience and knowledge, will be invaluable.'

He stood and shook her hand, accompanying her to the door.

As she walked back out onto the one street that made up the village of Ballycreggan, she was elated. Things were going to be all right after all. In the weeks after the bombing, when they were being put up by a colleague whose house wasn't hit, Elizabeth wondered what would become of them. The school was condemned, and any evacuated children that had come home to the city were promptly dispatched back to Wales, so there was nobody to teach even if they had a school. It looked bleak.

She was luckier than most, having a home in Ireland. The house was perfect, lovely in fact, and the way her mother kept all of her things... Well, she didn't know what to make of that. Her bedroom was like a shrine. All of her schoolbooks, her exercise copies – everything – was as she left them. Did it mean that despite two decades of silence, her mother did care for her after all? And if so, why hadn't she just written?

With a spring in her step over her new job, she went home to tell Liesl and Erich the great news. The August sunshine was warm on her face as she surveyed the village through new, optimistic eyes.

The Protestant church was up on the hill, at the end of an avenue lined with flowers on the approach, and the Catholic church was on the other end, with its imposing spire and ornately carved pillars. It always struck her that even the buildings were trying to outdo each other. The village school catered, unusually, to both the Protestant and Catholic communities, and while there was a mistrust and definitely a divide between both congregations, they managed to get along reasonably well.

She passed the grocer's, Ernie Davies' tobacco shop, Mim's bakery, Scott's draper's that sold everything from a needle to an anchor, and four pubs.

There was a gentle, safe feeling to the place, and Bridie was right – nothing much changed there as the years progressed. It felt like just what they needed after all the upheaval.

She picked up the newspaper as she shopped. More slamming of the South's reaction to the war. They were being stubborn on their position of neutrality. The Irish prime minister, de Valera, insisted that while he was seeking to normalise relations with Britain after centuries of acrimony, that did not go so far as to take the Allied's side in this war. They didn't even call it a war; they called it 'the Emergency'. There was palpable animosity now, and the refusal to even allow the British to use the ports in Ireland, or Éire as it was now called, known as the Treaty Ports, was the final straw. As a Catholic, she understood the Irish position. They were a newly independent state – a very hard-won freedom – and it would just not be acceptable to the electorate to immediately ally themselves to their centuries-long foe. But that wasn't how Britain saw it, and they never would. She kept her mouth closed on the subject; it was safer that way.

A stance she could never understand, however, was the Irish Free State's attitude towards Jews. They were neutral but they refused to take refugees. Entering Southern Ireland with Liesl and Erich would have been impossible, but the North was part of the United Kingdom, so carrying one small bag between them all, which contained the few bits of clothes they'd managed to borrow or buy and not much else, they boarded a boat and sailed into Belfast harbour. Getting tickets was tricky as civilian travel had been curtailed to a trickle, but the principal of her old school knew someone who knew someone, and eventually, they were given passage.

Having bought the groceries that were available – they were on emergency ration cards as theirs had been destroyed – she walked back home.

She had never anticipated this turn in events, but for now, whatever Ballycreggan held, at least she had a home and somewhere safe for Liesl and Erich to live. She put her key in the lock and called them.

They came running downstairs, their faces the picture of anticipation. They were happy to go to school now, especially as there were going to be other German Jewish children there as well, but if Elizabeth were the teacher, then that would be just perfect.

'So I start at the local primary school on Monday!' She put her arms around their waists.

'Oh, Elizabeth, that is wonderful!' Liesl was so relieved, and Erich whooped.

'You'll probably be able to speak German for a lot of the day again with your new friends, but we'll speak English in the classroom. Not everyone had a *mutti* who could speak English to them, you know.'

Liesl and Erich exchanged a glance, and then Liesl said solemnly, 'No, Elizabeth. Erich and I talked about this. I know the children on the farm speak German, but we will help them with English. We don't like to speak German now – it's not our language. Our *mutti* always spoke to us in English or French or Italian, we'll speak German only if we have to and if we ever see Papa again.'

Elizabeth paused. What should she say? Apart from the fact that Peter had been arrested, there was no further news.

'Do you think we'll see our papa again, Elizabeth?' Erich asked, and her heart broke for this sweet little boy. His big, brown, trusting eyes pleaded with hers to give him the reassurance he craved. What should she do? Liesl too was waiting.

'I don't know, Erich, and that's the truth. We know there are work camps they have taken people to, and your father was a big, strong man, right?'

They nodded.

'And so they would want someone strong for lifting heavy things, I'd imagine.' Elizabeth was improvising here, and she hoped Liesl didn't see through it.

'So the truth is, we don't know where they are, but I do know that your parents love you two so much that if there is any way on earth they can get back to you, they will do it. Things are so topsy-turvy these days, nobody really knows what's going to happen. Your *mutti* and papa wanted to keep you with them, I'm sure, but Ariella sent you to me so you would be safe, and I'm so glad that she did. I love you both so much.'

She had never said those words out loud before, and was worried for a second that she'd gone too far, but Liesl's smile reassured her.

'We love you, too, Elizabeth. Thank you for taking care of us.' Liesl's voice cracked with emotion.

Elizabeth tightened her arms around them and held them close. 'We'll be all right. I promise you, you will be fine.'

# CHAPTER 10

*D*aniel Lieber woke to the familiar sensation of wet feet. As he sat up, he realised his whole sleeping bag was soaked. The tent had leaked again. He was too big for the tent anyway, but it was all they had. He crawled out and stretched to his full height of six feet one, releasing the tension from his muscular shoulders that ached from sleeping on the hard ground.

Back in Vienna, the trees would be at the end of their summer bloom, the leaves beginning to fall, but it would still be warm enough to drink morning coffee outside. But here in the Ards Peninsula in Ireland, some days it felt very much like winter. For all that, though, he thought as he struggled out of the wet fabric, he was so grateful to be there and not in Vienna.

He tried to remember his beautiful home city as it was before Hitler came, before the people he considered friends, colleagues and neighbours showed their true colours. Before the scarlet flags with their black swastikas hung from every building. Before Kristallnacht.

Since his arrival at 'the farm' as it was optimistically called, people had been so busy trying to make it habitable and trying to keep the children's spirits up that the adults rarely talked about their own worries and fears for their families back in Germany or Austria.

Everyone dealt with it themselves because it felt wrong to unburden your fears onto others who were experiencing the same thing. If someone had asked him before how human beings would react against such adversity, he would have assumed they'd be united in their trauma, but in fact, the opposite was proving to be true.

He wondered about Lydia. All the pain he'd felt when she broke off their engagement was long gone. She'd met and married Hans within months of the breakup. It was hard for a long time, but he was over it now. The happy couple moved to Hanover; Hans's family had a nice Aryan business there.

He tried not to dwell on the dark memories of the night they came. He and Lydia were just about to go out when a Nazi official arrived at the door.

The official was insistent that Daniel was in breach of a directive that all Jews must register. Daniel had explained there must be a mix-up as he was Catholic, but upon further investigation, it seemed the Nazis were right. His parents were, in fact, Jews. They'd moved from Salzburg to Vienna in 1900, the year before he was born, and had decided to become Catholics on the way. They were both dead, so he couldn't ask them why, though he knew of the anti-Semitism that existed long before Hitler came to power, so he could guess. He and his brother had no idea they were Jewish. It had never occurred to them that their parents were anything but good Austrian Catholics. They went to mass; he and Josef went to Catholic school – first Holy Communion, confirmation, the whole thing. He and Lydia would have been married in a Catholic church if she'd not found out he was Daniel Liebermann, not Daniel Lieber, and that he was, in her words, 'a filthy Jew'. Her venomous racism still shocked him to his core. He'd thought he knew her.

Shaking those dark thoughts from his mind, he dressed outside quickly in his only dry clothes, stored in an old flour sack hung from the crossbar of the tent, then made his way to the dining hall. It was really just a byre, but they'd managed to set up some trestle tables and some benches. The steaming kettle on the two ring gas cooker perched on one of the tables was hissing out water to make tea –

coffee was not on the menu in Ireland, it seemed – and Daniel helped himself to a bowl of the grey pasty stuff called porridge that the Irish liked to eat for breakfast. It was kind of tasteless, but at least it filled him up.

'Not exactly the *Pfarrwirt*, eh?' Talia sat down beside him. She was Viennese too, and they had gravitated towards each other though she was twenty years his junior. He felt protective of her.

'I could never afford to eat there anyway.' Daniel smiled.

'Me neither,' Talia agreed, grimacing as she took a spoon of porridge. 'This stuff reminds me of the glue my papa used to wallpaper our apartment.'

'Any news of them?' he asked gently.

'Nothing.' She changed the subject quickly, it was too hard. 'So a new group of kids arrive today, I believe?' she said brightly, changing the subject.

Daniel scratched his stubbled face. He really needed a shave and a wash, but the boiler that was supposed to heat the water in the tank was broken again. His dark hair was longer now than he usually wore it, curling over his collar. 'Yes, and at least now we have a teacher for them, so that's great.' He drained his cup of weak tea and stood up.

'I'd better see how Levi is getting on with the boiler. It was freezing in the tent last night, and I can't imagine that where the kids are is much better. If we can get it going again, then at least there will be heat and hot water.'

The old boiler had been donated from somewhere else, and it wasn't one Daniel had ever seen before. He had the unenviable task of taking it all apart, trying to see how it worked and putting it back together. He drew diagrams of each section as he disassembled it so he would be able to rebuild it as the manufacturer intended. It was a long way from the mechanical engineering of his past, but he was the designated fixer of the farm.

'I'm in the kitchen today, so be prepared for dinner.' She rose too, and Daniel nodded. She was no more than nineteen or twenty, and she was tiny and dark haired, with pale skin and hazel eyes flecked with amber. She could be any race. She'd told Daniel once that her mother was Jewish and her father a gentile. She'd escaped when both her parents were executed by the Nazis for opposing the annexation of Austria. They had been putting up posters encouraging people to vote against the annexation. In the end, there was no vote, and the Germans walked all over Austria without a single shot being fired.

'I'll look forward to it.' He smiled, knowing whatever it was would be less than he needed and a far cry from what he was used to.

He crossed the yard to the large sheds where the children slept. The older ones were helping the younger ones to dress. Though it was summer, there was a chill in the damp air.

Daniel hated to see their innocence gone. These children became adults the moment their parents put them on the train and they had to fend for themselves.

'Good morning, everyone!' he called as he entered the large dormitory. Despite few of the children being bilingual, the language of the camp was primarily English. It was felt they would need it for the duration of their stay, so any adults who could speak it were encouraged to do so.

'Good morning, Daniel!' they chorused. Initially, they tried to call him Herr Lieber, but these were extraordinary times and this was an extraordinary situation, so he felt better when they called him Daniel. He was like a big bear to them, and the little ones liked to climb all over him. He kicked a football with the older kids, and to see their faces light up when they scored a goal, to see them behaving as children again if even only for a few minutes, did his heart good.

'Are you taking us to school today?' Viola asked him, a tall Polish girl with almost-white hair and pale-blue eyes.

'I will, but I'm going to try to get the boiler going first, so you all go have breakfast and get yourselves ready, and I'll meet you at the bus at 8:40, all right?'

He looked around. They were worried, sad and lonely, and his heart broke for them.

'I've met your new teacher, remember? Some of you were with me? She seems really nice and kind, and you'll all be fine.' He smiled.

'And if she's not,' he whispered, 'tell me, and I'll put a spider in her tea.' He winked and they all giggled.

He had studied at the university in Vienna and had his own engineering business that was doing well. At least it was until he was denounced as a Jew. Within weeks of the Nazi visit – and Lydia's departure – his shop was requisitioned, and his apartment too. He was lucky; he got out. An old college friend sponsored him. The friend was in the British Foreign Office, but Daniel had written to him at his address in Bristol.

Stephen Holland had studied in Britain but had come to Vienna for some post-graduate work in the area of hydraulics, and Daniel had been writing a paper on Blaise Pascal. The two young men hit it off and enjoyed all that Vienna had to offer together. Stephen had reluctantly returned to take over the family business in Bristol, but they'd maintained the friendship by letter. It was a relationship that saved Daniel's life. Technically, Stephen was to be responsible for him, but he'd explained that he was overseas so Daniel would have to make his own way. He was happy to do that.

On the boat from the Hook of Holland to Harwich, he met a frazzled woman who seemed to be in charge of lots of children. Daniel offered to help, and in the course of the conversation, she offered him a position with them in Ireland setting up a farm for the children of the Kindertransport. He had no better ideas, and anyway, doing so could salve some of the guilt he felt at getting out when so many didn't. If he was helping their children, at least he was doing something.

Days on the farm were long and supplies were scarce, but the Jewish community in Belfast were wonderful, and the Dublin Jews and the Quakers and some Christian groups were kind too, so he didn't complain. He did his best to get ancient rusted machines going, and so far, so good.

He turned his attention to the recalcitrant boiler.

Levi arrived soon after, and Daniel rolled out the large diagram he had made of the various component parts. Levi had been a general labourer at a large country house near Baden-Baden before the war, so he was good with his hands.

'I've taken this apart and put it back together twice, and I can't see where the problem is. But we need to get this going, so will we take it apart again?'

Levi shrugged and nodded. He was not one for chat.

Reading the diagram, they took each piece and placed it on the floor. Daniel used a piece of charcoal to mark the parts and filled in the corresponding number on his diagram. Finally, the entire thing was laid out on the floor.

'Now what?' Levi asked.

Daniel stood back and observed it. 'Well, this is a gravity-fed system, so we need to use gravity and convection to move water around the circuit. The tank is above us... Hot water has a lower density than cold, so it will rise up through the pipes...' He paused and ran his hands over his stubble.

'Thanks for the physics lesson,' Levi muttered, rolling his eyes, and Daniel suppressed a smile. 'There was a Bulex gas heater in the house where I used to work, but it looked nothing like this.'

'Hmm. I know. This is unique.' Daniel picked up his large diagram, explaining the valve and pump system to Levi and how he thought it should work. They discovered a hairline crack in the pump. Daniel repaired it, hopeful that would solve the issue.

An hour later, leaving Levi to clean all the parts and begin the reassembly process, he went down to drive the children to school.

Daniel cursed under his breath as he turned the key in the ignition of the old bus but the engine remained silent. The children were so excited, but if he didn't get the bus going, there was no way of transporting them there. They needed to get to school, to learn and to behave like children, not worker bees.

The first harvest was ripening nicely, and chickens, sheep and even a herd of cattle had been sourced, so while the farm was not totally self-sufficient, it was well on the way. The children all helped out, and it really was a case of many hands making light work. But now it was time for school.

He looked back at the stricken faces. 'Don't worry, I'll see to it!' he said, and a few of them relaxed. They saw him as a parent figure, and he took that responsibility seriously. If Daniel said it was going to be all right, then it was.

Some of the children had been reunited with parents who had managed to get out of the occupied areas of Europe, but the majority of them were alone and had heard very little from home. Letters were infrequent, but when the parents did manage to write... Well, there was just something so pathetic about adults begging their children to keep trying to find a way to get them out of Germany or Poland or Austria. Of course the children felt the pressure to do something, but there was nothing they could do. They were living on a remote farm in Northern Ireland.

He went under the bonnet of the vehicle. It had been donated by someone, but it was on its last legs. He dried off the spark plugs, sprayed a little oil and tried again. Nothing.

'OK, you might as well get off for a bit. Go back inside and tell the ladies I said you can have some cocoa. Leave this with me, and I'll call you when I get it going.'

There were cheers at the extra cocoa, and it worked in a small way to ameliorate the disappointment.

He fought the urge to kick the stupid vehicle, choosing instead to smoke one of his precious cigarettes. He leaned against the wall of the yard, going over what he knew about the internal combustion engine in his head. He was missing something, obviously.

'Hey, I thought you were supposed to be fixing the bus. They told me it won't start.' Talia emerged from the kitchen and leaned on the wall beside him.

'I'm at a bit of a loss, but I suppose I'll have to figure it out.' He exhaled a long plume of blue cigarette smoke.

'Well, everyone knows you are a genius with your hands.' Talia was flirting again.

Daniel knew she had taken a shine to him, though why was anybody's guess. He had nothing to offer anyone – the clothes he stood up in were all he owned, and he had the same uncertain future as everyone else on the farm.

Talia was a nice girl, and she was pretty, but Daniel just didn't see her like that. She was too young, and anyway, romance was not on his mind. He got along with everyone, and the children liked him, and that was enough. At first, he was sure it was just Talia joking around, but of late, he noticed how there was always a seat for him beside her in the dining room, or if they were going to pray, how she fell into step beside him.

He was a Jew by birth, but he'd never gone to a synagogue or eaten kosher. He was learning, though. Something about the faith fascinated him, and he'd asked Rabbi Frank to teach him. In the evenings, they had lessons, and the rabbi was patient and generous with his time.

It helped that life on the farm was very much in tune with the Orthodox Jewish way of life, and he found he liked it and was learning every day. The way they lived at the start, in tents and makeshift dwellings, was compared to Sukkot, the festival remembering the tabernacles the Israelites erected in the desert on their flight to the Promised Land. It seemed particularly poignant now. For some strange reason, it all made sense to him. He was a Jew, and he was happy to be one.

The community observed shabbat, from sunset on Friday until Saturday night. Daniel joined in, following the others' lead; he listened to the Rabbi as he recited the Kiddush and ate the blessed challah. He wondered what his father and mother would say if they could see their rebellious son, conforming so completely to the religion they abandoned.

He stamped out the butt of his cigarette and changed the subject. 'You got a letter two days ago – you want to talk about it?'

She sighed. 'No, not really. It was just a letter from my grandparents – well, my grandmother. It was to tell me that my grandfather had died. I loved him, so it was very sad, but he was old… The news of my father's death really finished him, as my papa was his only son.' Her voice cracked as she spoke, and her eyes shone.

'I'm sorry,' he said quietly, and opened his arms instinctively. He liked her as a friend and hated to see her sad. She stepped into the circle of his embrace, and he held her as she cried.

Her sobs subsided, and she gazed up at him, her face tear-stained. 'Do you have anyone? You never say.'

'No, my parents are dead, my brother also, killed in a road accident. I had a girlfriend, but she left me for someone else, and she's now a good *hausfrau* in Hanover. I'm lucky, I suppose.' He shrugged. He was honest about not being a practising Jew up to that point – so many of those deemed Jewish by the Nazis had never set foot in a synagogue – but he kept his parents' deception to himself. It wasn't anyone's business.

He smiled down at her, and she reached up and placed her hand on his face. Suddenly, as she went to kiss him, Daniel realised what was happening. He released her gently.

'Talia, stop. I'm sorry, I...' he began. She was a kid, and she didn't want him, not really, he knew that. It was just that he was familiar and from home.

'What? Don't you think I'm pretty?' she asked, and he hated to see the vulnerability there.

'It's not that. I... You're too young, and I'm too old for you, and besides –'

'I don't care about that, Daniel. I really don't...' she interrupted him.

'But I do. And I'm not the one for you, Talia, I swear I'm not. I'm an old man and you're a beautiful young girl. So let's just survive this, and hopefully, life can go back to normal and you'll meet someone the right age and have lots of babies.' He tried to bring a little levity. He didn't want her to feel rejected, but he needed to make clear once and for all that he had no interest in her that way.

'What's wrong with me?' Talia asked, and Daniel could hear the edge of resentment in her voice.

'There's nothing wrong. I'm just not... Look, we're friends, living this life none of us anticipated, and it's bound to play havoc with emotions...'

'I love you, Daniel,' she said, resting her head on his chest.

He sighed. 'You think you do because I'm from Vienna and I'm actually old enough to be your father. But you are looking for security, safety – of course you are – and I will be that for you. I'll look out for you, Talia, but not like that, all right?' Gently, he stepped back from her, and even though it was hard to see the hurt in her eyes, he kept her gaze.

'All right?' he asked again.

She nodded slowly, and he gave her a one-armed squeeze.

'All right,' she said, and she walked back to the dining hall.

# CHAPTER 11

*D*aniel pulled the bus up outside the primary school an hour late. He hoped the Catholic and Protestant kids and their families would be kind to the children; they had suffered so much already. At least the woman he'd met in the sweetshop had been appointed as the teacher, and she seemed lovely.

It was hard not to believe Jews were universally hated after everything that had happened. The Jewish organisations from Dublin and Belfast had visited and told them a little about life as a Jew in Ireland, and while they were a separate people – everyone in the South seemed to be Catholic apart from a handful of Protestants who had stayed after independence – they just got on with things and were generally allowed to live unhindered. An overzealous priest led a pogrom against the Jews in Limerick at the start of the century, which caused many Jews to flee the city, but apart from that, they were accepted. It was a source of deep shock to the Irish Jews that their government was refusing refugees, but they were. Apparently, the Catholics were afraid of the impact a huge influx of Jews would have.

There had been much discussion on the farm once the children went to bed. The Irish Jews were constantly protesting the apathy the neutral South was showing towards the fate of the Jews in

Europe. It looked like they just didn't care. Many of the Jews explained how they'd joined the part-time Army Reserve in Ireland, and there were many who had crossed to England to join the British Army to throw their weight behind the bid to rid Europe of National Socialism forever. Apparently, up until the war, Jews were just part of society. There was even the story of a young Jew from Cork, called Goldberg, who was silenced at a debate at the university there because 'only Irishmen could speak'. But the friends and relatives of the late IRA mayor, the republican Terence MacSwiney who died in a British prison during a hunger strike, insisted Goldberg be heard. It was hard to understand. On one hand, the Irish knew what it was like to be a persecuted people. They were subjected to terrible cruelty at the hands of the British by all accounts, so this stone wall of refusal on the subject of refugees was hard to understand.

Daniel was ashamed that he knew nothing of the conflict in Ireland before coming. He'd heard rumblings, of course, but it seemed so far away and utterly removed from his life. And yet there he was.

As he watched the children file off the bus, he gave them an encouraging smile. They were given asylum because they were Jews, but would the locals see them just as Germans? On the farm, they were protected, isolated and among their own. The director had visited the previous night and tried to warn the children without terrifying them about how people might react once they heard they were Germans or Austrians or Jews.

He was unsure if he should go in with them and was considering what to do when he spotted Elizabeth crossing the road to where he was parked.

'Good morning.' She smiled. 'Better late than never.'

'Good morning,' he replied. 'Bus trouble.'

'Well, you are here now, and I'm delighted. My two have asked about fifty times, "How long before they get here?"'

'Sorry to have made you wait. I think it is fixed now, for today anyway.' He smiled ruefully. He hoped his English was correct. He was learning it as fast as he could but suspected his Austrian accent was heavy. He wasn't a natural at languages, having more of a mathematical mind.

'Well done. I was hoping you could come in. It might help to settle them if they see one face they recognise. It's a big day for them – they must be nervous.' She smiled again, and Daniel relaxed. The kids would be safe with her; she cared about them already.

'Of course.' He switched the engine off and followed her into the schoolroom. His large frame seemed even bigger surrounded by little desks and chairs, and he tried to stand in the corner out of everyone's way. The children were aged from five to eleven, as the older ones stayed to work on the farm – some instruction in English was provided for them in the evenings. He was going to do some math and physics classes as well once winter came and there wasn't as much to do.

He stood beside a large bookshelf filled with brightly coloured books and noticed several of the children gravitate towards him as they waited for Elizabeth to arrange them into groups by age. He waved at Liesl and Erich, and they waved back. They looked in better shape than the kids from the farm – nice clothes and well fed.

He marvelled at Elizabeth's organisational skills. Within a few minutes, she had everyone sitting and sharing boxes of crayons to decorate their name tags, which she had stuck to the corner of each desk.

The classroom itself was makeshift. It had once been an outbuilding of some sort, but it was clean. Elizabeth had clearly gone to a lot of trouble to decorate with pictures and maps, and being September, it wasn't cold.

He noticed that one of the windows had no glass and that the teacher's desk was what looked like a door held up with blocks. Once the children were all busy, he approached her.

'Thank you for your kindness, Elizabeth. They were scared this morning, but now they are not. Thank you.'

She looked up and smiled. 'Yes, I can imagine they were. It's all been such an upheaval for them too, the poor little pets.'

Daniel looked into her kind, gentle eyes. There was something about this woman. He couldn't quite put his finger on it, but there was a goodness to her that was rare. Despite having several pressing jobs waiting at the farm, he found himself making an offer. 'I can perhaps help here? The desk, the window?' He pointed, just in case he had used the wrong words.

'Would you mind?' Her blue eyes lit up. 'There is a caretaker, but he's very elderly and I don't like to ask.' She seemed thrilled.

'Of course. I will go back to get my tools. And then I will return, if that is all right?'

'Wonderful! I really appreciate that.' She turned to the class and addressed them slowly and clearly. Thirty children watched and waited.

'Now, everyone, firstly, can I just welcome you all to Ballycreggan Primary School. Please do not be worried about anything, as we are going to have a wonderful time here together learning all sorts of things. And some of you have very good English and others don't, but that's all right. We'll fix that too. The most important thing is not to worry. Now, my name is Mrs Klein, and my husband, Rudi, was Jewish – he was killed in the last war – so that's why I have a Jewish name even though I am Irish. I grew up in this village, but I taught in Liverpool in England for a long time. The Germans bombed my house and the school where I worked, so I came home with my two foster children, Liesl and Erich.' She pointed at them and they smiled.

'Liesl and Erich's *mutti* and papa asked me to take care of them, and they came from Berlin on the Kindertransport, just like you did, so I hope you are all going to be very good friends.'

She scanned the room, and Daniel noted how every child was enthralled.

'Now, I know things have been very hard for you, and you are all worried about your families back at home, but I was saying to Erich and Liesl the other week, all we can do is trust Mr Churchill, do our bit for the war effort and hope. So we will make friends, and learn new things, and grow up strong and clever. Your parents wanted you to be safe and to be happy, so let's make them proud, shall we?'

Daniel saw the looks of trust and determination on the children's faces, and he thought again what a kind woman Elizabeth Klein was. She never said they would be going home to Germany or that their parents would come for them soon or anything like that – the possibility was less and less likely with every passing day – but she had managed to rally them and give them hope of a brighter tomorrow.

Yes, Elizabeth Klein was a remarkable woman, he thought as he walked out to the bus.

# CHAPTER 12

*R*uth Alger tried her best to fix her hair. She'd been chasing that donkey all afternoon – he'd escaped and was roaming the backroads around the Ards Peninsula. She had volunteered to go and find him, hoping someone would be around to drive her in the bus. But Daniel was down at the school again, and Levi was out in the fields repairing some fencing that had been trampled by the newly arrived heifers. The big old car, another donation, was in the yard, but she dared not take it – it was not the done thing for women to drive; the rabbi frowned upon that sort of modern idea – and there was no sign of any of the other men.

She had volunteered to come up from Dublin the previous summer and had intended to only stay a few weeks, but seeing the children and how lost and alone they were, she decided to stay.

As she checked in the mirror, she saw Talia behind her. Something about that girl irked her, although she couldn't say why exactly. Coming from safe, neutral Ireland, it was not really accepted to say anything bad about the refugees – they'd all been through so much – but she admitted to herself that she just didn't like her.

Talia flopped down on her bunk in the women's dormitory. 'I hate those bloody chickens, I really do.' The younger woman was examining her chapped hands.

'I do too,' Ruth agreed, trying to be friendly despite her reservations.

'Daniel is down at the school again. I wonder what the attraction is down there?' Talia flipped onto her stomach, and Ruth glanced over.

The young woman was beautiful, but she knew it. The other women worked so hard on the farm that they looked like bedraggled scarecrows most of the time, and while nobody could accuse Talia of not pulling her weight, she seemed to always look well. The overalls they'd been given were too big, as mostly they were for men, but Talia had rolled hers up and cinched them with a belt. She wore a shirt that was open at the throat, revealing her smooth olive-skinned décolletage – again, not too much, but enough to have the men notice. Ruth was sure she stuck her breasts out and swung her hips just for attention.

Talia was attractive in that she was small but curvy, and men seemed to want to take care of her. She tied her dark hair back with a flowery hairband, leaving a tendril or two around her face, and those hazel eyes of hers looked so innocent. Ruth suspected she was anything but.

She came from Vienna, like Daniel, though they didn't know each other until they arrived at the farm. Both Daniel's and Talia's family were secular Jews, which explained how they knew so little about their faith.

Like everyone who'd escaped, Talia was reluctant to talk about her family, and Ruth understood. She could not imagine how hard it must be for all of them, especially the children. But there was something different about Talia. She did what was necessary when it came to worship, but you could tell she didn't believe a word of it. She'd been heard to explain that she was only Jewish insofar as the Nazis determined it. One quarter Jewish – having one Jewish grandparent – made you Jewish, and she had one Jewish parent, but she claimed that she never felt Jewish before now. That was probably why Ruth didn't like her, if she were honest. The others, those brought up either

Orthodox or Reform, she had more in common with. She liked most of them and had spent a lot of time with Levi discussing scripture recently as they'd thinned turnips. He was quiet and some might say taciturn, but she thought he was a good, devout man. Her thoughts were far away when she realised Talia was waiting for an answer.

'Hmm?' Ruth dragged the brush through her tangled curls. She had no idea what the younger woman was on about.

'Daniel, down at the school. He's spending a lot of time there, isn't he? I wonder why?'

'Why don't you ask him?' Ruth replied nonchalantly. 'You two are good friends, aren't you?'

'Mmm, we are,' Talia said, her tone suggesting they were a lot more than that. 'He's so nice, but deep, you know. You wouldn't know what was going on with him.'

'The same as everyone else, I expect.' Ruth tried not to snap as she wrapped an elastic band around her hastily bunched ponytail. 'Trying to make do and manage until this awful war is over and Hitler and the rest of his henchmen are blown to kingdom come.'

Talia had taken out her sketch pad once more and was on her knees on the bed, drawing the scene out the window. 'I won't be holding my breath for that,' she said, holding her pencil horizontally and taking a measurement with her thumb with one eye closed. Then she returned to her drawing.

'Well, losing the war is unthinkable – it just can't happen. So we'd better pray Mr Churchill can convince the Yanks to join in.'

'Why should they?' Talia replied, though her attention was on the drawing book. 'It's not their war.' She took her eraser and removed some pencil strokes.

'Because it's the right thing to do, of course. There are lots of Jews in America – they'll just have to make their government understand.' Ruth found the other woman's intransigence irritating.

'I hope you're right, but I think in the end, the Americans will turn on the Jews just as the Germans and the Austrians did.' Talia flipped her drawing book closed and sighed. 'Now, I've a pile of potatoes to peel. Honestly, did you ever meet a nation so obsessed with one vegetable?' She rolled her eyes and threw her book and pencils into the locker beside her bed. Lots of sheets of paper were rolled up in there already. Ruth had seen some of her artwork before, and even she had to admit it was very good.

Ruth changed her dress. She'd have to handwash the one she'd been wearing later on, as it had chicken blood on it from when she'd had to decapitate that night's meal. She gave herself a quick wash under the arms.

'That wouldn't happen in America. They are civilised people who wouldn't behave like that.' Ruth tried to sound as sure as she felt.

'Oh, believe me, Ruth, you were never there. Germany and Austria are very civilised places. Opera, ballet, art, architecture... There is an ancient and proud culture in those countries. But they just had enough of the Jews – that's how they saw it – and wanted them out. Simple as that. If it can happen there, it can happen anywhere.' Talia shrugged and strolled out the door, and Ruth swallowed her fury. It was true she'd never been to Germany – or anywhere – in her thirty years, but she refused to believe that the rest of the world would behave as the Nazis had.

The use of the word 'them' annoyed her too. Maybe Talia didn't feel very Jewish and wasn't brought up in the faith, but she was here like everyone else, expelled because she was a Jew. So why would she say 'them'? Surely it was 'us'?

# CHAPTER 13

*allycreggan, June, 1941*
  The time had flown, and Elizabeth could hardly believe almost a full school year had passed. There had been Halloween decorations made, Hanukah and Christmas celebrated inasmuch as was possible with rationing, and now they were preparing to finish up the school year with a big concert. The people of Ballycreggan had been welcoming, if a little distant at the start, to the Jews at the farm, but the children had brought them together in ways only they can. As she watched Liesl and Erich blend into life in the sleepy Irish village, she wondered often how they could ever go back when the war ended. They were assimilated and loved their lives in Ireland. They had great friends among the refugee children as well as the locals and seemed to be constantly attending football matches and birthday parties.

  She could never have imagined during all those years on her own in Liverpool that she would ever feel at home in Ballycreggan, but she did. Everyone knew her by name, and they knew Erich and Liesl too. She was part of the community, and she found she liked it.

  The rabbi, with his short curly peyot and black hat, still caused a stir when he walked down the main street of the village. Daniel Lieber, on the other hand, had integrated much better than the others.

He helped out any local who needed it with farm machinery, and he'd been asked by both the Catholic priest and the Protestant vicar to remove the church bells and railings to be donated to the military's call for metal. Most of the able-bodied men of the village were in uniform, so a strong man was much in demand. Levi helped out too, as did the older boys, but it was Daniel they all sought out.

Daniel. She thought of him often, and sometimes she caught him looking at her as he did odd jobs in the school or at her house, but he never said anything. Besides, he and Talia were often together, so she assumed there was something between them. He was always most polite and proper, and so was she. He'd done full days getting the outbuilding she used as a classroom into better shape, and on those days, she brought an extra sandwich for him as well as three for herself, Liesl and Erich. They were relaxed and easy in each other's company. He was funny and kind, and she laughed at how precise he was when it came to even putting up shelves. Everything was measured and drawn to scale before he did anything.

She was marking tests and had sent Erich and Liesl home alone after school. She was determined to give each of the refugee children a report card so they could post it to their parents to show them how much progress they were making at school. The parents might not receive it, but the fact that they were able to send one meant a lot to the children. They were all growing up so fast, and despite the pain of the separation from their parents, they were thriving. Being surrounded by other children living with the same heartache seemed to have helped, or perhaps it was just the natural resilience of the young. Whatever it was, she loved to see them smile and laugh.

Ireland was the best place in the world as far as Liesl and Erich were concerned. There was more food, and though Belfast had been bombed last week, in general, it was safer. Some people remembered her, and whenever she met any of the old neighbours, they said nice things about her mother, which may or may not have been true. But independently of the fact that she was Margaret Bannon's daughter, she was beginning to feel like she fit in.

The principal and his wife – both teachers at the school – were lovely people. There was another woman as well, an elderly lady called Mrs Ashe who taught singing and music and could be heard warbling in a watery contralto all over the school. The children did not look forward to their singing lessons, and Elizabeth could see why. Though Mrs Ashe wasn't openly unkind, she acted as if she found the Jewish children distasteful. She seemed to stare and never addressed them directly. She asked Elizabeth questions about the children's ability to understand her instructions when they were taking singing classes, and though it irked the older woman to no end, Elizabeth simply redirected every question to the children.

Mrs Ashe had never met a Jewish person before, as she was fond of pointing out, and she acted as if it were really a most inconvenient thing that she had to meet some now, but Elizabeth bit her tongue and said nothing. If Mrs Ashe was the worst that they had to contend with, then it wasn't so bad.

Mr Morris, the master as he was called, and his wife were very kind to the refugees and encouraged lots of integration with the local children. They played sports together and of course took the dreaded singing classes together, and slowly but surely, the barriers of language, nationality and religion were being eroded. In a world so divided and harsh, it was good to see.

The children's English was improving week on week, some of them even developing Irish accents. Liesl was best friends with two sisters from Poland called Anika and Viola, and Erich was on the Ballycreggan football team.

Elizabeth had stayed behind every evening that week to finish decorating the little school hall for the concert that would be performed for the whole village on Friday night. Daniel was in the hall, putting the finishing touches to the stage, and it even had a curtain – four old sheets stitched together by Liesl's class. Each child – or group for the shy ones – was going to perform, so there were going to be uilleann pipers and tin-whistle players among the local children, youngsters performing traditional dances from Poland, Czechoslovakia, Austria and Germany, and singers and mime artists, home-grown and international. Everyone was looking forward to it, and the parents' association had offered to run a tea-and-bun stand to raise money for an outing for all the children on the last day of term.

People were so kind. The cinema owner in Donaghadee didn't charge the refugee children for the Saturday matinee, so Daniel made the trip every weekend with a busload of excited boys and girls. The local parents, though they hadn't much themselves, donated any clothing that was too small for their children to the Jewish little ones. It was hard to believe such hatred as they heard about on the news existed just a few hundred miles away in the face of such generosity and sympathy.

Elizabeth finished the last test and boiled the kettle in the little staff room to make coffee. Daniel had bought some of the precious beans from a shop in Belfast, and she had discovered a coffee grinder in her mother's kitchen. Elizabeth had never known her mother to drink coffee, but perhaps she developed a taste for it in the years they were estranged. Just another thing about her mother that she didn't know. She ground just enough coffee for two cups. In one of her first conversations with Daniel, he explained how he could not get into drinking tea no matter how often he was offered it.

She put the cups on a tray, cut two slices of the caraway cake a kind parent had dropped in for the teachers and made her way to the hall.

Daniel was up the ladder, attaching the pole, as she went in.

'I've brought you some coffee,' she called.

'Thank you. One moment.'

She watched as he fixed the pole in place and climbed agilely down. His shirt had ridden up, and she caught a glimpse of his taut olive-skinned torso. He was fit and muscular from all the physical work on the farm, and she felt a lurch in her stomach at the sight of him. It was an unfamiliar and not entirely welcome feeling. She felt herself blush, so she turned around and busied herself arranging paintbrushes.

*Pull yourself together for God's sake,* she berated herself. *And don't be taking mad old notions.*

Daniel walked to the table and lifted his cup. He inhaled its luxurious scent before sipping.

'Mmm...' He sighed theatrically. 'I miss coffee the most.' He grinned at her, and she felt the blush rise again. His dark-brown eyes were warm.

'You were lucky to get this. I'd enjoy it if I were you because I doubt you'll be able to get more. I don't think anyone here has had proper tea for ages, let alone coffee.' Elizabeth smiled at his enjoyment.

'I got it from a man who imports wine and fancy food. Even in wartime, if you have enough money, you can have whatever you want. I had to fix the whole electric system in his house and his shop to get it,' Daniel said ruefully. He sipped his drink and took a big bite of cake.

She found herself looking forward to his popping his head around the door every day as he dropped the children. Since that first day, he was in the habit of coming into the classroom to settle them in. Elizabeth or the Morrises sometimes had a job for him to do, and he was always happy to help. He waited in the bus at the end of the school day as the children filed out of school, always giving Elizabeth a friendly wave as he loaded up his charges.

'Thank you for all this work,' she said, gesturing to the stage. 'The children are so looking forward to it all.'

'Yes, they are. Every night at the farm, it is music and dancing in preparing... Is this right? In preparing?'

'In preparation,' she corrected with a smile.

'Yes. This. In preparation. You make them happy, Elizabeth. You know that is not easy, as they have much sadness. But coming here to you, it makes them happy. That first day, I was so...not feared... nervous – yes, I was nervous. They are not my children, but we are all together here and they don't have parents, so I feel like...' He shrugged. 'Anyway, I am so glad it was you.'

'I'm glad it was me as well, both for the children from the farm and for Liesl and Erich too.'

She took her cup and sat down on the old chair that they used for standing on. Daniel leaned against the wall.

'No word from their parents?' he asked.

Though they'd had lots of chats in the past year, this was the first time they were alone together and could talk properly about the situation. There were always small ears around, and so the adults spoke in a kind of code.

Elizabeth sighed. 'Their father was my cousin – Peter was his name. I never met him. According to Liesl, her mother explained that the Germans needed him for work, so they'd taken him to a work camp. I don't know exactly, but it doesn't sound good. That would have been in early 1939, sometime before the war was declared. Ariella, their mother, was the one who wrote to me, asking that I take them. I've written several times to her last-known address telling her that Liesl and Erich are here, and the children send something every fortnight, a card or a picture, but we've had nothing in response.'

'They're from Berlin?'

'Yes.' Elizabeth looked at him and their eyes met. 'It's difficult to keep coming up with excuses as to why she's not been in touch, you know?' she asked, knowing his answer.

He nodded.

'And I want their parents to come for them, of course I do. But every month that goes by, the more I... Well, I would hate to lose them.' She was surprised to hear herself admit that, especially to him. 'I find myself trying to prepare to hand them over...'

Daniel put his coffee cup down and turned to face her. He went down on his hunkers in front of her. She caught a waft of the distinctly masculine scent of him, soap and oil and something else. She was close enough to see the shadow of stubble on his jaw.

'I don't think you'll need to worry about that any time soon,' he said quietly.

'But we don't know. Ariella could get a visa – I hope she can. Peter could come back from wherever it is they are holding him.' Elizabeth was trying to be realistic.

'She was Jewish, alone in Berlin, her husband arrested.' Daniel sighed. 'Things are bad, and I'm only hearing this on the grapevine, as Rabbi Frank still has some contacts there. But, Elizabeth, your care for these kids might be a lot longer than you think. It might be forever.'

She tried to process what he was saying. 'But Peter isn't even Jewish...' What he was suggesting was horrible – poor Liesl and Erich!

'He was arrested defending a Jew, though, wasn't he?'

She nodded.

'Well, they hate that. If he was taken away, who knows? And his wife alone in Berlin... They would have rounded her up by now, I'd imagine. Unless she could go into hiding, if someone would hide her, but if she had such a person, you would think she would have hidden the children rather than send them away.'

She could see Daniel hated to be the bearer of such a terrible prospect, but she also knew he was telling the truth. She felt pain for the little girl and boy she considered her own. She assumed from the start that it was just a matter of time before their mother and father would come for them, but from what Daniel was saying, it wasn't a guarantee.

'At least they have you. It was a lucky day for them when you agreed. It was a big thing to take total strangers into your home. It was a great kindness.'

She smiled. 'They've given me more joy than I could ever have imagined. I was nervous at first, as I was very set in my ways. After Rudi died...' She paused. She used to think and talk about Rudi all the time, but she realised she'd not mentioned him in months.

'How did he die?' Daniel asked.

'That last war. He was shot in the early morning of the 11th of November. The armistice was at eleven a.m., and he was killed around nine. He survived the last bloody months of that thing and then...' To her horror, her voice cracked and her eyes stung.

'I...I'm sorry...' she began.

Daniel reached into his trouser pocket and pulled out a clean handkerchief. Gently, he wiped her tears.

'I'm sorry…' she began again, and he shook his head slightly.

'You're sad – don't be sorry about that. It was such a waste. The war was over. He should have lived.'

'Exactly. I just feel silly, as it was so long ago…'

'Don't feel silly. It is the price of love, this sadness. You were lucky to have known such love.'

She nodded.

'And you had no children?'

Nobody had ever dared go there with her over all the years she spent in Liverpool, but there was something about Daniel that made her not just want to know about him but to open up to him as well.

'I was pregnant when Rudi left in June of 1918. I wrote to tell him he was going to be a father. I don't know if he ever got the letter – I hope he did. When I got the telegram to say Rudi was dead… I don't know. It was such a shock or something that I had a miscarriage.'

The silence hung easily between them, the big schoolroom clock ticking on the wall.

Eventually, Daniel spoke quietly. 'You would have been a wonderful mother. I see you with Liesl and Erich and all the children – you *are* a wonderful mother.'

'Thank you.' She gave him a watery smile. 'How about you, Daniel? Did you have someone?'

He looked so sad sometimes that she thought there must have been someone he'd had to leave behind or someone the Germans got to.

'There was someone. Lydia. I thought I loved her.' His sad smile surprised her. 'But she left me for a man with a lot of money and a big house in Hanover – someone who was not a filthy Jew.' He shrugged and smiled.

He paused, as if contemplating what to say next. 'I've told nobody here my story except Rabbi Frank. I was raised Catholic. My parents didn't officially convert or anything like that. They were Jews in Salzburg, and when they moved to Vienna in 1900, they lived as Catholics. It wasn't until the Nazis checked and accused me of not registering that I realised I was, in fact, Jewish.'

Elizabeth didn't know what to say.

'It's strange, I know, but funnily enough, I like Judaism, and I'm learning. Rabbi is teaching me privately.'

'So they just changed without doing anything official? Did you ask them why?' It was unlike her to be so inquisitive, but she wanted to know about him.

'My parents are dead long ago, thank God. My brother, Josef, was killed in a car crash. So there's just me. An old college friend from Swindon helped me by sponsoring me into Britain. Otherwise, I would be in a camp by now, or worse.'

'It's hard to believe, isn't it? I mean I know it's happening, but that German people are just going along with it...' Elizabeth still found the situation in Europe difficult to comprehend.

'It is. I never knew what it was like to be a Jew. I suppose I wasn't one, not really, but I'm so shocked at the way people are behaving. I find it hard to reconcile the country I know and love – or at least I did love – coming to this, but it has.'

He took another sip of his coffee, draining the cup. 'This is strange cake to me, with these seeds, but I like it,' he said, polishing off the last mouthful. She was permanently hungry herself, so she couldn't imagine what existence on the small rations was like for a man as large as him.

Suddenly she blurted, 'Would you like to come and have dinner with the children and me? It's only shepherd's pie, and the meat is scarce, so lots of potato and carrot, but if you'd like to, you're welcome.'

His dark-brown eyes held hers, and she noticed how long his eyelashes were – most girls would love to have lashes like that. A smile played around his lips. His dark hair, longer at the top and short on the back and sides, was streaked with grey at the temples and flopped over his face, which was expressive; every emotion he had was there for all to see. There was something so exotic about him. She should have looked away, but something about his gaze was compelling.

'I would love to,' he whispered.

The mood was broken by the sound of doors opening. Mr Morris was still around the school.

They finished up and walked back up the street to her house. Liesl knew how to put the pie Elizabeth had prepared the previous day in the oven, and so a delicious aroma met them at the front door. Erich was at the table shelling peas freshly picked from the garden to accompany the pie.

'Hello, Daniel,' Erich called, as if Elizabeth bringing men home for dinner was the most normal thing in the world.

'*Hallo, mein Schatz.*' Daniel ruffled his hair.

'Where's Liesl?' Elizabeth asked.

'Upstairs.'

'Can you call her? We need to set the table.'

Erich took a deep breath and bellowed, 'Liesl! Set the table!' without ever moving from his seat.

Elizabeth leaned over and started to tickle him. 'I could have done that myself!' she said as Erich screamed with laughter.

Daniel smiled. Erich and Liesl Bannon had surely landed on their feet.

# CHAPTER 14

$\mathcal{T}$he children looked on in amazement as Talia sketched Viola, who was perched on Elizabeth's desk. The drawing looked just like her.

'So now I will show you all how to do this.' Talia smiled, and they eagerly pulled their drawing pads and pencils towards them.

It had been Daniel's idea to invite Talia to give a few drawing lessons, and it was working out wonderfully, though there were only a few weeks left in the term. Elizabeth had feigned insult when he first suggested it one evening as he popped in to say hello while the children enjoyed a few extra minutes of playtime before getting on the bus back to the farm and chores.

She pointed to the picture of the cat she had drawn on the blackboard. 'And you think my drawing is not up to standard, is that it?' she said, hands on her hips in indignation.

'Well, no, I think this is a very good elephant you draw here.' He pointed at the board with a cheeky grin.

'That's a cat! How dare you!' She swiped at him with the cloth she was using to wipe the board, but he ducked out of her way.

Elizabeth found she was very relaxed around him these days. He called to the house in the evenings sometimes, although he didn't stay long. Liesl and Erich loved his company, and he was building something with Erich, using a Meccano set he had bought the boy for his birthday.

The children were invited to partake in religious ceremonies with the rest of the Jewish community from the start, and Daniel often collected them and dropped them home afterwards. They were practising Jews back in Berlin, so she was glad to be able to keep that up for their mother.

Liesl had unearthed a box of old dolls and busied herself making dresses for them with the Singer sewing machine in the parlour. Elizabeth's mother had kept the dolls too, but then, she kept everything, if the tins of buttons and boxes of mouse traps she had on every shelf and in every cupboard were anything to go by.

Life had settled into a nice rhythm. Elizabeth loved teaching, and Liesl and Erich were thriving. They spoke about their parents often. Elizabeth encouraged it. Sometimes they got upset, but it was better out than in, she believed.

Daniel had done a lot of odd jobs for her, but usually during the day when she was at school. There were tins of paint in the shed, there since God was a child, she imagined. Daniel managed to resurrect them with turpentine, and the brown paint that had been on every single surface had been replaced with whites and creams and even a few pastels. The whole house was so much better for it, bright, airy and welcoming.

Despite their closeness and the way they teased each other, nothing romantic had happened between them, though she knew the neighbours noted his comings and goings.

To him, she was probably just the old schoolteacher with the sensible clothes, and he was likely being kind. He never mentioned Talia, but Talia often dropped his name into conversation, so Elizabeth assumed there was something there.

Daniel Lieber did attract attention among the women of Ballycreggan, though, and Elizabeth had seen the way the mothers looked at him as they dropped their children to school. He was so much more exotic looking than the locals, and so many of the women were lonely.

They had not seen their men for a long time. She'd heard Juliet Maddox – mother to the incorrigible Maggie – remark after he passed one day, 'Just 'cause you're on a diet, girls, doesn't mean you can't look at the menu.'

She hoped Daniel hadn't heard them. She did not want to be one more middle-aged woman ogling one of the only eligible men for miles.

Still, she had to acknowledge in the small hours of the morning when she tossed and turned in bed that she'd not had feelings like this since Rudi.

Daniel was nothing like Rudi, physically or in terms of personality. Rudi had been slight and boy-like, but then, she supposed he had been just a boy of nineteen years. She often wondered what sort of man Rudi would have become, but he never got the chance, just like so many others. She tried often to remember Rudi's face, but Daniel's smile kept floating in front of her eyes, and she found herself wondering what it would be like to kiss him. Immediately, she dismissed the thoughts; she was behaving like a lovesick schoolgirl.

Talia was more his scene. She was so pretty and full of life and fun despite everything. The children loved her, though Elizabeth got the impression that Liesl had some reservations. She couldn't put her finger on it exactly, but something about the girl's demeanour every time Talia turned up made her think the girl wasn't too keen on her. Elizabeth suspected it was about Daniel. Liesl really looked up to him, and in lots of ways, he'd taken her under his wing, so perhaps she resented the closeness he seemed to share with Talia.

Talia held the others in the palm of her hand as she explained about light and shade. Every child was totally focused. Elizabeth noticed Talia had that effect on people; they gave her their undivided attention.

The young artist made the little ones giggle as she showed them how to draw funny animals. It had been a good idea to invite her, and the children looked forward to her Friday morning classes.

While the children had their undivided attention on Talia, Elizabeth used the opportunity to tidy the classroom. They were breaking up at the end of the following week for the summer holidays, and she would normally make up a bundle of artwork and crafts that her pupils had done for the year for them to take home and show their parents. But these children had nobody to show them to, so she was arranging a little exhibition in the school hall instead. The local children's work would be on display as well, so her hope was that their parents would come and at least some adults could admire the masterpieces. The adults from the farm were going to come too. It wasn't perfect – she knew every single one of her class wished that things were different – but it was the best she could do.

Talia explained how they should avoid trying to draw hands at first, as they were so difficult to get right, as Elizabeth pottered about the room.

That evening, she was invited with the children to the farm for Shabbat for the first time. She was a little nervous, but it was a big honour and she wanted to see how Liesl and Erich observed their faith with other Jews. Liesl would be preparing for her bat mitzvah, so the rabbi thought it would be a good idea for Elizabeth to at least have seen what Judaism was all about. She tried at first to keep a kosher house, but it proved too difficult with rationing and it was so complicated, not mixing meat and dairy, having to have two sets of dishes so she gave up. She said their prayers with them, as she didn't want Ariella and Peter to think she had allowed them to abandon their faith and culture while in her care.

Rudi had been a practising Jew, but it was so long ago and he did it on his own, so she had no idea how she should be. Daniel assured her there was nothing to be worried about. There would be prayers and a blessing as they lit candles a little before the sun set, then a meal. Shabbat lasted until three stars appeared in the sky on Saturday night, but she and the children would come home after dinner. Daniel was going to drive them, which was outside of the rules – no work, including driving, was to take place during Shabbat. But he'd explained that while he did his best to observe the faith, as far as he was concerned, allowing a woman and two children to walk three miles in the dark was a much greater sin than driving, so he insisted.

Liesl's upcoming bat mitzvah had caused a bit of contention. She was adamant that if she was being singled out by her government for being Jewish, then she should at least be a full member of that faith. Rabbi Frank was Orthodox and had not really been in favour of it – it was more a Reform idea that girls mark this milestone – but Liesl found an ally in Daniel. He'd spoken to the rabbi on her behalf, once he'd discussed it with Elizabeth, of course, and he made the point that the girls as well as the boys were being persecuted for their faith. Should they then be discriminated against within that faith? They were all in this together. And finally, the rabbi relented. He'd never performed a bat mitzvah before, but he was willing.

She was only eleven, and she would celebrate her bat mitzvah at the age of twelve. Perhaps the war would be over by then and she could go home, or Ariella and Peter would turn up, but since either of those was unlikely, it was best to be prepared.

The lesson finished, and each child produced a portrait of the child sitting beside them with varying degrees of success. Talia helped the children put the art things away before cycling back to the farm. Elizabeth had offered her tea, but she had to get back – she had to help prepare the Shabbat meal.

The rest of the day went by in a blur of hectic activity for Elizabeth as most school days did.

When the bell rang, she walked the students out as she did every day, and there was Daniel, waiting at the gate.

'I'll collect you at 8:15? I cannot believe how bright it is here at this time of year. Sunset is going to be around nine thirty this evening, so we will be in plenty of time.'

'Thank you, Daniel.' Elizabeth smiled. 'We'll be ready.'

As he drove off, she remembered the care Rudi used to take with his appearance before Shabbat. He would shave and wash thoroughly, often getting a haircut, and he always wore his best clothes, freshly laundered. She was determined that she and the children would not let anyone down, so she rushed them home to prepare.

By seven thirty she had both of them sitting on the sofa, looking beautifully turned out. Liesl was in a white dress and had a pale-pink ribbon in her hair; Erich wore a short-sleeved pale-blue shirt and navy short trousers. Their shoes were polished and their socks were brilliant white. She was so proud of them, it almost broke her heart. She went to get herself ready after giving a dire warning – to Erich in particular – not to move a muscle. That boy could get dirty in one second if she turned her back.

In her own bedroom, she wondered what to wear. All of her old dresses were hanging in the wardrobe. She pulled out a dress of midnight-blue silk, with a high collar and a row of seed-pearl buttons down the front. She had worn it to a piano recital she had played at when she was fifteen, but she knew it would still fit. It was very elegant, and she'd never normally wear an outfit so decadent, but something made her consider it.

The other dress in the wardrobe was red, and she dismissed it; it was a little too frivolous for a night of prayer. The last thing she wanted to do was scandalise the rabbi.

She put on the blue and was pleased when she saw how it looked. The bodice was fitted but not tight, and the flared skirt fell nicely. On a whim, she took her hair out of its bun, shaking it loose. She felt the familiar headache she got every night when she removed the elastic band and hairpins. She smiled as she recalled the first time Liesl had seen her hair down.

'Oh, Elizabeth, you're so pretty,' she'd gasped.

Of course, the child was biased, and 'so pretty' was stretching it, but as she brushed her long chestnut hair, she had to admit she did look younger with it down. As she picked up her elastics to tie it up again, she stopped. She'd leave it down. She would need to cover her head for the prayers, and she had found an old lace mantilla of her mother's that would do the job perfectly, but for the meal, it could be down.

She patted some cold cream on her face and plucked one or two stray hairs from her naturally arched eyebrows. She put on a little powder and a slick of pearl-pink lipstick.

Before she had a chance to change her mind, she walked downstairs and into the sitting room where Liesl and Erich were sitting quietly. She stopped, just watching them, her heart bursting. Liesl was reading a story to her brother. They were the best thing to ever happen to her, she knew, and though she prayed for the day she would return them to their parents, if that never happened, she would care for them with a heart and a half.

Liesl stopped just as Peter Rabbit was about to do something dastardly to poor old Mr McGregor and just gazed.

'Elizabeth!' Erich recovered first. 'You look like a beautiful fairy.'

Elizabeth blushed. 'Ah, don't be daft. I just decided to leave my hair down. Does it look all right?' She was suddenly not so sure.

'It looks so lovely, Elizabeth, so pretty. And your dress is beautiful too. You look really nice tonight.' Liesl was sincere.

'Well, you two look smashing as well.' Elizabeth smiled at her two young charges.

They stood up and walked into her outstretched arms. She hugged them and kissed the tops of their heads.

'Now, one last check – let me look at you both.' She settled a stray hair on Erich's head and smoothed the sleeves of Liesl's dress.

As they'd measured Liesl for the dress, Elizabeth had noticed a curviness that had not been there before. Liesl was a tall girl for eleven, and her body was developing. Elizabeth had wondered if she should have the conversation with her about puberty and what was going to happen, and decided there and then that she would. Her own mother had never mentioned anything about her body or anyone else's, and Elizabeth remembered vividly the horror of getting her first period. She thought she was dying, and if it were not for a kind teacher, she didn't know what she would have done. As for boys and where babies came from, well, that was a total mystery. She never imagined it would be her job to inform a girl about such things, but now that it was, she was determined to do it right.

She applied her teaching technique – the facts with no frills, but not so much information that would make the child anxious. Liesl listened as Elizabeth explained about women's bodies and how they worked, and then about men's bodies and how they worked, and finally, how babies were conceived and born.

Liesl listened and had some questions, and neither she nor her young charge was mortified as Elizabeth had feared. Afterwards, they sat in the kitchen and had a cup of cocoa, and Elizabeth realised she had never felt as close to another female in her whole life as she did with this little girl.

'Your *mutti* and papa would be as proud of you as I am if they could see you now,' Elizabeth said to the children as they sat on the sofa. Their eyes were suspiciously bright, and she was glad when they heard a beep outside. Daniel was there to collect them.

She opened the door and waved. He was in the car this time. He always drove the school bus whenever she met him, so to see him in a big black Austin was unusual. He got out and opened the back door theatrically for Liesl and Erich, giving them a low bow. They giggled as they got in. He was dressed in dark trousers and a snow-white shirt. His hair was brushed and he was clean-shaven. He took her breath away. She took one last glance at her reflection in the hallstand mirror before going out the front door and pulling it closed behind her.

In her nervousness, she fumbled with the lock. When she turned, she found Daniel at the gate. He was leaning against the pillar, a look of astonishment on his face.

'Elizabeth. You look lovely.' There was such sincerity in his words, she didn't want to dismiss them and brush off the compliment. She forced herself to just accept it.

'Thank you, Daniel.' She prayed she wouldn't blush.

He didn't move; he just stood there, staring at her.

'We'd better go?' she asked, feeling uncomfortable.

'Of course.' Daniel snapped out of it. 'We mustn't be late.' He went around and held the passenger door open for her and smiled as she sat in.

'I hope it doesn't smell too bad?' he said, sliding into the driver's seat.

She looked at him in confusion. The car smelled of beeswax polish and leather. 'No, it smells nice, actually. Why?'

'Earlier today, someone took this car to the market with lots of chickens. I spent the evening cleaning feathers and worse from the seats.' He chuckled, a lovely gurgling sound that came from the back of his throat.

'Well, thank you. I don't think I'd like to arrive for my first Shabbat dinner smelling like chickens.' She smiled.

'Nobody there would notice.' Daniel gave her a wink. 'I think we all smell like chickens by now.'

He put the car into gear and drove along the narrow country lanes. There was a lot of construction going on at the RAF base on the coast, and army trucks were everywhere.

'They are expanding the RAF base, that's why there are so many more trucks and things,' Erich announced. 'Marcus Bridges told me.'

'His father is in the RAF, isn't he?' Elizabeth asked.

'Yes, but I was worried it would make Hitler want to come.' Erich seemed to lack his usual confidence.

There was no point to saying it wouldn't happen. There was every chance of a bombing raid, but she wanted to reassure him. Before she could say anything, Daniel spoke. 'If they come, we will be ready. They won't hurt you because I will build you a bomb shelter in the garden.'

'Really? Do you think you could?' She had been planning on having one built anyway. 'I'd pay you, of course.'

Plans were in motion in the village to use the crypt of the Catholic church as a communal bomb shelter. All the men were volunteering to remove the decades of furniture, broken pews, boxes of old hymnals and all the other stuff that currently occupied the space, but it was taking time.

Daniel refused to take any money for the work he did for her in either the house or the school, and he had a full workload on the farm as well, so she didn't want to impose further.

'Yes, you can pay me in meals, and in the clothes you find and repair for me, and in the friendship. That is my payment.'

She sighed. She'd found some old shirts and jackets of her father's hanging in a wardrobe, and she had freshened them up and offered them to Daniel. She'd felt a bit awkward at the time, as food and clothing parcels generally were delivered to the farm and distributed evenly, but she gave them directly to him one night after he'd stayed for dinner. He accepted them gratefully.

He turned up the rutted lane to the farm, and Elizabeth felt a pang of sadness. She loved time with him alone or with the children. The idea that they were going to be surrounded by beautiful young women who all seemed to have eyes for Daniel made her feel old and frumpy.

Liesl and Erich ran off to find their friends the moment he parked.

Daniel showed Elizabeth around. The land had been leased by the Jewish community for the refugees, and they were doing a wonderful job of turning it into a productive business. Elizabeth knew from the children's stories how hard everyone worked, even the little ones, and they were rightly proud of their new sanctuary home.

'How many people are here?' she asked as Daniel led her towards the main living area.

'At the moment, fifty-five – ten adults and forty-five children.'

They entered a large room where people were beginning to gather. Several freshly washed children, wearing old and worn but spotlessly clean clothes, greeted her and welcomed her to their home. As dusk settled on the summer's day, the entire community had arrived and the singing in Hebrew and the lighting of the candles began. Elizabeth watched in wonder as Liesl and Erich participated fully, and she paid very close attention to the proceedings.

She saw them in a new light as they integrated easily with the rituals of their faith. She vowed to do everything she could to keep it going for them; it may well be all they had left of their parents.

The evening was a wonderful experience, and the discovery that her late husband was Jewish was met with warmth. There was eating, and even a little wine was found for the occasion. After the meal, the children went to play, and Elizabeth and Daniel sat and conversed over weak tea with the adults.

Ruth and another woman who was introduced as Rosa came to clear the tables, and Elizabeth insisted on helping.

'We would normally not even do the dishes at home,' Ruth

explained, 'but we don't have enough crockery or cutlery for breakfast in the morning if we don't, so we have to wash up.'

'Well, I'm happy to help,' she said.

'We never refuse a helping hand, so here, throw this on. You don't want to ruin your beautiful dress.' Ruth handed Elizabeth a worn apron that was grey from washing; it was impossible to tell what colour it might once have been.

'Thanks.' As she wrapped the apron around her, she asked, 'You're from Dublin, aren't you?'

Elizabeth had met Ruth once or twice and seen her around, but this was the first conversation they'd ever had. Rosa was in the dining room, gathering dishes.

'Yes. Dublin born and reared. We live off the North Circular Road – do you know it?' She began to wash the dishes as Elizabeth dried them.

'I don't, I'm afraid. I've never even been to Southern Ireland.'

'How come? It's only a hundred miles south?' Ruth seemed surprised.

'Well, my parents weren't much for travel, and I moved to England to train as a teacher when I was just seventeen. I met my husband there, and we married, and I never returned.'

'And someone said your husband was Jewish?'

'Yes, Rudi Klein. He was originally German – well, his family were, I think, going way back – but his great-grandfather came over to Britain sometime in the last century. Rudi was a lot more Liverpudlian than German.' She smiled at the memory of his Scouse accent. 'He was killed in the First War.' Elizabeth dried the beautiful silver platters carefully, placing them on the shelf Ruth indicated.

'And you never remarried?' Ruth certainly was inquisitive, but Elizabeth didn't mind; everyone knew her story anyway.

'No, I never did.' She tried to shift the focus from herself. 'How about you? Are you married?'

Ruth looked to be in her late twenties, or thirty at the most. She was dark featured, and while she wasn't heavy, she would be as she aged. 'Solid' was how Margaret would have described her, and she had big hazel eyes and thick almost-black hair tied back in a heavy plait down her back. She was attractive in a way, Elizabeth thought, but there was a sharpness to her that was hard to describe. She seemed a little on edge, belligerent or something.

'No, not yet, but I'm hoping to be.' Ruth paused as if weighing what she was going to say next. She looked like she was about to say something else when Talia stuck her head around the door of the makeshift scullery.

'Need any help?' she asked, smiling. 'Ah, you're almost finished. Sorry. I should have come sooner.' And she was gone.

'Typical,' Ruth muttered. From body language alone, it was clear there was no love lost between the two women.

'Talia is doing a wonderful job with the children in school,' Elizabeth said to lighten the mood.

'I'm sure she is. Though I suspect the bus driver is more of an attraction for her than the kids.'

Elizabeth was taken aback at the other woman's tone. Talia had more or less said she and Daniel were more than just friends a few times, but Ruth did not seem to be happy about it.

'But Talia and Daniel are close, aren't they?' She couldn't stop herself.

'Well, if by that you mean she's always hanging around him and trying to make it look like they are together, then yes. Just because they're both from Vienna... I mean, they didn't even know each other before coming here. Daniel has no interest in her, despite her less-than-subtle efforts,' she said as she wiped the sink. Elizabeth felt a slight relief.

Ruth looked to Elizabeth for a second. 'You've no idea, do you?'

'About what?' Elizabeth asked, confused.

'Daniel.'

'What about him?'

'He doesn't like Talia, not like that. He likes you. It's obvious – anyone with eyes can see the way he looks at you.'

Elizabeth blushed but was spared answering by Erich's arrival. 'There you are! I was looking everywhere,' he said.

She saw that his eyes were suspiciously bright. She put down the cloth, and immediately, he ran into her arms.

'I thought you were gone, and one of the boys said that you'd leave us here because we were Jews and you're not...' He was sobbing now, a combination of anxiety and relief.

She crouched so she was eye level with him. Her hands gently cupped his head, and their eyes locked. She didn't care that Ruth was still there.

'Listen to me, Erich Bannon. You are my son until one or both of your parents arrive. Only then will I be willing to let you go, my darling boy. You must believe this, no matter what anyone says. You and Liesl are my and Ariella's and Peter's children. And until you can live with your *mutti* and papa, you stay with me and I will never, ever leave you.' She looked into his eyes and whispered, 'Do you trust me?'

As she searched his distraught little face, he nodded slowly.

'So there is nothing to worry about. I won't ever leave you. Never. No matter what.'

'And what if Hitler's men come and take me and Liesl away?' Erich asked, not for the first time.

'Didn't you hear Mr Churchill last summer? If the Nazis try to come here, we will fight them on the beaches, in the fields, on the streets. We will never surrender.' Her eyes blazed with passion and love.

'None of us – not me, not you and Liesl, not Ruth here, or Daniel or Rabbi Frank, or any of the boys and girls in the school or their families – none of us would let that happen, so we'll stick together, and he will not win, Erich.'

'But people didn't want to give in in Germany, and they had to because the Nazis are too powerful...' Erich was still unsure.

'The good people in Germany didn't know what he was going to do – it took them by surprise. By the time they knew what he really was, it was too late to stand up to him. But we know what his plan is over here, and we'll be ready for him if he does try to come. Isn't that right, Ruth?'

Ruth looked startled to be included, but she took her cue from

Elizabeth. 'Absolutely, Erich, and you know what? Here in Ireland, we've been fighting the English for years and years, and we're really good at it, so we'll be more than a match for a silly little man with a silly little moustache.' She giggled, and Erich gave a ghost of a smile.

'Now, we'd better get home, I think.' Elizabeth gave Ruth back the apron. 'It was lovely to meet you, Ruth.'

Daniel was waiting to drive her home, and once again, he held the door open for her. Ruth's revelation loomed large in her mind. Was the other woman right? Did Daniel have feelings for her? Terrified this new information would be somehow evident on her face, she chose to sit in the back seat with Erich and Liesl. Within a few moments, both children fell asleep leaning against her. She held their warm bodies close, kissing their heads. In the silence, she mulled over what Ruth had said again.

They had driven a mile or two before Daniel spoke, his eyes on hers from the rear-view mirror. 'You love them,' he said, his voice a low rumble.

'I do,' she whispered.

'They love you too.'

Once at her home, he carried the sleeping Erich up to his bed and Elizabeth helped Liesl. He was just about to leave, as both children were settled, when she made a split-second decision. 'Would you like a drink?'

He turned and smiled.

'There's some whiskey in the cupboard. It's been there years, but I don't think it goes off?'

'I believe it improves with age. Yes, I would like some, please.'

He sat on the big sofa in the sitting room, which no longer had one trace of brown on the walls or doors, and she handed him a crystal tumbler with a generous measure of Irish whiskey. She had poured a sherry for herself. She considered sitting on the armchair beside the fire but impulsively sat beside him instead.

'I enjoyed it tonight. I think that pair of scallywags upstairs did too.'

He turned so his body was facing hers. 'It was nice to have you there. We're an odd bunch, I suppose, but we are managing, and the children stop everything becoming too...*rührselig*... You know what is this?' His brow furrowed as he tried to think of the English word.

She shook her head.

'Like sad and crying and always seeing the bad future?'

'Maudlin?' she suggested.

'Yes, maybe this. Maudlin. We have to stay cheerful for them, and so it is better, I think. Every day, the news is not good, so keeping knowledge of what's happening in Europe to a minimum is best, I think. It is very bad, but I am just grateful that I got out and that I came here...' He paused, his face inscrutable. 'I am glad I met you, Elizabeth.'

She held his gaze. His dark eyes reflected pools of emotion she had never seen before. Ruth's revelation gave her the confidence she needed. 'I'm glad I met you too, Daniel,' she whispered.

He leaned closer, their faces only inches apart, but as he did, they both heard footsteps on the stairs. She jumped up and went into the hallway.

'I'm thirsty, Elizabeth.' Erich was standing there, his hair on end.

She led him to the kitchen and gave him a glass of milk. When she returned to the sitting room, Erich beside her, Daniel was standing with his coat on.

'I'd better get back...' he began uncertainly.

'Of course. See you tomorrow, Daniel.' She smiled. 'And thank you for the lift.'

'*Danke schön*, Daniel,' Erich said sleepily.

'*Bitte, kleiner Freund.*' Daniel ruffled his hair and was gone.

# CHAPTER 15

The following Monday, Elizabeth burned the toast and was about to go out the door to school with her cardigan on inside out. Liesl pointed it out, and Elizabeth acted furtive and guilty. She couldn't sleep the previous night. What would have happened if Erich hadn't appeared looking for a drink? They would have kissed undoubtedly, but would it have been a friendly kiss or a passionate one?

They walked up the street to school together, Erich talking happily about a football tournament all the boys were planning once they got their holidays.

'Do you think we'll be allowed to use the school pitch even though the school is closed?' he asked.

She barely heard him.

'Elizabeth! You're not paying attention.' He giggled. He did a wicked impersonation of her in the classroom.

She smiled. 'I'm sorry, Erich. I was just thinking about lessons. You wanted to know about using the school field? I think it would be fine, but you better check with the master.'

The boy seemed happy with that suggestion.

One of the local boys caught up with them, and he and Erich ran on.

'Did Daniel go straight home yesterday?' Liesl asked.

Elizabeth shot her a look. That child was too perceptive by half sometimes.

'No, he...he came in for a drink,' Elizabeth admitted, and hoped she sounded nonchalant.

'He likes you,' Liesl said.

'And I like him. He's a very nice man.' Elizabeth sounded prim even to her own ears.

'No, I mean I think he really likes you, like he loves you, actually.' Liesl kept her gaze straight ahead.

'Well...I...I think he's very nice, as I said and...' Elizabeth was flustered. How did everyone but her know this?

'Talia is always saying how Daniel likes her, but I don't think so. Talia says a lot of things that are hard to believe,' Liesl said ominously.

'You don't like Talia, do you?' Elizabeth asked, glad to change the subject.

'It's not that. It's just she's always going on like she and Daniel are together, and she says some nasty things about the others too, like Ruth and Levi especially. Ruth is really nice and really kind to the children, and Levi is a bit quiet and can be a little bit grumpy, but he fixed Viola's bike last week and it took ages. And he works so hard on the farm so they have enough food. And they are really nice. The Irish Jews are trying to help, but she can be a bit – I don't know – catty or something.'

Elizabeth was surprised. She liked Talia. The young woman was always upbeat and cheerful, and the class loved her art lessons. She knew Ruth felt the same about her as Liesl; perhaps Ruth was influencing the child.

The newspaper boy passed, offering her paper to her rather than cycling the length of the street to her house. She took it with a disapproving glance. That Joey Foster was a lazy boy and constantly trying to pawn his newspapers off on others to deliver. She'd had words with him last week when she discovered Liesl carrying all the papers for their whole end of the street and instructed the children to refuse if he asked them again.

She let herself in and made a cup of tea before the school day started. Part of her wanted to see Daniel when he dropped off the Jewish children, but a larger part was shy. She would invite him to dinner, but not in front of everyone. Perhaps this afternoon he might pop in when he came to collect.

She opened the paper. The war was raging and showing no signs of turning against the Nazis. Everything was scarce, but the spirit of 'keep calm and carry on' was valiantly trying to defeat any doom and gloom. It was deemed unpatriotic to dwell on the negative, and people instead were focusing on Roosevelt's insistence to the American government that they would need to step up their efforts to defeat Hitler. Charles Lindbergh and the America First Committee were fighting him. Lindbergh had just addressed a rally of 30,000 in Los Angeles, lashing out at what he saw as a very pro-war government, but the American president's fireside chats seemed to be swinging the American public towards participation in the war on a bigger scale. They really needed American boots on the ground.

Apart from that bit of cheer, the rest of the news was depressing. The Germans had reached the Spanish border, so the capitulation of France was complete and Hitler was swanning about like the cat who'd got the cream. She couldn't bear to even look at him. She folded the paper in bad temper and threw it in the bin. She did not need that to start her day. It was hard enough to keep the children positive without that news swirling about in her head. She vowed to stop reading the paper first thing in the morning.

One of the Polish children had received a letter a few weeks ago, smuggled out of Warsaw, and had showed it to the children in her class, explaining that all Jews in Poland now had to wear a yellow Star of David. It was terrifying, as they were now marked men and women. Had Elizabeth intercepted the letter first, she would have asked the child not to share it, as its contents had the entire class petrified for their families back in Europe. Erich wondered over dinner if his mother was having to wear a star, and Liesl explained that it was Poland and not Germany. But Elizabeth knew it was probably only a matter of time.

She'd spoken to Rabbi Frank, and they agreed to avoid discussion of the war as much as possible with the children. It would not do them any good. So the child with the letter was allowed to vent her fears and anxiety about her family, but Elizabeth then implored her not to bring it up again or to go on about it too much because it would just frighten everyone further. The girl, a friend of Liesl's, agreed and never raised the matter again.

The children filed in and took their places. There was no sign of Daniel, and Elizabeth tried not to feel disappointed.

Later that morning, Elizabeth was in mid-flow explaining long division when the master knocked on her classroom door. She looked up in surprise. He hardly ever came to her classroom during the teaching day, as they both had classes of more than thirty pupils and to leave them could spell disaster.

'I'm sorry to interrupt, Mrs Klein, but I wonder if I could have a quick word?'

Something was wrong. His whole demeanour was different.

She set a particularly difficult sum for the children to do, and instructed them to do their best with it while she went outside to speak to the master.

'Mr Morris?' She was worried.

'I'm sorry, Elizabeth, but the police are here. They want to speak to you.'

Liesl and Erich were in the classroom, so it couldn't be them.

'What about?' she asked.

'They're in my office. It's best to let them explain, I think.' He walked quickly ahead of her, negating any possibility of conversation.

In the tiny organised office were two uniformed policemen and a man she assumed was a plain-clothes officer.

He spoke first. 'Mrs Klein, my name is Detective Inspector Gaughran, and these are my colleagues, Officer Barnes and Officer Topper. I'd like to ask you some questions if I may?'

She recognised his accent as Belfast; he had the hard vowels of the city. He was tall and thin, was dressed in a grey suit and a beige trench coat and wore a pencil moustache. His thinning hair was combed back from his high brow. He had intelligent hazel eyes and a calm demeanour, but something about him unnerved her.

The master left her in the room, and the detective gestured that she should take a seat.

'Of course, what's this about?' she asked.

The detective didn't answer but pulled a roll of paper from a large buff envelope. He unrolled the paper, which was around two feet wide by a foot long, on the desk in front of her.

Elizabeth peered at it, instantly recognising it as from a roll of drawing paper one of the children's fathers had managed to procure from the offices of the Belfast Telegraph. He brought it in, knowing the school was short of paper. Elizabeth had taken it gratefully, asking no questions.

On the paper was a map of some description, but at various points, numbers were written in pencil. It was like an architectural drawing or something. The rest of the drawing showed a coastline with a variety of inexplicable symbols at seemingly random points.

'Have you ever seen this before, Mrs Klein?' the detective asked.

Elizabeth had no idea what she was looking at. 'No. Well, the paper looks like the art paper we use in class, but the drawing, never. What is it?'

Gaughran gazed intently at her, as if determining her guilt or innocence. 'It's a map.' He was clearly only telling her the bare minimum. 'And you are a hundred percent positive you've never seen it before?'

'No. I said I hadn't.' She was getting impatient now, and she didn't like the accusation in his tone.

'But you do recognise the paper?'

'Well, yes, it's newsprint. We use it for artwork. I have a roll of it in my classroom.'

'And did you give this paper to anyone?'

'Well, the children obviously,' she responded, her voice sharpening. He surely wasn't suggesting one of the children did this?

'And do you ever give them blank paper to take home?'

'No. They use it in school only, and they get to take their artwork home at the end of term.'

'And you've only given this to children, no adults?'

She racked her brain. Had Talia taken some, or Daniel? They would be the only adults in the classroom apart from herself and Mr Morris.

'Well, I don't know. Talia Zimmermann and Daniel Lieber from the refugee farm spend some time in the room. Talia teaches drawing, and Daniel does a lot of maintenance. I suppose in theory they could have taken some, though I must say it's unlikely, not without asking me anyway.' She had no idea what was going on, but she did not like the turn this was taking. 'Where did you find it?' she asked pointedly.

Gaughran's eyes fixed on hers. 'At the refugee farm.'

'But why assume I'd know anything about it?'

'Because it is newsprint being used as school art paper, as you correctly point out, and you, Mrs Klein, are the only person in the village with any.' He spoke as if that instantly made her guilty of whatever he thought was going on.

'Well, I've no idea how it got there, but why is it a matter for the police anyway?'

Gaughran looked grim. 'Because, Mrs Klein, it is a map of the Royal Air Force base out at Ballyhalbert that opened last month, complete with coordinates. The Luftwaffe would be very happy to have such a map. There are many service personnel stationed there, not to mention a lot of vital equipment. And what we want to know is why someone other than the military would have a map of the area?'

'I've no idea. I swear to you.' Elizabeth's mind was racing.

'Who, apart from yourself – what adults I mean – has access to your classroom?'

'Well, as I said, there's me, Talia and Daniel. I mean, there's only one key, and I lock up every evening. Mr and Mrs Morris teach in their own rooms and rarely come to mine, and when the children go to singing class, it is held in the hall with Mrs Ashe because that's where the piano is.'

'And this Talia Zimmermann, what do you know about her?'

'Well, not much, just that she's Jewish. But she's just a girl...'

'You don't know her family history?'

'Not really. Her parents were executed for opposing the annexation of Austria, I think. She's from Vienna, and she went to art college, I believe... I don't know much else...'

'And Lieber?' Gaughran's voice cut through her recollections like a knife. 'What do you know about him?'

'Um...Daniel is also Viennese. He was raised Catholic, but his parents were Jewish...' The moment she said the words, she realised she was betraying his confidence. He'd not told anyone else about that out of loyalty to his deceased mother and father.

'Go on,' Gaughran said.

'And he...he came here. A friend of his from university, I think, a British man, helped, sponsored him, I think. He met the people and children from the Kindertransport on the boat, and he helped them, and then was offered a position here, so he came. I... He is an engineer,' she finished weakly. The map was almost pulsating on the desk. She felt like she was betraying him, but she had to answer the policeman's question. 'But honestly, I don't think either of them –'

'And he has access to the classroom alone?' the detective interrupted.

'Well, yes, he does some odd jobs from time to time, but he –'

'And what is the nature of your relationship with Mr Lieber?' Gaughran asked, slightly more aggressively now.

'We... Well...we're friendly, I suppose you'd say...' She struggled to describe it.

'And you're not romantically linked then?' Gaughran's eyes bored into hers.

'No...no, not at all...'

'Hmm.'

'Look, neither Daniel nor Talia could possibly –'

'Mrs Klein.' Gaughran interrupted her once again. 'The future of our country is at stake. We cannot rule anything in or out at this stage. There is no reason anyone would need a map such as this for civilian purposes, so we must assume, since the RAF know nothing of its existence, that it was created with some kind of nefarious intent. Do you know anyone who exhibits skills such as those?' Gaughran pointed to the drawing.

Elizabeth hesitated but looked more closely at the drawing. Daniel was an engineer, and he was capable of a drawing like this, but she was sure he would not try to undermine the British war effort. He hated the Nazis with more personal passion than most British people. He fervently hoped every follower of Adolf Hitler would be annihilated in this war. Perhaps he did the drawings for another reason, though what that might be, she couldn't guess.

'Well, as I said, Daniel Lieber is an engineer by profession, and Talia is a talented artist, but I can assure you, Detective, I am sure neither of them is doing anything nefarious, as you put it. They just wouldn't have any reason to do that.'

'And your background – I understand your late husband was German?' Gaughran spoke softly, his tone almost conversational, belying the gravitas of his question.

Elizabeth was incensed – how dare he? She'd had enough of him and his insinuations. 'My late husband, Detective,' – she emphasised every word – 'was killed by a German bullet on the last day of the war. His family had origins in Germany, it's true, but generations ago. And I am from Ballycreggan and lived in Liverpool for twenty years before returning here. So if you are asking me if I am a German spy, then I'm afraid you are barking up the wrong tree.'

'But you do have German relatives, those two children you care for?'

Elizabeth felt her blood boil. The cheek of the man. 'Yes, my father's brother married a German, and their son Peter is my foster children's father. They are *Jews*, Inspector Gaughran. Their father is missing, presumably in a German prison or worse, arrested for trying to defend an elderly Jewish woman on the street. And their mother put her children on a train because she feared for their safety. So yes, I do have German relatives who, believe me, have far greater reasons to hate Hitler than you or I.'

She was breathless and knew her face was flushed, but she didn't care. Something about the way he mentioned Liesl and Erich caused her hackles to rise. 'Now if there's nothing else, I have a class of refugee *Jewish* children waiting for me. Children whose stories would give you nightmares. Good day to you.'

As she left, the detective spoke again. She spun round to face him.

'It is of vital importance that you do not discuss the nature of this conversation with anyone else. Am I making myself very clear, Mrs Klein?'

'Crystal,' she replied coldly.

Elizabeth stormed out and fumed as she stomped across the yard. The cheek of the man. Daniel and Talia were no more spies than she was. Honestly, what a suggestion.

The rest of the day passed slowly, as she found it hard to keep her mind on the job. She wanted to speak to Daniel, to ask him straight out if he had done those drawings, and if he did, why? The clock crawled slowly to three o'clock, and finally, the bell rang and school was over.

She went out with her class, and there was the bus in its usual spot, but as she approached it, she realised Daniel wasn't behind the wheel.

'Levi, hello.' She tried to hide her disappointment. 'Daniel isn't here today?' *What a stupidly redundant question*, she silently admonished herself.

'No. Daniel has been arrested.' Levi looked shaken.

'What? Why?' Elizabeth could guess but wanted to hear what Levi had to say.

'Nobody knows, and the members of the refugee aid committee are stunned. They're trying to find out more, but the police have said nothing so far.'

Elizabeth could barely swallow.

'Do you know something?' Levi's eyes bored into hers; her face must have given her away.

'The police were here this morning, but I've no idea... I'm sorry, Levi, I have to go.' Elizabeth didn't even wave goodbye to the children, which was unusual; instead, she hurried back across the road.

Mr Morris was in his office. She knocked gently.

'Come in.'

She entered the office, and the usual cheery greeting was notably absent.

'I'm sorry to interrupt, but we must do something. The police have arrested Daniel, and they are holding him. I just know –'

Before she could go any further, Mr Morris raised his hand to stop her. 'Mrs Klein,' – he'd called her Elizabeth at her insistence since the first week – 'I do not know what was going on between you and Mr Lieber, but I would suggest that you keep your distance from him from now on. I do not want the school involved in this in any way. I am sure the authorities will do whatever is necessary to determine why a civilian would create such a drawing, but until such time as they do, I think it might be best to have the refugee children split between myself and my wife. Most of them can speak reasonably good English now, and they will be able to participate. I'll be in touch when I know more.'

He returned to his writing, leaving Elizabeth stunned. Was she being dismissed? For what?

'But why? What have I done? Please, Mr Morris, I don't understand. Do you think I had something to do with –'

He sighed. He was not a bad man; in fact, he'd been very kind to her since she arrived, and she could tell this had shaken him.

'Mrs Klein, I'm not doing this lightly. I just want the police to get to the bottom of this as quickly as possible. And in the meantime, because of the situation, I think it might be best for you to take some leave.'

'I can't believe this. We don't even know that there is anything sinister about that drawing. It might be perfectly innocent! But even if it's not, I can promise you the first I saw of it was today in this office –'

'Mrs Klein, please. Just take some time off, and the police will figure it out soon enough, I'm sure.'

Elizabeth knew he was not for changing. He wasn't asking; he was telling.

'Mr Morris, please don't do this. I swear to you, there is nothing going on between Daniel and me. I know absolutely nothing about this. We were friendly but nothing more, and of course I have helped the police. I'm on their side.'

He looked up and took off his glasses, cleaning them with his tie.

'Mrs Klein, Elizabeth...' His voice softened. 'This is a very difficult situation, and if you are associated with –'

'But I'm not. I swear to you, I'm not. If you dismiss me now, you might as well tell the whole of Ballycreggan I'm guilty of something. Innocent people do not get suspended from their jobs. It would be devastating, not just for me, but for Liesl and Erich as well. Please, Mr Morris, don't do it.' She knew she was begging, and denying any relationship at all with Daniel was hard to do, but she needed to prioritise the children.

'Do you give me your solemn word that you know nothing of this business and that you and Lieber are not involved in any way?'

'I give you my word we are not.' She felt like Peter denying Jesus.

He looked conflicted and did not speak for a long minute, obviously weighing the right thing to do.

'I am deeply sorry for everything that happened, but in the light of the discovery... Well, I was advised by the police to put some distance between you and the school until it could all be cleared up. In these times, you can't be too careful. I hope you understand?'

Her eyes pleaded with him. She knew he was a decent man, and the children liked him and his wife, and she supposed he had to do what the police advised.

'I do.' She had no choice but to be magnanimous. 'And to be honest with you, I was as shocked as everyone else. I...I got to know Daniel, and I still can't believe that he would do something like that...'

Mr Morris's face flushed. 'I'm sorry to have to say this, Elizabeth, and please understand that your private life is just that and nothing to do with me as such, but if I were to allow you to continue in your capacity as a teacher here, I would need to be sure that there would be no contact between you and the man in custody.' He appeared mortified now, but obviously her remark about Daniel's innocence had changed things. 'Now or in the future. The police seem very suspicious that he is an enemy agent, and whether you believe him capable or not...'

Elizabeth knew her future was on the line. She needed this job for Liesl and Erich as much as for herself.

'Mr Morris, there never was a relationship between me and Daniel Lieber, and I give you my word, I will not have any contact with him from now on.' She felt such a traitor saying the words, but she was backed into a corner, and she could see how it would not go down well in Ballycreggan if the man they suspected was a German spy was on close personal terms with the local schoolteacher.

'Well, if you tell me that's the case, I believe you. We can't do without you is the reality, but I was just trying to do what was best...'

'I understand, Mr Morris. This is a difficult situation. Thank you for giving me the benefit of the doubt.'

His smile was kind, and she could hold no grudge against him.

# CHAPTER 16

$\mathcal{I}$n her classroom, Liesl and Erich were waiting patiently. She would explain as best she could, but not now, not there. She put on a bright smile, gathered up her things, locked the door and ushered the children out of the school ahead of her. Once home, she gave them a very rough outline of what had happened but left out that the police thought Daniel was guilty. She said they just needed him to help them with their enquiries. The news upset them, she could tell. Another adult they loved and trusted had been taken away by the police. They didn't cry but went to their rooms, and she didn't see them until dinner time. They ate in silence, and then they went to bed.

The rest of the week went on uneventfully. There was no word of Daniel or what was happening, and though she desperately wanted to hear news of him, she was afraid to ask in case it made her look guilty. She battled feelings of disloyalty but rationalised them by telling herself that she had to protect Liesl and Erich, and that if all the evidence suggested it, then she had to face the fact that perhaps the police were right. She had slept badly every night since the police came to the school, pitching between being totally sure Daniel was innocent and convincing herself he must be a spy. It was exhausting.

A week after Daniel's arrest, having finally fallen asleep at two a.m., Elizabeth woke to the sound of screaming. She sighed – this was happening most nights now. She crossed the landing to Erich's room and went to him, holding him until he woke up properly, soothing him.

'It's all right. You're safe. You're here with me. Don't worry, Erich. Don't worry, my love...' She crooned the words until he was awake and his sobs had subsided.

'I dreamed they took you away. They took Papa and *Mutti* and now Daniel. They always take people away from children, and there is nobody to take care of them...'

Almost every night, they had the same conversation. Whatever progress the Bannon children had made since the move to Ireland was gone; they were back to square one again. Daniel's arrest had shaken them both.

Liesl, who normally calmed Erich down, was equally upset. She had a special bond with Daniel, especially since he had backed her request to have her bat mitzvah, and she felt his loss keenly, Elizabeth could tell.

'Erich, my darling, please believe me, I'm not going anywhere. I won't let anyone –' She tried again.

'But Papa was bigger and stronger than you, and they took him. Daniel is even stronger than Papa, and they took him too. If they want to take you, they can! You can't stop them.'

She couldn't argue with the logic of a nine-year-old. The argument she had used at the start, that the police didn't just come and take people away in Britain, held no water now.

'But, my love, I haven't done anything wrong...' She was tired but realised immediately she'd said the wrong thing.

'But Papa did nothing wrong, and you said Daniel did nothing wrong...' Erich was becoming distraught again.

'And they didn't,' she agreed wearily.

'So not doing bad things doesn't mean they can't take you away...' Erich disintegrated into another series of sobs that racked his body.

His cries woke Liesl – or perhaps she was already awake. Either way, she was now in his room too.

'Daniel didn't do anything wrong, so why is he in prison?'

She would have to tell them the truth. She pulled the covers back on Erich's bed and got in beside him, making space for Liesl on the other side.

'All right, I'm going to tell you as much as I know, which isn't much, but you mustn't talk to people in school or in the village about it because people love to gossip.' She inhaled, praying she'd find the right words. She wasn't disclosing any classified information, and as was the nature of things in a small Irish village, everyone seemed to have a version of the story anyway.

'The police found a map at the farm, and they think Daniel might have made it. It's a map of the air force base out at the coast, and they are afraid whoever made the map wants to give it to the Germans.'

'But why do they think Daniel did it?' Liesl asked.

'Because, as you know, back in Vienna, Daniel was an engineer, and he's able to do drawings and make them very accurate. So he is one of the people who could do this.'

'But Daniel wants Germany to lose the war, just like we all do, so why would he do something to help them?' Erich asked.

Elizabeth knew what she said next was going to be vital. She would have to reassure without giving false promises, exactly as she'd done on the subject of Ariella and Peter. Daniel was an important part of their lives now. They saw him as theirs, and he spent a lot of time with them. He read them stories and made things with them. They trusted him and so did Elizabeth, but what if she was wrong? The facts were stark. He was the only one who could have done the drawing, and if it was him, why would he do it if not for counter-espionage?

'I don't know,' she said quietly.

'Do you think he did the drawing?' Liesl asked, and Elizabeth knew she would have to be honest.

'Perhaps. It certainly looked like something he would be able to do. But if he did do it, I don't think he drew it to give to the Nazis.'

'But you don't know for certain?' Liesl's brown eyes were pools of worry.

'No, my love, I don't know for certain,' Elizabeth had to concede.

'I don't think Daniel did anything wrong – I know he didn't – I don't care what the police or anyone else says,' Liesl said with quiet determination.

The following days were heavy on her hands, and she knew the people in the village were talking about her. Small places like Bally-creggan thrived on gossip and hearsay, and the idea that the local Catholic black sheep, who married a Jew, maintained a rift of two decades with her mother (a walking saint by everyone's reckoning) and then turned up out of the blue with two German kids in tow was enough to set all the tongues wagging, leaving aside entirely the prospect of her being somehow connected to a German spy. She tried to ignore the looks and the sudden silence whenever she entered the grocer's or the butcher's.

A German plane had been shot down two nights ago by the RAF, who scrambled at a minute's notice, but not before it managed to drop bombs very precisely on the fuel silo. It also hit a hangar and destroyed a lot of expensive equipment. Two British airmen were killed. A local girl who was on her third day there as a typist was injured so badly she would never walk again. The word around the village was that they knew exactly where to drop the bombs. Where the Luftwaffe got such information seemed to be common knowledge – Daniel Lieber was to blame.

She tried to keep busy, and she tried to find out what was happening at the farm, but she didn't want to just turn up there. While she was the Jewish children's teacher and Erich and Liesl's foster mother, she had no real place at the farm in her own right. If she showed up there, it would look odd. She and Daniel were not a couple, and she wasn't Jewish, so she had no grounds on which to go there, no matter how much she longed for information.

The impression she got from the older children, however, was that the Jews too had put two and two together and made five when it came to Daniel. She was fearful that her association with him, however innocent, made her guilty, but she dismissed that thought. If that was the case, everyone he came into contact with was a potential accomplice.

She was so torn. It seemed impossible that the man she'd come to know so well, the person she'd become so close to over the past few months, would be a spy for Hitler's hateful regime. She just didn't believe it.

So often, once Liesl and Erich were asleep, she and Daniel discussed the war, and the way he spoke about the regime in Germany and Austria – and increasingly, every country in Europe, it would seem – made her believe he hated the Nazis for what they'd done to his homeland. He had such compassion for the little Jewish children who'd come on the Kindertransport...and his dedication to the farm...and his Jewish faith – none of it made any sense.

But then, a voice in her head spoke. Why would he have done such drawings of the RAF base? And why hide them? He was the only one with the training to do such technical drawings. They looked very professional, and the detective assured her that the notations were something that all engineers would understand. She wished she could speak to him. She'd started so many letters but hadn't posted any.

The little voice in her head that kept her awake at night insisted that there could be no other possible reason. She desperately didn't want to accept it, but if everyone on the farm believed the police and there was no evidence to the contrary, only one conclusion could be drawn.

And if Daniel was a spy, it meant he was a supporter of Hitler, and he would, by that token, support Hitler's treatment of Jews. Did Daniel look at Liesl and Erich and the others and want them dead? She shuddered.

She watched each day for the bus, and to her relief, one day it was Talia behind the wheel and not the taciturn Levi. She went out to greet her young friend; Talia had not been in school or called to the house since Daniel's arrest.

'Hello, Talia.' She smiled as she approached the bus. The children were playing in the yard, knowing Talia wouldn't mind giving them a few extra minutes. When Levi collected them, they went straight to the bus, as he had no patience for idling around. The June sunshine was warm, and watching the children having fun together, one could be forgiven for thinking all was right with the world.

'Coffee?' Elizabeth offered. She knew, as with Daniel, it was Talia's weakness. The little bag Daniel had managed to get his hands on was almost gone. Suddenly, a thought struck her – did he really get coffee from a grateful shop owner in return for work, or did he get it from somewhere else?

'You have some?' Talia's face lit up, and Elizabeth had to smile. She looked so young.

'I do, a little.'

'Ooh, Elizabeth, I would love a cup of coffee.' Talia jumped out of the bus and followed her into the school. The classroom was deserted and had a holiday air. There were a lot of finishing-up and clearing-away projects happening to make space for the new school year. It struck her how the children just assumed they'd be back in September. The prospect of the war being over any time soon wasn't to the forefront of anyone's mind now.

They made idle chit-chat as Elizabeth brewed some of Daniel's coffee; she managed to find a biscuit to go with it.

Talia sipped her drink gratefully. 'Mmm…that is so good. It tastes like Austrian coffee – I could almost be in Stephansplatz.'

'Well, it actually belongs to Daniel. He left it here.' Elizabeth was glad of a way to move the conversation around to him. The voices of the chatting and playing children wafted in through the open window. The older girls were sitting on the grass outside making daisy chains.

'Well, he won't need it now, I suppose,' Talia said with a sigh.

'Do you think he did it?' Elizabeth asked her straight out.

Talia shrugged and took a bite of the plain biscuit. 'Look, I don't know what went on, but the police don't just go around arresting people, do they? I mean, what does anyone really know about him, Elizabeth? He hasn't any family, it seems, not one person here could verify he was who he said he was, and he doesn't even look very Jewish…'

Elizabeth tried to hide her frustration. 'But lots of Jews don't look Jewish, whatever that means, and there are many people scattered all over the globe on their own with nobody to vouch for them – it's the nature of the thing – so I don't think that's very fair.'

'Look, Elizabeth, do yourself a favour and let the police handle it.' Talia fixed her with a gaze. 'You don't want to look any more guilty.'

Elizabeth was nonplussed. Did the people at the farm think she was somehow implicated? 'What do you mean, "not look any more guilty"? Why would anyone think I was guilty of anything?'

She froze. Liesl was standing in the doorway.

'Elizabeth isn't guilty of anything and neither is Daniel!' the girl blurted, and Talia spun around, all colour draining from her face.

'And you were supposed to be his friend, and now you're saying he's a spy when you know he isn't!' Liesl's chest was heaving and her cheeks were flushed. Elizabeth had hardly ever seen the girl so angry.

'Liesl, I was just –' Talia began, walking towards the girl.

'Get away from me! I hate you!' Liesl ran outside, leaving the two women standing in the classroom alone.

'I didn't mean that, Elizabeth. It's just we are all suspects, I suppose, anyone who had anything to do with Daniel, so...'

'Do the Jews think I'm involved?' Elizabeth asked directly.

'Look, it's hard. We all loved and trusted Daniel, and now it seems he's one of them. And you and he were close, so...'

Talia didn't need to say any more.

'I need to go to the farm. Can you take me in the bus?' Elizabeth cut through the younger woman's attempts at reconciliation. If the refugees thought she was somehow involved in some wrongdoing, she needed to clear her name. Her career, Liesl and Erich's future, their friendships and membership in that community all depended on it. This was getting out of hand.

'Of course, but I don't think...'

Elizabeth glared at her and Talia stopped.

'Let's go,' the younger woman said with a sigh.

Elizabeth sent Liesl and Erich home and got on the bus with the children. Somehow, she managed to chat with them and hoped she gave no indication of the turmoil she felt inside. If the Jews thought she was involved, then so would Mr Morris, the people of Ballycreggan, and even the police. She needed to nip this in the bud.

As the bus pulled in, she spotted Rabbi Frank. He was dressed as a farmer, and his small wiry frame was moving quickly. She got off the bus and followed him.

'Rabbi, please, I must speak to you.'

Daniel had explained that the rabbi escaped from Germany and his English was virtually nonexistent, but he had been eager to learn and within a matter of weeks was having rudimentary conversations. Soon after that, he was conversing freely.

'Ah, Mrs Klein. You have spared me a journey. I was going to call on you later.' His blue eyes were small and penetrating, and there was a serenity to him that belied his lean, sinewy body.

She assumed he wanted to talk to her about Daniel. She gave him a moment to collect his thoughts.

He had been assaulted by thugs on the street in Germany in 1938 and as a result was physically frail, but somehow he managed to pull his weight like everyone else on the farm. He was an inspiration to them all.

Apparently, he had family in Scotland, but he ended up in Ireland because he heard of the farm community and decided he would be more use there. He had tried to get more children over – he was a personal acquaintance of Florence Nankivell, the woman who organised the first Kindertransport out of Berlin – but all borders were closed once war broke out. Some Czech children did get out of the Netherlands towards the end, before that country fell under the Nazi jackboots, but despite their best efforts, the fate of the millions of Jewish children and their families still left in Europe was precarious to say the very least.

Rabbi Frank thrust his hands into the pockets of his trousers. He still wore his hat and had his curly peyot tucked behind his ears, but in his work clothes, he looked less imposing than when she'd seen him for Shabbat.

'I have some news for you. And it is not good. It concerns your cousin, Peter Bannon.'

Elizabeth felt her mouth go dry. 'Go on,' she managed.

'It is difficult to be certain, but it seem this man was arrested along with another gentile friend of him, and they both taken away. But these men, both is Roman Catholic, but only one, he comed back and told that this Peter Bannon is dead. I don't know more details. Someone tell this man when he goes to the Bannon's house that the children are in the Kindertransport, so he pass it on to the organiser in Berlin. I only get this now. Maybe it happen long time ago, I don't know.'

Elizabeth tried to remain composed. How could she tell the children this? 'And his wife?'

The rabbi looked blankly at her.

'Peter's wife? Did he pass that information on to her?'

'I don't know.' He shrugged sadly. 'But I think maybe he don't find her, if he try to get message to children by Kindertransport.'

Elizabeth felt tears sting her eyes. The idea that she would have to inflict such pain on Liesl and Erich by telling them what she knew was horrible. For the time, all thoughts of Daniel Lieber were gone.

She paused and looked into the rabbi's blue eyes. He was no more than five feet tall and looked ancient. Erich said once he thought the rabbi looked like a tortoise, and she could see why. It was hard to tell what age he was. He had several teeth missing and many scars on his head and neck.

'Should I tell them?'

He nodded sadly. 'Yes. You must. Then take them here and we will say Kaddish for him. His son is not yet bar mitzvah, no?'

'No, not yet... Erich is only nine. Liesl is eleven. She will have her bat mitzvah in two months' time,' Elizabeth replied.

The Rabbi didn't comment on that but nodded. 'Well, we will all say it for him, all the men, and his boy. So many now, we say Kaddish for so many.' He nodded his head slowly again. 'This prayer, you know it?'

Elizabeth shook her head. 'I'm not Jewish...' she began.

'Yes, but you know what is this prayer?'

'Well, it's a prayer for the dead?' she answered, unsure if that was what he was after.

'Yes. But don't say dead. Only to praise God. When you tell this to the children, say this. Their father is with God, and he is safe.'

Elizabeth envied him his pure, simple faith. The dead are gone to God, that was all there was to it. They were relieved of the suffering of this mortal world to enjoy the presence of God. There was comfort in it, if you believed it.

Did she believe? She hadn't practised any religion for most of her adult life. Rudi's faith didn't make any demands on her – he practised, but it was nothing to do with her – and her mother could practically say mass herself, so Catholicism just meant long boring hours in the draughty chapel with the priest wittering on in Latin and old people rattling their rosaries.

So she had no religion, but did she believe in God, heaven, all the rest of it? Did she think Rudi was somewhere else? She spoke to him often – less so, admittedly, since she'd come home – so on some level, she must believe the dead go on, mustn't she? She didn't know.

'Do you want I come to children with you?' The rabbi's eyes were kind, and she knew he meant well, but she needed to do this on her own.

She wished Daniel were here. He was of their faith and culture, and he'd be so much better at explaining than she would be.

Suddenly, not caring how it looked, she blurted out, 'Do you think Daniel Lieber is a German spy?'

He gave her a slow, sad smile. 'No. I do not think this. But...this world, I don't understand it. All this murder and suffering for why?'

'I don't know.'

There was nothing more to say. They stood in a silence of mutual understanding and empathy. Eventually, the rabbi placed his hand on her shoulder, patted it and walked away.

# CHAPTER 17

*L*iesl and Erich were on the village green when she returned. She'd walked all the way back – she needed to clear her head and try to compose the words that would crush their little hearts.

She called them and let herself into the house.

They burst in the door full of a story about how a dog had run into the schoolyard when everyone else was gone and how Mr Morris had to chase it and how the little Jack Russell did a wee in the hall. Erich was in fits of giggles describing the puffed-out principal and the puppy's antics, and she let him finish.

'What is it, Elizabeth?' Liesl knew by her face something wasn't right.

'Sit down. I have something to tell you.' She tried to keep her voice even as she patted the sofa on either side of her.

'Do we have to leave you?' Erich asked, stricken.

'No, darling, of course you don't. I told you, I won't ever let someone take you away, except your *mutti*.' She swallowed.

'Or Papa,' Erich added for clarity, relaxed now that his worst fear was not to be realised.

'My darlings, the rabbi gave me some news today about your papa.'

Oh God, how was she going to say those words? She offered a silent prayer to Rudi. *Please help me.*

'What about him?' Liesl asked, almost physically recoiling from her and her news.

'He is dead, my loves. Your papa is gone to heaven, and he is with God now.' The words dropped like stones.

'Did the soldiers kill him?' Liesl asked quietly, her face ashen.

Elizabeth nodded and whispered, 'They did, my darling girl. I am so, so sorry.'

'No!' Erich's high-pitched sob broke the silence. 'No, my papa is strong! He could fight them! He would not leave me and Liesl and *Mutti*! He wouldn't do it, Elizabeth, he wouldn't. You are wrong, and the rabbi is wrong... It's a lie!' He pummelled her with his fists, sobs racking his body, and she just held him tight and waited for the grief and anger and confusion to subside. Liesl was like a statue beside her.

'Did someone tell our mother?' Liesl asked, her voice leaden.

'I don't know, my love,' Elizabeth answered, dreading this line of questioning even more.

'But how did the rabbi know...and you... How did he find out?'

Elizabeth exhaled. 'There was a man with your father when he was arrested, and he was released or escaped or something, I don't know. He brought the news to someone involved with the Kindertransport. He must have known somehow that you two came on that, I suppose.'

'But did he tell our mother? Did he go to our apartment and tell her about Papa?' Liesl's voice was rising, the shock wearing off and panic setting in.

'I don't know, darling. I swear if I did, I would tell you...' Elizabeth tried to comfort her, but the girl shook her off.

'He must not have told her, because if he had, Mutti would tell us, not the Kindertransport people?'

Elizabeth had shielded the children from the worst stories coming back from Europe, but even they knew that life was close to impossible for Jews now. What should she do? Was it best to prepare them? They'd not heard from their mother, and they both seemed convinced the reason they had not received a letter was no letters were allowed in or out of Germany. That was probably true to an extent, and it was the best way for the children to come to terms with the silence. Nonetheless, they wrote religiously every two weeks. Surely if Ariella was there, she would find a way to get in touch?

'You would think so, Liesl, so I'm not sure, but I think he may not have been able to make contact with your mother. We've written often, telling her we're here, and we've not had a reply, which must mean your mother is no longer at your apartment.'

'So where is she?' Erich asked, his cheeks tear-stained and his breath ragged. 'Where is *Mutti*, Liesl? Where is she?' He began to sob again.

She said nothing, just let him cry into her chest as she smoothed his hair. Liesl caught Elizabeth's eye over his head, and in that instant, there was an unspoken sentence, a depth of understanding far beyond what eleven-year-old Liesl should have had to comprehend.

A single tear leaked from the corner of the girl's eye, and Elizabeth squeezed her hand. No words were needed.

The days afterwards were a blur, and Elizabeth did her best to comfort them. She fed them and held them and talked when they wanted to talk, but mostly they crept about the house like a pair of little ghosts. It broke her heart. They ate and slept and went to school, but it was as if the life had been drained out of them.

She tried to get more information, but the contact in the Kindertransport knew nothing further, and despite writing again to Ariella, there was no news from Berlin.

\* \* \*

ELIZABETH TOOK the children to the farm for the prayer service for their father and for so many others as well. It was a solemn occasion, and the Kaddish would be said for Peter every day for thirty days. Liesl and Erich didn't go every day, but they were frequent visitors. She encouraged it; she thought it gave them comfort to be around people who understood.

That night she went to Shabbat with Daniel seemed like a lifetime ago. She had tried to bring his name up in conversation with the others when she accompanied the children, but nobody wanted to talk about him. It was as if this were yet another betrayal, and they were meeting it with steely stoicism as they had so many others. She'd managed to glean that he was awaiting trial – he'd been charged and was in prison in Belfast. It was all kept very quiet, no mention of it in the papers, but the sentence for espionage was always death, and it could be carried out at any time.

Everyone seemed to believe he was guilty. She knew Rabbi Frank didn't believe it – he'd said so when he told her the sad news about Peter – but even he would not be drawn.

Talia drove the school bus now, and the children, apart from Liesl, liked her very much. She hadn't popped in since the day she told Elizabeth to stay out of it, and while she always said hello and was pleasant, there was a distance that wasn't there before.

The children were playing football in the yard after school as usual. A match, the locals against the refugees, had been going on every day for weeks. The score was currently eighty-seven goals to ninety-four.

Talia sat in the bus, waiting patiently. Elizabeth decided it was time to break the ice. She crossed the playground.

'Tea?' she offered with a smile. 'I'm afraid all of the coffee is gone.'

'Thanks.' Talia grinned and her face lit up. She must have been feeling bad about the rift as well. She jumped out of the bus and followed Elizabeth. As she sat on a desk, she examined her nails. 'Farming hands was not my plan,' she said with a rueful grin. 'I imagined by now I'd be swanning about the salons of Europe being lauded as the next van Gogh, not chasing bloody chickens and weeding turnips.' Despite her grumbling, she was good-tempered.

'So how are things at the farm?'

'All right.' She sighed. 'We are working hard though, the tractor is out of action, and this time we have no Daniel to fix it.'

The mention of his name hung between them.

'He feels so bad about everything. This is just another problem.' Talia took the cup.

'You've heard from him?' Elizabeth asked directly, trying to sound more casual than she felt.

Talia looked at her, but her hazel and amber eyes gave nothing away. 'Yes, he wrote to me. He just wanted to say he was sorry for... well, for everything, I suppose. We were close, both being from Vienna and all. He was afraid he'd made trouble for everyone.'

'So he admitted it?' Elizabeth's heart was thumping in her chest, cold sweat prickling between her shoulder blades.

'Well, more or less. He is sorry, that's all he said really.' Talia sighed again and gazed into the middle distance, lost in thought.

Elizabeth was taken aback by her reticence, as she was normally chatty and open.

'And the case against him?' Elizabeth was determined.

'He'll be tried under the new Treachery Act, I suppose, and the only sentence if found guilty is death, either by hanging or firing squad.' Talia's voice was flat.

The two women sat silently, neither one willing to show her hand.

'You think you know someone, don't you?' Talia said, suddenly looking very young.

'I don't know. I just... It's all so...so strange.'

'It is,' Talia agreed. 'I don't know what I expected, but he's from my city. I... Well, it doesn't matter now.' She shrugged. She looked like she had the weight of the world on her shoulders.

'I know you didn't know each other, but surely you must have had some mutual acquaintances even? Put two Irish people together for five minutes and they'll have found at least ten people they both know.' Elizabeth smiled. She wanted the conversation to remain casual, but she couldn't just leave it at that.

'No, but Vienna is a big place. He lived in Floridsdorf in the north part of the city, and I was from Liesing in the southwest. My parents – well, my mother, she was Jewish, but my father was agnostic. My mother used to go occasionally to temple in her younger days, I think, and once her parents died, she wasn't really practising, so I didn't know any Jews. We didn't live in a Jewish neighbourhood, so...'

Daniel had told her that Talia's parents were dead, two more victims of the hateful regime that was crushing Europe.

'I'm sorry about your parents. Daniel told me.' Elizabeth tread carefully, as it was not the done thing to raise with the refugees the fate of those left behind, but Talia was different to them; she was more open.

She nodded, acknowledging the sentiment but saying nothing.

'Have you been to see him in prison?' Elizabeth had been toying with the idea before this revelation. She didn't even know if she could, and if she did, would it bring doubt over her involvement? If it was just herself she had to worry about, she would have tried, but she had Liesl and Erich to think about. She could do nothing that might result in them being taken away from her. They'd lost so much already.

'No. I didn't. I think maybe the rabbi has, but I'm not sure.' She put down her cup. 'I'd better get them back – homework and chores and all of that.' She smiled. The conversation about Daniel was over.

'Elizabeth.' Talia turned back, her hand on the door. 'In class the other day, when I was drawing people, Erich came up and asked me if I could draw someone from a description. I didn't really know what to say, but he told me that they lost their photographs of their parents when your house in England was bombed and that he wanted to look at his father and mother's faces.'

Elizabeth inhaled raggedly. 'It's true they lost everything. So did I. I wish they had even one photograph. It's so hard for them. It's all just so...'

From nowhere, the tears came. Throughout the entire process, she hadn't cried – Peter, Daniel – but now, hearing Erich's simple request, it was the last straw.

Talia came back into the room and put her arms around Elizabeth. She rubbed her back as she cried, making soothing sounds.

'It is so hard, I know... I lost my parents too, and I know I'm older, but it's so difficult. And it all seems so senseless. If it is all right with you, I will try to do what Erich asks. I will get him to tell me about their parents and see if I can make a likeness. For Liesl too if she wants, though she doesn't like me much. It won't be as good as a photo, but it might be something.'

'Would you do that for them?' Elizabeth asked, drying her tears. 'It would mean so much if you could...'

'I can try.' Talia smiled.

'I would be so grateful, and I'll pay you of course...'

Talia raised her hand. 'No...nothing. We are together, we are the same, and we must help each other when we can.'

'Thank you, Talia. It would mean so much to them.'

The younger woman smiled again. 'You are a kind woman, Elizabeth. You didn't know these kids, nor even their parents, and yet you took them. And not just that, you love them like they are your own. It takes a special person to do that. Daniel saw that in you, and I see it too.'

Elizabeth looked down; she did not want Talia to see the devastation in her eyes.

'He talked about you a lot,' Talia said quietly.

'Well, that's all water under the bridge now, isn't it? If he's guilty, then he will hang.' Elizabeth heard the hard edge in her voice at the thought of Daniel being led to the gallows. Sweet, funny, kind Daniel. It was hard to accept.

## CHAPTER 18

*July, 1941*

'Do you think we'll be allowed to use the beach tomorrow? It's getting very hot now,' Erich said to Elizabeth as they sat down to tea and Irish stew. Meals were heavy on potatoes and carrots, which she grew in the back garden, and very light on meat. 'I'd love to go for a swim.' He sighed wistfully.

Elizabeth thought for a moment. 'I don't think so, not the main beach anyway, where I used to swim as a child. But I think they're talking about allowing access to the shale beach on the Ards road, you know the one? Where you caught the crabs last summer?'

'Oh, but we want to go to the sandy beach,' Erich complained.

'I know you do – we all do – but the RAF need all of that for the base, so we'll have to let them. Remember, everyone must do his or her bit, and if it means giving up our lovely beach, then that's what we must do.'

'Do you think the Germans will come again to bomb Ballycreggan?' Erich asked, his eyes worried.

With the ever-expanding RAF base not five miles away, the answer was obvious, but she would temper her response. The reality was the entire coastline, with all of the military activity, would be a very attractive German target.

'No, darling. This is only the countryside. I know we think it's a big base, but compared to the ones in England, it's not, so I doubt nasty old Adolf wants to waste his bombs here.' She smiled and piled his plate high with vegetables in stock. She was going to use the top of the milk for some strawberries from the garden for dessert.

After tea, Erich went to the village green to play football with the local boys and Liesl helped to wash up.

'I think they might try again to bomb the RAF base out at Ballyhalbert, though?' Liesl knew not to voice such opinions around her younger brother.

'Well, if they do, they'll get plenty of response.' It was all Elizabeth could say to reassure her.

'If the war is still on when I'm a grown-up, I'm going to sign up to fight Hitler.'

Elizabeth dried her hands and placed them on Liesl's shoulders. Since the news of her father's death, the child had become even more solemn. Elizabeth knew she believed her mother was dead too, and it was all too much pain to bear.

'I will pray every single night that by the time you're a grown-up, this mad world will be at peace once more. It will happen, I am convinced of it. With the Russians over in the east, we have help, and it is only a matter of time until it's over.'

'But even if it ends, nothing will go back to how it was.'

'No, it won't, but you can go home...' She was treading very carefully. There was a tendency to treat Liesl as older than she was because she was such a diligent, serious child, but Elizabeth had to keep reminding herself that she was only eleven. She would be twelve next month.

What would become of the Bannons when the war was over was never discussed, but Elizabeth wanted Liesl to understand that if she wanted to go back to Germany, then she could.

'Will we have to?' the girl asked, suddenly looking so much younger.

'Well, it depends.' Elizabeth wondered what the best thing to say was. Since that night when she told them about Peter, and Erich had asked where Ariella was, Liesl had not mentioned her. Before that, their *mutti* had been a regular feature of their conversation.

The same was true with a lot of the refugee children. They just stopped talking about their parents. Liesl and Erich had been with Elizabeth for two years now – a long time in the life of a child.

Elizabeth spoke slowly, watching Liesl's reaction to the words carefully. 'It all depends on your mum, doesn't it? Maybe she'll want to stay in Germany, and then you will want to go back to her. Or she might even want to come here. We have lots of room. But the decision will be yours, my darling, and for as long as you and Erich want it, you will always have a home with me.'

Liesl seemed to relax. 'Some of the others are saying that we'll be put back on trains and just dropped off at the station where we got on the Kindertransport.'

Elizabeth drew her into a hug. 'No, my love, that won't happen. Of course, those children whose families are back in Germany or Austria or wherever they came from will go home and be reunited. But those who don't, well, they'll have to stay here, I would imagine.'

'But we don't have to go back?' Liesl wanted to be sure.

'No, Liesl, you can decide for yourself.'

'I don't think I'll be going back. Do you?'

Elizabeth pressed her lips to Liesl's dark hair. 'I don't know, darling. I really don't.'

'Elizabeth?'

'Yes?'

'Was Daniel your boyfriend?'

The question caught her unawares. When Daniel was arrested, she explained as best she could what the police thought, and they had not asked about him since.

'No, no, of course he wasn't. Why do you ask?' Elizabeth prayed Liesl would not see that the question flustered her.

'Viola said that she overheard some of the adults talking about him up at the farm and that one of them said you were his girlfriend. And then the rabbi came in and got cross with them for gossiping.'

'No. Daniel and I were just friends,' she said firmly.

'But you think he is a spy?' Liesl asked, her gaze never leaving Elizabeth's.

She recalled Talia's revelation that Daniel had written and apologised. He had as much as admitted it.

'I really don't know what to think.' The child deserved for her to be honest. 'I can't imagine him as a spy, but then… I…I just don't know.'

'Could you just ask him?'

'But Daniel is in prison, pet…' Elizabeth had thought she understood.

'So why don't you visit him then, if you're friends? Or at least ask if you'd be allowed or even write to him. If someone said something about me or Erich, you wouldn't just accept it without question, would you?'

The child had a point.

'Well, Talia had a letter from him…' she began.

'But you only have Talia's word for that. You didn't see the letter, did you?' Liesl demanded, more forcefully now. The mention of Talia seemed to set her off.

'No,' Elizabeth admitted. 'But she has no reason to lie, and she said Daniel apologised for what he'd done –'

'Did he admit it?' Liesl interrupted. 'Did Talia say Daniel confessed?'

'No, not as such, but, Liesl, my love…' Elizabeth was desperate for her to understand. 'I can't just walk up there, demand to see him, you know. What he's accused of is extremely serious, and anyway, I promised Mr Morris I wouldn't have anything to do with Daniel now,' she finished miserably.

Liesl sat at the kitchen table and Elizabeth sat opposite. Liesl reached over and held Elizabeth's hand in hers. 'He's our friend. I don't think he did anything wrong, and deep down, neither do you. You could go and hear what he has to say, or at least write. I know you are probably trying to protect us, but we'd like you to go to see him.

We hate the idea of him being all alone in prison with nobody. After everything Daniel's done for us, doesn't he deserve that much?'

'Well, as I said, it's complicated...' Elizabeth began.

'But if I were put in prison for something, even if I did it, you'd visit me, wouldn't you?' Liesl said bluntly.

'Yes, I would... It's just –'

Before she could continue, Erich burst in. 'A Yank kicked the ball with us. He's from Mississippi, but he's in the RAF 'cause his mum is British, and he came over to join up. He said loads of other Yanks were trying to join up too, and a lot of them pretended to be Canadian so they could get in, but he didn't have to, and he gave me this.' The little boy spoke without taking a breath, such was his excitement. He held a stick of chewing gum aloft triumphantly as if it were the FA Cup, his eyes glittering with excitement.

The arrival of even more RAF personnel in the village certainly caused excitement, and the children, the boys *and* the girls, were mesmerised by their smart uniforms and confident swaggers. According to Talia – who attended the village dances with some of the other girls on the farm – and the village grapevine, there were quite a few romances going on with the local girls when the men were off-duty.

'Well, that was very kind of him. I hope you said thank you. And people from America are called Americans, not Yanks.' Elizabeth smiled at his excitement.

'I did.' He nodded, stuffing the pink gum in his mouth and ignoring her admonishment. 'And he asked me where I was from, and I told him, and he said he and the other chaps were going to bomb Hitler to hell for what he's doing.'

Elizabeth hid her disapproval. That was not the kind of talk she wanted around Erich, as he was quite riled up enough as it was.

'I told him to come over to meet you and to have a cup of tea. He's on the way,' Erich announced cheerfully.

'What?' Elizabeth said exasperatedly. 'Why?'

'Because I told him you were pretty and you had no husband, so he said he'd like to meet you. His name's Bud.' Erich couldn't understand the problem. 'He has chocolate and all sorts of stuff,' he said, as if to seal the deal.

Before Elizabeth had time to remonstrate with him further for inviting total strangers into the house, there was a knock on the door.

Erich ran out to the hall to answer it. 'That'll be Bud!'

Sure enough, a tall, slim, very young man in RAF blues, cap under his arm, was standing at her front door. He looked to be around six feet tall, and his dark-red hair was Brylcreemed back from his open face. He had freckles and a crinkly smile.

'Good evening, ma'am, I hope I'm not disturbin' y'all?' Elizabeth shot Erich a glance but smiled at the man.

'No, not at all. Erich was just saying how you played football with the boys.' Elizabeth struggled for something else to say.

'I sure did, ma'am.' He grinned. 'It's not like our football, but I'm getting the hang of it.'

'Good… It's…um…' Elizabeth allowed her voice to trail off.

'I'm sorry, ma'am, where are my manners? My name is Corporal Thomas Smith. But everyone calls me Bud.' He stuck out his hand and she took it.

'I am Mrs Elizabeth Klein, and this is Liesl. And you've already met Erich.' She smiled.

'Erich was tellin' me that he was from Berlin, Germany?'

She suppressed a smile. Americans always seemed to need to clarify both the city and the country. As if there were another, equally well known Berlin someplace.

'That's right.' Elizabeth wondered where this was going.

'And I thought maybe y'all could tell me a bit about it there?'

'About Germany?' Elizabeth was confused.

'Well, yes, ma'am. My daddy's family came from Germany, on my grandma's side, I think, way back along, sometime in the 1800s, I reckon. Anyway, since we are gonna invade at some point onto mainland Europe, and my mama told me to be as prepared as I can be for any situation, I was hoping that maybe Erich could teach me some German – if that's OK with you, of course?'

Elizabeth looked down at the boy she considered her son. It was the first time she'd seen him really happy since the news of Peter's death.

Bud mistook her silence for reticence. 'Or maybe you need to check with someone, ma'am? I can get you a reference from my CO saying I'm a decent guy if that would help?'

She knew the kudos Erich would gain at school from being friends with not just an RAF airman but an American to boot, but she didn't want to draw any further attention to herself. People in Ballycreggan were only just thawing after the Daniel episode, and she wanted to maintain her position within the community. Having a handsome albeit very young airman hanging around immediately after the departure of an alleged German spy wasn't going to do anything for her reputation, however innocent the reason.

Erich pulled on her hand. 'Please, Elizabeth, I really want to.' His eyes were pleading, and after all he'd been through, she couldn't refuse him.

'All right.' She addressed Bud firmly. 'But only once a week, OK? And it has to be here. He's only nine, and I need to keep an eye on him.'

Bud's face lit up. 'Thank you, ma'am, I really appreciate it. Erich told me how he can speak French and Italian as well as English and German, so I thought to myself, this is the teacher for me. I could come next Wednesday, around this time?'

His enthusiasm was infectious, and she had to stifle a smile.

'Elizabeth got a German dictionary in case she needed it for the refugees,' Erich announced, as if he weren't one himself. 'But you won't need that because I know all the words in English and in German.'

Liesl caught Elizabeth's glance and rolled her eyes slightly. Elizabeth knew Liesl had a much better grasp of languages than her brother, but she also knew that Erich needed Bud to be his friend. She smiled. If this Bud character was going to put a smile on their faces, he was as welcome as the flowers in May.

All that night, she tossed and turned, unable to sleep, Liesl's admonishment going round and round in her mind. If Daniel was her friend and she believed he was innocent, then why did she abandon him? Because Mr Morris told her to? Because of something Talia suggested? Because of what people would say? Because everyone else believed he was guilty? None of those reasons was good enough.

She assumed Daniel was allowed to write and receive letters – Talia had written and he'd replied – though they were no doubt heavily censored, and yet he'd never written to her. Maybe she imagined the closeness? Maybe if she wrote to him now, he would wonder what on earth the local schoolmistress was thinking by getting in touch with him? Nothing had ever been said or acknowledged between them, so maybe she imagined the growing closeness because she wanted it to be true. She could feel her cheeks burn at the thought of him believing she was chasing him like some pathetic old spinster.

As the weak dawn spread across the inky sky, she got up and pulled her mother's old beige flannel dressing gown around her. She got a shock when she passed the oval mahogany mirror on the landing. Wrapped in her mother's old robe and with her hair tied back in a bun as usual, she could have been Margaret. Had she turned into her own mother without realising it? Bitter, unfeeling, only willing to see her own side of any situation? She shuddered at the thought.

Elizabeth crept downstairs so as not to wake the children and started to make a cup of cocoa. She'd made a decision – she was going to write to Daniel and at least give him the opportunity to tell her the truth if he wanted to. She owed him that at least.

Of course, the moment the letter arrived at the prison in Belfast, word would undoubtedly come back to Ballycreggan. What if Mr Morris dismissed her for breaking her word? Perhaps she should tell him of her plan? Instantly, she put that idea from her mind. She was a grown woman who did not need his or anyone else's permission to write a letter.

She stirred the last of the cocoa into her mug and filled it with hot water and a little milk. It would be another week before she was entitled to get any more, so the children would have to survive without their bedtime drink.

The mug was one she'd bought her mother for Christmas one year when she was around Liesl's age. She'd found it in the sideboard with all the 'good ware' that was never used in the whole of her childhood.

It was white china and had pink roses on it. She remembered saving up her pocket money to buy it, thinking it was so pretty. Her mother opened it on Christmas morning and said, 'China is so hard to keep.' And that was it. No mention of how expensive it was, or how Elizabeth had saved up so hard to buy it. Nothing. Just a complaint about how hard it was to wash and stop from chipping. Typical Margaret. And yet she kept it safe all these years, alongside her most treasured possessions. Her mother was a conundrum, that was for sure.

Since coming home and eradicating all the dark-brown paint, the house of her childhood felt totally new, not at all like the one she grew up in. Having the children meant she had little time for reminiscences or sad lonely strolls down memory lane.

But now, at three a.m., the same clock ticking on the dresser, the sepia photograph of her parents on the shelf, it all felt eerily familiar and she was suddenly ten years old again. Her father was gone – he had died two weeks before her tenth birthday – and she could still recall the pain of his loss.

Jeremiah Bannon was a blacksmith, and his forge was at the other end of Ballycreggan. Her mother didn't like her being there, but Elizabeth loved the smell of the furnace and the leather, and she could sit for hours watching her daddy shoeing horses in his big leather apron. Skittish colts and mares, big old cart horses and even one or two racing horses were brought to be shod, and all of them relaxed under Miah Bannon's gentle hands. He would whisper into their ears, blow his breath into their nostrils and then expertly run his hands down each leg, from knee to fetlock. And without exception, the animals raised their hooves and allowed him to shoe them.

He made farm implements as well, along with all sorts of other things. At the end of the day, he would wash up at the cold tap in the forge yard, and she would run down the street to meet him. Her father would carry her home, and she would bury her face in his neck, savouring the smell of him.

She disliked her mother for as long as she could remember because of the way she treated her daddy. Nothing was ever good enough: He was too dirty coming home from the forge, he was too late, he didn't know the local gossip, he had ruined his trousers. All she ever did was complain, and all he did in return was take it. Elizabeth was convinced her mother nagged him to death.

One evening, as she was doing her homework at the kitchen table – her mother had forbidden her from running to meet him because she would ruin her dress – the local grocer knocked on their door to say that Miah had taken a turn (a euphemism for a heart attack) in the street. He had just been in Bridie's little sweetshop buying her a lollipop. It was still in his pocket when they laid him out, and her mother had taken it and thrown it in the bin. Her last present from her father, and Margaret threw it away.

Elizabeth blinked back the tears.

There was no cake or any reference to her tenth birthday as they were in mourning, but she didn't care; she just wanted her daddy back.

Margaret never cried once throughout the endless days of people calling to the house with cakes and sandwiches. Elizabeth recalled the long hours in the days after he died, sitting beside her mother on the front pew of the church as the entire village and every farmer for twenty miles passed by and shook her hand to say they were 'sorry for her troubles'. Throughout it all, Margaret was stoic. Elizabeth remembered thinking that her mother was actually enjoying it.

The old priest's housekeeper, Miss Tanner, died at the ripe old age of eighty, three months after Miah Bannon's death, and Margaret stepped into her role temporarily. She arranged flowers, cleaned the brasses, laundered the priests' vestments, and protected the priests from the parish. If you wanted to see Father O'Toole about anything, you had to first get through Mrs Bannon, a task close to impossible. The priests were minded like prize pigs, and the way she fawned over them made young Elizabeth cringe. But the priests called her a treasure and a godsend, and the temporary appointment inevitably became a permanent one.

All through school, Elizabeth had been such a good girl, studying hard, never giving an ounce of trouble. But still, nothing pleased her mother. Why was she never good enough? Liesl and Erich were not her children, but she loved them so much, and she tried in every way to build them up and give them confidence; she couldn't bear to see adults cut children down.

When the Reverend Mother suggested she go to England, her enthusiasm had little to do with an interest in teaching or a love of England and a lot to do with getting away from Margaret and Bally-creggan.

Little did she know on that day she left, at the ripe old age of sixteen and a half, green as grass, what life held in store. For twenty-one years, England had been good to her. It had given her a career she loved, a man she'd adored for the short time they were allowed, and a home.

Rudi. She wished she still had his photograph. From that first evening she met him in the chip shop, he'd been the only boy for her. He was so full of life and fun. He thought her very serious, but up to the time she met him, that was all she'd known. Rudi brought light and laughter into her life. He made her feel special and loved and beautiful.

Did she do it to defy her mother? She didn't think so. She had wanted her mother to accept him, but she was foolish even to try. Margaret would not have accepted anyone – well, maybe the local doctor's son or something like that. But Rudi had no qualifications, not even a trade – he just worked in his uncle's chip shop – so he wouldn't have been good enough anyway. The fact that he was Jewish just put the tin hat on it.

What would they say now if they could see her? Her father, Margaret, Rudi? Back in this house, with two Jewish German children.

She liked to think her father and Rudi would be proud of her. They'd never met, but they were both men who stood for something. She knew they would have liked each other. They were decent and hardworking and kind. Just like Daniel. Daddy and Rudi would both have liked Daniel too. They would have seen those qualities in him, that decency and goodness, and they would see how he made her feel.

She stood and went to the sitting room, opened her writing bureau, a lovely old piece that her mother had hated because it came from her father's home in County Cavan, and extracted her writing pad and a pen.

By the light of the lamp, she began.

*Dear Daniel,*

*I hope this letter finds you well and healthy. I am sorry for not writing before; I didn't know what to say. You have been on my mind since you left, and I wanted you to know...*

She paused. What did she want him to know?

*...that my experience was that you are a good man. I don't know any of the details, and I cannot explain why that map was where it was or who made it, but if you want to get in touch, I would be happy to hear from you.*

*Best wishes,*

*Elizabeth*

She folded it and placed it in an envelope before she had time to change her mind. It was a short letter, and nobody could accuse her of anything from reading it. He might not reply, and that was fine, but at least she'd reached out to him and felt like she'd done the right thing.

The following morning, she put the letter in the postbox in between two other letters she needed to send, and nobody was any the wiser.

# CHAPTER 19

*B*ud and Erich sat at the kitchen table, and Erich was explaining how the definite article changed in German depending on whether the noun was masculine, feminine or neutral. The weekly German lessons consisted of about fifteen minutes of German, followed by lots of joking around and, finally, Bud eating with them.

At first, Elizabeth was wary. Why would someone like Bud want to be friends with two German children? But she soon realised Bud was homesick. He wasn't cut out for the military life, and he missed having a family around.

'But, Erich, how am I supposed to know what gender every single thing is?' Bud complained. 'Like, if I say the dog is brown, then it's *der Hund ist braun*, but I can't say, "*Ich sehe der Hund*"?' He ran his hands through his copper-coloured hair in frustration.

'No.' Erich giggled. 'It's *Ich sehe den Hund*.'

'But why, lil' man?' Bud leaned back and groaned. 'This is sure one hard language you got here. I ain't never gonna get it.'

'I dunno,' Erich admitted. 'You just don't say it that way.'

Liesl looked up from her homework. 'It's because in the first sentence, the dog is masculine and is the subject of the sentence, so it takes *der* as the definite article. But in the second sentence, the dog is the object, and it is accusative case, so *der* changes to *den.*'

Bud looked over at her and grinned. 'How come y'all are so smart? When I was your age, I could jes' about catch a fish or say my prayers, but y'all know so much.'

Liesl and Erich giggled. They loved to hear Bud speak with his drawling American accent. He would tell them about Biloxi, where he was from, in the state of Mississippi.

'Tell us about the beach,' Erich begged, bored with the grammar lesson. He also hated to be outdone by his sister – Bud was *his* student. The stories of the seaside fascinated Erich; he'd never seen a beach before he left Germany.

'Oh, the beach in Biloxi is the most beautiful beach in the whole wide world.' He told the story the same way each time. He'd get all wistful and the children would giggle. 'You can sit and watch the sun set over the Gulf of Mexico and eat an ice cream and swim in the sea, and I tell you, it's God's own country. It's so lovely that I hated to leave, but I knew there was a job to be done. And I used to watch the seagulls and think to myself, boy, imagine what it's like to fly. I went and told my daddy I was gonna be a pilot over here in Great Britain, and you know what he says to me?'

The children knew this story by heart but loved hearing it. They parroted back, in a perfect Mississippi drawl, 'Boy, the only way you's gonna fly is if you stick some of them there turkey feathers where the sun don't shine and take a long run off a short pier.'

The story always ended with Bud and the children in paroxysms of laughter.

Life had fallen into a pattern of school and friends and trying to make do on the rations. The children usually went to the farm on Friday nights for Shabbat, and Liesl was preparing with some of her friends for her bat mitzvah.

The ceremony was to take place on the first Shabbat after her birthday. She was excited and knew her prayers from the Book of Psalms and the siddur perfectly.

The rabbi was conservative but had come round to the idea of girls being treated just the same as their brothers. After Daniel spoke on Liesl's behalf and convinced him to allow her and the other girls to have their rite of passage into adulthood, the rabbi had softened his attitude and Daniel had earned Liesl's unwavering loyalty. There was a sense that they were all in it together anyway; they might as well be completely in it. Rabbi Frank insisted that girls did not read aloud from the Torah when there was a quorum of ten men to do so, and while it rankled with Elizabeth that Liesl would be discriminated against like that, it wasn't her business. All churches, including the one her mother was so devoted to, were the same in her opinion – run by men, favouring men and trying to denigrate women. She had no time for any of them, but she hoped she was doing the right thing by the children for Ariella and Peter.

Talia called often in the evenings as well these days, she and Liesl falling into a kind of grudging acceptance of each other. Liesl was quiet when Talia came round and generally went off to read a book, but she was reasonably polite when she had to be.

Talia seemed to have taken a bit of a shine to Bud, and he to her. They met one evening at Elizabeth's, and Talia admitted shyly that he'd taken her to the pictures at Donaghadee and was even talking about a trip to Belfast when he got some leave.

It was nice to see the young woman with something to look forward to. Talia and everyone on the farm worked so hard, and they all lived in such a constant state of fear about their loved ones and the future, that it was hard to inject any joy. Bud seemed to cheer Talia up to no end, and he'd told Elizabeth that he really liked her.

Daniel never replied to her letter, and she'd given up hope that he would.

'Are you going to come to the dance?' Bud interrupted her reverie.

'Sorry?' Elizabeth had no idea what he was talking about.

'The dance, Elizabeth, on the base. Remember I told you all the girls from the farm are going, and all the locals too. It's going to be wonderful. I wish I were old enough,' Liesl sighed wistfully.

'Well, you are definitely not old enough, and I'm much too old, so we'll keep each other company while the rest of them go dancing.' She grinned.

'You're not too old, ma'am,' Bud said respectfully. 'I know lots of our officers would love to see a pretty lady like you at the dance.'

Elizabeth blushed and shooed him away. 'Go on out of that with your American sweet talk. I've no intention of going anywhere near a dance at this hour of my life.'

'Talia said that lots of ladies are going...' Bud tried again. 'I'd like a dance with you.' He winked at Erich, who giggled.

'Now Corporal Johnson, I think you might have your dance card full with a certain Viennese beauty, so you'd better keep your attentions there and not be worrying about old ladies.'

'You're not an old lady!' Erich was indignant. 'Mrs Morris is old and Mrs Ashe, but you're lovely and you are really young.' He placed his arm around her, and she squeezed him affectionately.

'I'll tell you what, Erich. Let's wait until you're old enough to go to a dance, and then I'll go too and you can dance with me. Is that a deal, as the Americans say?'

'All right,' he said doubtfully, taking her suggestion seriously, 'but by then you really would be an old lady. But I'll still dance with you.'

* * *

WORD ABOUT THE DANCE SPREAD, and the excitement around the village was palpable. There had not been a dance in years, and it was something to lift the young people out of the gloom and drudgery of war.

When word got out at the farm through the ever talkative Erich that Elizabeth was handy with a needle and thread, Ruth, Talia and two other girls arrived one afternoon begging for help. Armed with only a bag of mismatched work clothes, they had pitifully little to potentially turn into a party frock.

Abandoning the bag of rags they had brought, Elizabeth went rooting in the overstuffed cupboards upstairs and found some dresses. They were in a very old style as they'd belonged to her mother, but the material was good and hardly worn, and if she could take them apart, she could remake them into more fashionable dresses. The girls were thrilled, and Elizabeth was happy to bring some joy into their lives.

All evening, she had them carefully unpicking seams, then she remodelled the outfits, pinning them to fit and instructing the girls to sew them up in a different style. Liesl was her tailor's assistant, and eventually all four girls had something new to wear.

'Have you heard from Daniel?' Talia asked. She was standing in Elizabeth's bedroom in her underwear as she was fitted into her new dress. It was a lovely dark-red crushed velvet. Elizabeth could never have imagined her mother wearing something so decadent, but it accentuated Talia's dark features and curvy figure. She'd made a red lipstick with beeswax and cochineal, and the overall effect was lovely.

'No, I haven't,' Elizabeth said as she straightened the hem. She wondered if she should mention that she'd written. When she collected the children after Shabbat the previous week, she asked the rabbi for news of him. Rabbi Frank said that Daniel was doing all right, considering. He had no idea, though, when his case was going to be heard. It would almost certainly be held in private, and he feared that the next news could be that he had been executed.

She did not mention to him that she'd written. The rabbi never raised it, so she wondered if Daniel ever got her letter. If he had, he may not have mentioned it to the Orthodox rabbi, in case he was scandalised. The old man admired her, she knew that, and was grateful for the help she gave the children at the farm, but he would not have approved of a gentile and a Jew being involved in any way.

To say she and Daniel were ever involved would be to overstate the case anyway. A possible near kiss weeks ago hardly constituted a romance, but she found herself still thinking about him and worrying for him. The new Treachery Act enacted by Churchill in May was necessary, she supposed. Foreign spies could not be charged with treason because they weren't British, so this measure had to be introduced to deal quickly and effectively with enemy agents operating on British soil. The fact that anyone found guilty of treachery against Britain was executed was something she could not dwell on.

'Have you?' she asked as nonchalantly as she could.

'No. Nothing since that last letter. He just wants to be left alone, I think. His fate is sealed now anyway.'

Talia sounded sad but resigned. Elizabeth didn't want to be drawn on the subject.

'There, you're done.' Elizabeth led the younger woman to the full-length mirror on the huge mahogany wardrobe door. 'You look lovely.'

The two women stood, side by side, staring at their reflections.

'Thank you, Elizabeth. I...' Talia was pleasant and friendly but emotional exchanges made her uncomfortable. 'I...I'm grateful to you for this dress. It's the best thing I've ever worn. I...' She paused. 'I'm sorry that things didn't work out for you and Daniel. You would have been good together.'

Elizabeth was surprised. She knew Talia had feelings for him – it was obvious from the start – but she was now willing to concede that perhaps Daniel's affections lay elsewhere. They had never had a conversation about it, but she knew from others that Talia liked to make out that she and Daniel were more intimate than they were. But now that he was facing death, perhaps she was less inclined to peddle that notion. Elizabeth admonished herself for thinking so badly of Talia, but it did strike her as odd how easily the girl had put aside her affection for him.

Elizabeth did not acknowledge her remarks about her and Daniel but said instead, 'I don't think he's guilty, Talia. I don't know why, as I don't have any evidence, but I just don't believe he's a Nazi.'

The younger woman didn't flinch. 'I know how you feel, but whether he is or he isn't doesn't matter, though, does it? Nobody but him could have done those drawings, and he doesn't have anyone to vouch for him. He'll be tried and most likely convicted and sentenced to death. Everyone on the farm hates him, as they all believe he's guilty. And if I say anything to defend him, they'll think it's just because I have feelings for him.'

'What does Rabbi Frank say?' Elizabeth asked.

'I don't know. He's not very... Well, he doesn't say much.' Talia sighed. 'I just wish this was all over. I'm so sick of it all.'

It was so unlike Talia to react emotionally. Elizabeth tried to comfort her. 'It's been hard, and I know you loved him,' she said gently.

'I did. I do. But he doesn't want me. We both know that.' The younger woman sighed again, and it sounded like it came from her toes. 'It's hard to keep going, you know? I don't really have friends. Daniel was the closest person to me, and now...'

'That's not true. The girls downstairs are your friends, and the children in school love to see you coming, and Bud is crazy about you, as he'd say himself. You have your art... You have a lot going for you.'

Talia gave a small smile. 'I am selling some paintings, so that's nice.' She'd explained a few weeks ago that she had approached a gallery in Belfast and they were stocking her watercolours. She'd only sold a few – money was tight and frivolities like art were low on people's list of priorities – but it did allow her a little money, and she was generous with it. She bought sweets for the children, and even a scarf for Elizabeth.

'There you go. And you have a fabulous dress and a handsome American on your arm, so it's not all bad, is it?'

Talia gave what Elizabeth thought was a sad smile, turned and went downstairs. As Elizabeth was packing up her things, Liesl came into the room.

'She's gone, is she?' Liesl was talking about Talia; only one person caused the girl to be so bitter.

'Liesl, why do you dislike her? She likes you and Erich very much.'

The girl snorted. 'Talia likes me? No. Definitely not. She can't stand me and the feeling's mutual. She knows I can see through her. She pretends like she's like the rest of the Jews, but she's not. And she complains all the time about having to do the chickens, but everyone has to take their turn. She thinks she's so much better than everyone else.'

Elizabeth was taken aback. She knew Liesl didn't like her, but she'd never realised there was such animosity between them.

'I don't know, Liesl. I think she's all right. She loved Daniel, you know. This is hard for her too.'

'She didn't love him, or you or us – she only loves herself. She wanted people to think she was with him, but she wasn't. Daniel loves you and me and Erich. This is where he belongs, not with her.' It was all very simple to Liesl.

Elizabeth let it go. The child was hurt and grief-stricken about everything. Admonishing her about her feelings for Talia wouldn't improve anything.

# CHAPTER 20

*E*lizabeth and the children cycled along the coast road in the hot August sunshine. She had a picnic lunch in her basket, and Liesl had a blanket, towels and their swimsuits on her carrier. Erich insisted on balancing buckets and spades on his handlebars. They were so excited to go on their first beach picnic of the summer. The RAF had taken pity on the local children and allowed a small section of the public beach to remain open. It was a tiny section and more shingle than sand, but it was better than nothing. School was out for holidays, and four more weeks of freedom stretched in front of them.

Liesl's bat mitzvah had gone off very well, and she and several other boys and girls were now considered adults in their faith. The event was conducted at the farm in the little synagogue they had created, and a feast was held afterwards. Seeing the look on Liesl's face as she earnestly said her prayers in Hebrew and English filled Elizabeth with such pride.

She had offered a now-familiar silent prayer to Ariella and Peter as she sat on the hard seat listening to Liesl's confident tone. *She's a wonderful girl – they both are such special children. Thank you for trusting me, for giving your most precious gifts to me to care for. I hope and pray you will see them again one day, in this life or the next. In the meantime, I will do my best.*

The adults laid on as good a spread as they could after the ceremony. Liesl explained what would have happened back in Berlin if the war had not changed everything; there would have been a big party, and friends and neighbours would have come and celebrated the day with her family. The Jews understood how hard it was for the children – their parents should have been there, aunts, uncles, grandparents – but they did their very best to provide nice food and a cheery atmosphere.

As they turned down the road to the beach, they spotted Talia and Bud. He was sleeping on the beach, and she was sketching him as he slept. It was his first day off in two weeks. The children waved and Talia beckoned them over.

'Why didn't you say you were coming here?' Erich asked. 'We would have brought enough picnic for you.'

'Thank you, Erich, you are so sweet, but we must get back. We just came out for a swim, as it's such a lovely day.'

Bud stirred as Talia put away her art things. Their wet swimsuits were drying on a flat rock beside them.

Talia had remained true to her word and had done a portrait of Ariella and Peter that now hung in the hallway. Erich loved it, and Liesl said a polite thank you but never looked at it like Erich did. She did it from their descriptions of their parents, and apparently it was an excellent likeness; she really was gifted.

'What did you paint?' Erich asked as Talia rolled up the sketches and put them in her leather satchel that seemed to never leave her shoulder.

'No, you can't, nosy!' She tapped Erich on the nose playfully. Then in rapid German, she said, '*Es ist ein Geschenk*,' and glanced quickly in Elizabeth's direction.

'Oh...' Erich grinned.

'Hey, lil' man,' Bud drawled sleepily as he stretched. 'Hi, ladies. You're both looking beautiful today.' He smiled and got to his feet, agile as a panther. He planted a kiss on Liesl's head, and she blushed.

'So you can't join us for a picnic either?' Elizabeth asked. 'We can share what we have.'

'No thanks. We'd better get back. I'm back on duty at thirteen-hundred.' Bud groaned.

They stood watching as an army vehicle passed by on the narrow road above the beach. The surface was pockmarked and uneven now, as so many vehicles passed there daily on the way to and from the RAF base.

'It's really busy there now, isn't it?' Elizabeth mused.

'It sure is, ma'am, and I better get myself back there toot sweet.'

'What?' Talia looked at him in puzzlement.

'Liesl taught me – it's French for "right now", ain't it?' He looked to Liesl for confirmation, and the girl blushed to the roots of her hair again.

'That's right.' She smiled shyly.

'Anyway, I better go,' Talia announced. 'There's a pile of peas to be shelled and it's my turn, but at least it's not the bloody chickens!'

Liesl and Elizabeth shared a glance.

'See you all soon!' Talia called as they walked off the beach.

The day passed quickly. Liesl and Elizabeth spent most of it lying on the warm sand reading their books, while Erich watched the various military vehicles and even a few aircraft. He had been given a book by Mr Morris of all the various planes and was studying the shape and features of each one. For boys like Erich, these were just big exciting machines, and of course Bud filled his head with all kinds of stories of heroics. But Elizabeth saw the bombs and the bullets and the destruction they could cause. She tried not to think about her house in Liverpool. It was gone, along with everything in it she held dear. Still, they were only things. Liesl and Erich were her priority, keeping them safe and well.

She never allowed herself to think beyond the end of the war. It was too complicated. If, by some miracle, Ariella survived, then she would obviously want Liesl and Erich back. And that would be a joyous day, for them and for their mother, but the thought of letting them go tore at her heart. She loved them every bit as much as a natural mother would, but she would have no claim to them, and rightly so.

At around five o'clock, they began to pick up their belongings. The bread and jam had been devoured, the end of last year's blackberry and crab apple jelly spread on soda bread Elizabeth made with flour she bought directly at a small mill on the Donaghadee road. She used sour milk to raise it, and though she couldn't spare any butter or eggs as the recipe called for, it wasn't too bad.

They had strawberries from the greenhouse and pears from the tree her father had planted when she was small. She noted with relief that while neither child was heavy, they didn't look gaunt. Many of the children in school did, as the rations were barely enough to survive, but because her parents had the sense to plant fruit trees and her mother had a large greenhouse, they were able to supplement the ration with home-grown produce.

They cycled back, happy and tired from the sun and swimming, and she didn't notice the letter on the mat as she went directly to the kitchen to unload the remains of the picnic lunch and hang out the wet towels.

'Elizabeth, there's a letter here for you,' Liesl called, handing it to her.

It was handwritten and the envelope felt flimsy.

'Who is it from?' Liesl asked hopefully. The stamps were familiar, so it didn't come from abroad.

'I don't know, pet, but it's local.' She hated to dash Liesl's hopes it was from her mother.

She sat at the kitchen table and opened it, extracted the single sheet and began to read.

*Dear Elizabeth,*

*Thank you for your letter. It was wonderful to receive it. I hope you and the children are well and are managing as best you can in these troubled times.*

*I have something to say to you, but I need to say it in person. Because of my circumstances, I cannot come to you, so if it is possible, could you come to visit me?*

*The address is at the top of this page. If you feel like you can come, you will need to write to the governor for permission. I think he will allow it, as I asked him before I wrote. This is why my response took so long.*

*If you do not wish to see me, I understand, but please know that I hold you in the highest regard always.*

*Yours faithfully,*

*Daniel*

'Who's the letter from?' Erich asked, peering over her shoulder.

'It's from Daniel,' Elizabeth said. Her initial reaction was delight – he had contacted her – but the familiar doubts that plagued her at three a.m. came crashing in.

'Is he coming home?' Erich asked eagerly. He really missed Daniel.

'No, darling. He's still in prison.' She hated to see Erich's sad little face.

'Can I visit him then?'

'I don't think the prison authorities will allow children in.' She was lost in thought.

'But they'll let you?' Liesl asked, reading the letter over her shoulder.

'Yes, I suppose so, but I don't know...' She wished she'd opened it in private.

'But you have to go. You said that you didn't think Daniel did anything wrong. He's not a Nazi, Elizabeth – he hates them.' Liesl burned with passion. 'He does, he told us he does. He couldn't be like he was with us and be a spy for Hitler at the same time.'

'I don't think so, either, but the police would have let him go if they thought he was innocent, and they're not doing that. He's going to stand trial.'

'And then what?' Erich asked. 'If they say Daniel did something bad, will he have to stay in prison until the war's over?'

Elizabeth looked into his innocent eyes. For the thousandth time, she deliberated about what to tell him. Inwardly she raged; a little boy shouldn't have to face these grim realities all the time. His life should be carefree, and instead, it was a series of traumas. She couldn't bear to tell him that the crime Daniel was accused of carried the death penalty. Anyway, he was innocent until proven guilty, so she decided to postpone telling him yet another dark truth.

'We'll just have to wait and see.' She pulled them both into a hug.

'Go to see him, Elizabeth. He must be so lonely in that horrible place all on his own,' Liesl said.

'So will you go?' Erich asked.

'I don't know...' She was not going to be drawn and have to back out of it later. 'Maybe. I'll have to think about it.'

That night she tossed and turned, but by morning, she knew what she had to do.

\* \* \*

As DANIEL PREDICTED, the governor replied favourably to her letter requesting a visit. Sitting on the bus to Belfast, she tried to quell the feelings of terror, dread and excitement that threatened to bubble up inside her.

She longed to see him. She had finally admitted to herself that her feelings for him were more than friendship, but if the trial went against him, it would all be irrelevant anyway.

She tried to imagine what it was he needed to tell her in person. That he was guilty? That he wasn't? That he had feelings for her? That he didn't? Elizabeth tried to be rational. She was a middle-aged schoolteacher with two vulnerable children to care for. Apart from that night when they almost kissed, nothing indicated their relationship was anything other than friendship. Looking back, perhaps she'd imagined the 'almost kiss'. Daniel was a very attractive man, and she saw how women looked at him. He could have had anyone. Even the much younger, much prettier girls seemed to simper and blush around him in a way they didn't with the other men, so she was probably being a foolish old widow. She hoped she didn't meet anyone she knew today.

She had eventually decided to tell Mr Morris her plan. He would no doubt hear it anyway, as nobody could do anything in Ballycreggan without it being common knowledge within minutes, it seemed.

Sometimes, she longed for the anonymity of Liverpool, where everyone minded their own business.

She was nervous telling him, as he'd made his feelings about Daniel very clear. But in her heart, she knew he was a decent man, so she hoped as she knocked on his door that she could convince him she wasn't behaving like some silly lovesick girl.

'Ah, Elizabeth.' He smiled and looked up from his desk. Several children were out in the schoolyard playing despite it being summer holidays. A big rounders match was planned for the afternoon, so Talia had driven the children from the farm into the village. He stood up and looked out his window.

'I see the refugee children are settling in so much better now. There are lots of little friendships springing up between them and the locals, so that's a good sign.'

'Yes, they get along well, and it's good for the Irish children to see not all Germans are monsters.'

'Indeed.' He thrust his hands in his pockets. 'Please have a seat. Did you just pop in for a chat, or did you want to speak to me about something?'

Elizabeth's mouth went dry. The Morrises had been so good to her and to Erich and Liesl, and she hated feeling like she was going to disappoint him, but she needed to see Daniel.

'Well, I got a letter from Daniel Lieber,' she said quietly.

Mr Morris sat back in his chair, his hands in his lap, and said nothing, his face inscrutable.

'And he said he needed to tell me something, and asked that I visit him. The rabbi on the farm goes to the prison every week, but apart from that, I don't think he has any visitors, and so I would like to go. The children became very fond of him, and so did I, and I...' – she felt herself colour with shame – 'I just want to give him a chance to tell me what really happened.'

Mr Morris fixed her with a stare, his normally jovial expression gone. 'Elizabeth, do you not think that if Lieber were innocent, the police would have released him by now?'

'Well...I don't know. I just... I...' She faltered.

'Look.' He leaned forward and was kinder now. 'I understand. He came across as a very nice chap, and all the children loved him – I saw it myself up at the farm when I visited. He was invaluable up there, and he did a lot of great work here in the school as well. It's hard to imagine him as a German agent, but there is no earthly reason he would have been drawing such detailed maps of an RAF base, complete with coordinates and all the rest, if he didn't have orders from the Germans. An RAF base, I might add, that was bombed recently with targeted precision. Why else would anyone do that?' He paused and waited for her to answer.

'I don't know,' she admitted.

'And so, Elizabeth, must we not assume that the most logical explanation is the correct one?'

She didn't have any words of defence. Mr Morris was right, but she still felt she wanted to see him. 'I'm not proposing to interfere with due process. What will be, will be, and if Daniel is found guilty, then his fate is sealed. But I would like to speak to him nonetheless.' She tried to sound forceful rather than pathetic.

'Why?' She could tell he was trying to understand but couldn't.

'I'm not sure. I just want to see him, hear his side of things for myself. That's all really.'

Mr Morris sighed. 'As I said before, your private business and your personal life are just that, but unfortunately, the situation here is precarious. This village has accepted what many would see as undesirables because of their German or Austrian backgrounds – and though we don't say this out loud, let's face it, because they are Jews – into this community. The situation is far from simple, as you know. Catholics and Protestants here have their own issues going back centuries, and they are both united in their...if not mistrust of the Jews, certainly ambivalence towards them. Mistrust of Jews is one of the few things they can both agree on, if truth be told. However misguided that may seem, Elizabeth, it is the reality. And yet here we are.

'So when one of those that we welcomed is seen to be operating on behalf of the enemy, the enemy that is killing men from this country, this village even, well, I don't need to tell you, it could be a tinderbox.' He sighed. She could see he wanted to understand, and she knew he liked and admired her, but his priority was always going to be the community in Ballycreggan.

'You're a teacher,' he went on. 'The children of Ballycreggan are in your care. I know you are primarily with the refugees, but still... I think if it got out that you were visiting Lieber, it would reflect very badly, not just on you personally but on the school as well. Very badly indeed.'

'And if it didn't get out? If I was very discreet and it was only one visit? I do not intend to make a habit of this.' She could see what Mr Morris was saying and why he was saying it, and he was right. But what about Daniel's right to say his piece, or at least see one friendly face before he faced his fate?

'You don't think he is guilty, do you?' Mr Morris asked directly.

'No.' Elizabeth sighed. 'I suppose I don't.'

The silence was heavy between them. The voices of children playing and having fun outside belied the tension in the principal's office.

'Well, obviously, I can't stop you,' he said eventually. 'But I would rather you didn't go. So if you insist on visiting Lieber, I would ask that you be as discreet as is humanly possible.'

'I promise you I will.' She got up, and as she placed her hand on the doorknob, he spoke again.

'Thank you for coming to me, even if I couldn't convince you. You're a kind woman, Mrs Klein, even if in this instance, I believe that kindness is somewhat misplaced.'

She nodded and gave him a small smile.

True to her word, she didn't get the bus from Ballycreggan, choosing instead to go to Donaghadee and catch a bus to the city from there. Bud was off-duty so offered to take care of the children. He said he thought Talia would stop by once her chores were finished. Elizabeth told them she had a hospital appointment. She assured Liesl and Erich there was nothing wrong, but that she needed a check-up. Luckily, she'd wrenched her back a fortnight ago carrying a heavy box of school supplies, so she told them she was going to have it checked. Everyone had seen her hobbling about with a stick, so a doctor's appointment was perfectly plausible. She had not given them a decisive answer as to whether she was going to visit Daniel; she knew Liesl in particular was watching her every move.

She arrived at Belfast Central Station and walked to Crumlin Road Gaol. Her path took her along the banks of the Lagan, and she remembered coming into the city as a child with her father and him buying her a toffee apple. Like all cities across the United Kingdom, the toll of war was everywhere. The strategic bombing of the city in April and May just gone was not as catastrophic as the London or the Liverpool blitz, but nonetheless, the city was a mess of boarded-up buildings, sandbags and warnings to keep your mouth shut.

Servicemen and servicewomen made their way busily around, intermingling with the locals. The fact that 900 lives were lost and over 1,500 people injured in the bombing raids would not cause people to cower. Not for the first time, she marvelled at the resilience of her fellow countrymen and women. Mr Churchill had a lot to do with that, she knew. He was always making speeches, rallying everyone not to be downhearted or beaten. This was as much a war of ideas as anything. The deeply held belief of peace-loving nations in which people had a right to be whoever they wanted, practice whatever faith they wanted, was horribly juxtaposed by the horrors of what Hitler was trying to do. So often, out of earshot of the children, Daniel would tell her of the atrocities against the Jews he witnessed in Vienna before he got out – the public humiliation, the violence, the utter disregard for their civil rights – and she recalled how his dark eyes burned with intensity, with horror, at what he'd seen. She could never reconcile that Daniel Lieber with a Nazi spy.

As Elizabeth hurried along the river's edge, she saw for herself the gaping holes where buildings once stood, the general air of decrepitude that hung over the city like a damp grey blanket. Belfast was battered and bruised but soldiering on regardless.

Lord Haw-Haw, through his chilling propaganda broadcasts from Hamburg, promised 'Easter eggs for Belfast', and true to his macabre word, the Luftwaffe came and bombarded the city. The broadcasts, delivered in his plummy accent sometimes several times a day, opened with the sinister line, 'Germany calling, Germany calling'. The fact that he had predicted the attacks gave the awful man even more notoriety. The children in school talked about Lord Haw-Haw's broadcasts. Their parents listened, though it was forbidden by the authorities, because he sometimes gave lists of British prisoners of war. Anyone who had someone missing in action tuned in faithfully. He was a fascist and an anti-Semite, and Elizabeth refused to allow him into her home. His accent was completely contrived, and in lots of ways, he was a ridiculous character, but his pseudo-aristocratic tones crackling down the airwaves gave people the creeps.

She shook off thoughts of Germans; that was not the mindset she needed. She crossed Nelson Street, and as she did, she spotted someone very like Talia on the other side of the road. She did a double take. Bud had seemed sure Talia would drop by Elizabeth's house that day, and Talia had never mentioned going to Belfast, though she had popped in to Elizabeth's the previous day for a cup of tea. Shielding her eyes from the sun, Elizabeth saw the woman go into what looked like a small gallery. She had several rolls of paper under her arm. That made sense. It probably was Talia. Elizabeth knew she was selling some of her artwork in a gallery in the city – that must be the place. Elizabeth hurried on, glad she'd not run into her; she didn't want anyone to know where she was going.

As the large limestone building grew closer, she felt the warm sun on her face. She had dressed carefully in her mother's best dove-grey coat and black and silver cloche, both two decades old. It was an outfit her mother had bought specially for a trip to Knock Shrine in Mayo after Elizabeth's father died. It was one of the many anomalies of Margaret Bannon: Though she was so religious, she was quite frivolous too; she loved make-up and clothes. The outfit was a bit dated, Elizabeth was sure, but nobody had anything new any more, so fashion was taking on an eclectic flair. Figure-hugging dresses and skirts were all the rage, young girls claiming it was because of a shortage of material – and it was true clothing was hard to come by.

But Elizabeth knew they loved showing off their svelte figures, made so by rationing, in the new clinging styles.

She took off her coat, as it was too warm and she didn't want to perspire. Under the coat, she wore a pink blouse with red roses carefully embroidered on the collar by Liesl as a gift, and a dark-red pencil skirt, which hit below the knee. She'd pinned her chestnut hair in its usual way, though she did soften the look by framing her face with gentle waves. She wore no make-up, despite finding a whole box of the stuff among her mother's things. Margaret Bannon certainly didn't mind putting something as sinful as lipstick on her sour face.

What would it be like? She'd never set foot in a prison. Would he look different? A moment of panic threatened to make her turn on her heel as she got closer and closer. What on earth was she doing? She swallowed down the lump in her throat. It was just a conversation. Nothing more. She forced her breath into a steady pattern, raggedly inhaling, holding and slowly exhaling. Bit by bit, her heart rate returned to normal.

As she approached the black railings that formed the perimeter of the prison, she took her letter of invitation from the governor out of her handbag with shaking hands and showed it to the guard on duty. Her stomach churned, and she was too hot.

He examined it closely, taking the letter into the guard's hut, and then looked at her. 'Follow me,' was all he said. They walked up to a heavy wooden door.

The Crum, as HMP Belfast was known, was notorious. Women, and even children had been incarcerated there over the years, and up until the early 1900s, public hangings were the norm. She'd read somewhere months ago that now they had an internal death cell, where inmates sentenced to death were hanged, their bodies buried in unconsecrated ground inside the prison walls – only their initials scratched on the wall gave any indication who they were. The image in her head made her blood run cold. Was this going to be Daniel's fate?

She followed the guard through the main entranceway, where she was instructed to wait. He left. The building was a grey stone on the outside, and inside, it was painted uniformly a pale green. Doors, walls – everything got the same colour. It had been warm outside, but standing there, she shivered. The air was dank. The flagstones on the floor were eroded from generations of feet – those of the condemned, and those employed to guard them. Several officers milled about, but there were no signs of any prisoners. Eventually, another officer approached her.

'This way, please, ma'am,' he said, indicating a nondescript corridor off to the right. Green walls again, but there the floor was covered in beige lino that was lifting in the corners. This new officer showed her into a small, sparsely decorated room with just a battered table and two chairs. A high window let in a little light, though the bars on it obscured any view even if one were tall enough to see out.

'Have a seat, please,' the officer instructed, and he left, closing the door behind him.

She tried not to shudder. The room was terrifying, not to mention the prison itself. She felt like she was struggling to breathe, and a sense of claustrophobia she had not experienced since childhood threatened to engulf her. She forced herself to inhale deeply again, her breath raspy and ragged on the exhale.

She was startled as the door opened a few moments later. An officer entered, with Daniel behind. He looked much thinner than the last time she'd seen him, that night they drank whiskey in her sitting room beside each other on the couch. He wore a prison-issue grey shirt and trousers. The officer stood in the corner of the tiny room, his eyes on the opposite wall, as Daniel sat down. He was handcuffed, and the officer made no move to remove the shackles.

He smiled slowly, and his eyes crinkled up as they used to. 'You look lovely, Elizabeth. Thank you for coming.'

'How are you?' she asked, very conscious that the officer was listening to every word.

He shrugged. 'All right. I am kept alone so I do not speak to others. I think these are the first words I say since Rabbi Frank came last week. Forgive my English. I have been in German in my head.'

'That must be so lonely, but at least you can send or receive letters.'

He shrugged. 'Not really. I asked to be allowed to write to you, and they gave me your letter, but that was the only one I ever got in here. Nobody would write to me anyway – why would they? They all think I'm a Nazi.'

'But you wrote to Talia?' she asked, on some level wanting to catch him in a lie.

He shook his head. 'No, I never wrote to anyone else, just you.'

'She said you did.' The words hung between them. 'She said you apologised.'

His brow furrowed and he sighed. 'I didn't. Even if I want to, I would not be allowed. The rabbi ask that I be allowed to reply to your letter. They were not really even willing for that. He must have convinced them, I don't know how.'

'But why would she lie?' Elizabeth was confused.

'I don't know, Elizabeth. She...she told me once that she loved me. She wanted us to be more than friends. And I refused, as she is too young, and by then anyway... Well, I wasn't interested. Maybe she wanted... I don't know...' He stopped.

He was telling the truth, she was sure of it, but speculation would get them nowhere at this point.

'What about your English friend?' Elizabeth asked. 'Could your legal people contact him to vouch for you?'

He smiled. 'I don't have legal people. I have one man, he works for the British government and is convinced I'm guilty. He is a solicitor, but even he doesn't believe me.' He sounded so sad; she wanted to reach over and hug him.

'Though they did say they would be questioning Stephen. I hope he is not in trouble now for bringing what they think is a spy from Austria. I am embarrassed that he will get the blame.'

Elizabeth's heart broke at the raw pain and grief behind his words. 'Would you like me to contact him on your behalf?'

Daniel just nodded. 'Yes, please, if you would. I just want to apologise to him for all the problems, and to say thank you... He saved my life.' His voice was barely a whisper.

'Are you... Are they treating you properly?' she asked, not caring what the officer thought of her question.

Daniel's hair was much greyer than it was last time she'd seen him. He had been dark before, with a little grey at the temples, but now his thick hair was streaked with it. He'd shaved, and his face had some small nicks.

'Yes. I'm all right. How about you and Liesl and Erich?'

'They're fine. They say hello. They got bad news that their father was killed – well, he was murdered actually.' She was not going to sugarcoat it. 'It is so difficult for them, especially since we have not heard anything from Ariella.'

'Oh, that is terrible. How did they find out?' He looked genuinely anguished, and she had to remind herself that she could be speaking to a German spy, a man who supported the regime that murdered Peter Bannon.

'A witness,' she said simply.

Daniel seemed to understand her reticence, nodding sadly.

She did not speak, but waited for him. She would not make this easy for him, no matter how much she was confused about her feelings.

'I wanted to tell you, Elizabeth,' he said eventually, his eyes blazing with intensity, 'that I did not make these drawings. I know it look like it was me, and nobody else can do drawings like this, I know that. And nobody else had that paper. All of the evidence says it was me. But whatever happens – and I think I will hang – it is important that you know it was not me. I never saw those drawings until the day the police come to arrest me. I swear to you.'

He never raised his voice, and his tone was neutral, but she held his gaze and knew, as sure as she was of anything, that he was telling the truth.

'But have you told the police this?' she asked.

He smiled. 'Yes, many times. But they say, if not you, then who?'

'But you're Jewish, so why would you support what Hitler is doing? It makes no sense...'

Daniel placed his shackled hands on the table, and she placed hers on his. He smiled and closed his eyes for a moment until the officer barked, 'No touching!'

She removed her hands, and he spoke.

'I am by birth, but as I told you before, I was raised a Catholic. Though looking back, my parents were not very enthusiastic Catholics.' He gave a rueful smile. 'I suppose they felt they would do better in Vienna if they were not Jews, who knows? They were unusual, an odd couple really. My mother was a suffragette. I remember the day they passed the law, in 1918, that women could vote. I was only a schoolboy then, but she was so happy.' He smiled at the memory. 'My father was an engineer – I followed him – and he was more interested in the machines of this world than whatever awaited him in the next. To be honest, I think they were probably both atheists.'

She wished she could touch him again, but she didn't dare.

'When my brother and I were born, they did not circumcise us, as would be normal with Jewish boys. So this is another reason the police think I am lying.'

Elizabeth tried to process this newest piece of information. 'Oh, I see...' She flushed red at such intimate knowledge.

'I'm sorry. I do not mean to embarrass you, just to explain...' It was his turn to look shy.

'No, please go on,' she said. This was too important.

'Very well. I told Rabbi Frank about not being circumcised, but only since I was arrested. If I had mention it before, then perhaps... But I did not. I only told you about what my parents did, nobody else, as I didn't want people to think bad of them, I suppose. The rest of the community on the farm thought I was just raised secular, and that was why I don't know about the Jewish faith. With everything else going on, I didn't think it was so important...' He sighed. 'Now, it doesn't matter. There is nothing anyone can do. I don't blame them. If I were a policeman, I would think I was guilty too. So many Jews are dead now, more to come I'm sure – I'm just one more.'

He gazed longingly in the direction of the barred window – a glimpse of blue sky could be seen outside – then dropped his head once more. 'Do you believe me?' he asked, avoiding her eyes. He picked at one of his fingernails.

'Look at me,' she said, her voice barely audible.

He looked up, and his intuitive eyes locked with hers.

'Do you swear to me, on the lives of every one of those children on that farm, that you are not a German spy?'

'I swear to you, Elizabeth. I am not.' He held her gaze and she didn't flinch. In that moment, it was as if she could see into his soul. He was innocent.

He was resigned to his fate, she could see that. He wasn't trying to get her to campaign to have him freed or anything like that; it was just important to him that she believed him.

'Then I believe you,' she said simply. 'How can you stand it, to be facing trial for something you didn't do?'

'I've had a lot of time to be angry, to feel frustrated, but in the end, I don't know...' He ran his shackled hands through his hair. 'So many of my people are dying, worked to death, beaten, attacked... I'm just one more. I want to live so much. I have so much I want to do. But you believing that I did not – could never – do such a thing is very important to me. More than you can know. That night, when we... I wish I could have kissed you...' He stopped.

'Time's up.' The officer moved in Daniel's direction and yanked him up roughly.

'Can I come again?' she asked, frantic now. Surely this would not be the last time she saw him?

He shook his head. 'No. The governor only allowed me one visit. My trial will be soon, I think, and then...well...' He shrugged again. 'Be happy, Elizabeth. You're very special to me.' Unshed tears shone in his eyes.

And then he was gone.

# CHAPTER 21

*E*lizabeth was shaken as she found herself escorted back out onto the street. She just stood there, unable to move. Daniel was possibly only days away from being executed for something he didn't do. She had to do something. But what?

Her mind worked overtime. What was going on? If Daniel didn't draw those things – and she was sure he didn't – then someone else did. Who could it have been?

She was lost in thought as she retraced her steps back to the train station, going over and over everything in her head. At the corner of Fredrick Street and Nelson Street, she saw the gallery again. She crossed and stopped outside, looking at the pieces in the window. Two of the three paintings on display she recognised as Talia's.

She peered in. There was nobody but an older man inside. On a whim, she pushed the door in. It made a little tinkle, as there was a bell attached. The man appeared from the back, wiping his hands on a cloth.

'Good afternoon, madam. Can I help?' he asked. He was tall and straight-backed, with a muscular build and hair that grew almost to his shoulders, luxuriously wavy and grey. He had a large waxed moustache. He wore a cream suit and a purple shirt and had a black silk scarf tied at his throat. He looked distinguished, bohemian and certainly unforgettable.

'Oh, yes, please. I wanted to buy a painting for a friend as a birthday present, and I liked the ones in the window.' She had no idea why she was lying, but she went with it.

'The oil or the watercolours?' he asked, his eyes never leaving her face. He smiled, but it wasn't a warm smile. There was something guarded about him. He had a Belfast accent, cultured, from the wealthier suburbs, not the heart of the city.

'Oh, the watercolours – they're lovely. How much are they?' she asked.

'They're sold, I'm afraid,' he said, with another insincere smile.

That was odd.

'Oh, what a pity. What about those?' She pointed to three other paintings she knew were Talia's mounted on the left-hand wall.

'Sold as well.' He didn't offer her anything else. Surely Talia's paintings could not have all been sold that quickly? She'd seen her with a bundle of them under her arm not an hour ago. Something was definitely awry.

'Oh dear. I really like this artist. Is he local?' she asked.

'Aye, he is. I'm afraid I don't have any of his work for sale right now, but if you pop back in a few weeks maybe?'

She got the distinct impression he was trying to get rid of her. Also, why was he pretending the artist was a local man? There were other paintings in the gallery too; surely any normal businessman would try to sell her one of those.

'What's the artist's name?' she ventured. 'If he's local, perhaps I could contact him myself?' She smiled innocently.

The man held her gaze a second longer than was necessary. 'Frank O'Doherty,' he said silkily, 'but he's a Donegal man, lives out there on an island, a recluse, you know? You won't be able to contact him, I'd say, but you can try if you like.' He started to turn away. Clearly the conversation was over.

'Oh well, thanks anyway,' she said as she left. He didn't say goodbye or wish her a good day.

All the way home, she reflected on what had just happened. So many questions. Was something going on? Did this peculiar situation in the art gallery have anything to do with Daniel's arrest? Why would Talia lie about getting a letter from Daniel? Were those things connected?

She was glad she never told the children she was visiting Daniel so she was spared the barrage of questions. They were friends now with all of the local children and had adopted their strong Northern Ireland accents. Hearing 'Oi! Pass the ball, Pawel,' or 'Elizabeth, can Simon and Viola come to our house to play?' was commonplace. Even the boys and girls from Poland, Austria, Germany and Czechoslovakia, who by now all spoke English fluently, used local colloquialisms and spoke with a County Down accent.

She went through the motions of the evening once she was home, her mind only half on the job of preparing supper. Amid the children's chatter, round and round the ideas went in her head, but there was no manner in which she could even try to protest his innocence.

Whatever about Talia, Daniel did not draw those plans. He was not a German spy, despite the evidence pointing to the contrary, and with each passing day, it was looking more likely that he would hang.

Once the children were in bed, she wrote to Stephen Holland, as Daniel had requested, and relayed the information that she believed him to be innocent and that Daniel was sorry for any pain he'd caused his old friend and wanted to express thanks for his help in getting him out of Austria.

The next morning, Elizabeth bumped into Talia in the post office where Elizabeth had just bought some more stamps, one of which she affixed to Stephen Holland's letter and the remainder she put in her purse. The children wrote to Ariella every two weeks, regardless to the fact they never got a reply. Elizabeth had no idea whatever became of the letters and cards, but it did the children good to write to her and tell her their news, and for as long as it gave them comfort, she would supply paper, envelopes and stamps.

'Hello, Talia, how are you?' Elizabeth greeted the girl as nonchalantly as she could.

'Busy.' Talia grinned. 'It's harvest time, so we are picking and bottling for the winter, and it's all work and no play. I'm trying to get some painting done, but I've no spare time.' The young woman's beautiful open face was the picture of honesty.

'How is that going? Are you selling many at that gallery?'

Talia shrugged. 'One or two, but not really. I suppose people have better things to do with their money at the moment.'

More lies if the man in the shop was to be believed. Elizabeth gave nothing away. 'Are you in a hurry, or do you have time for a cuppa? I still don't have any coffee, but I can offer you a cup of weak tea?'

Talia posted her letter as they went out into the sunshine. 'Sure, that would be nice.'

The younger woman groaned as they walked along. 'I so miss coffee. I swear at night I can smell the beans roasting. There was this café on Leopoldstrasse – Otto's – and oh my goodness, the aroma. Baking pastries, coffee, fresh bread... The others say I am driving myself and them mad going on about it all the time, and of course, I should be grateful to be alive, but I think if I have to eat one more bowl of porridge, or that hard brown bread, I will scream.' Talia sighed dramatically and Elizabeth grinned.

'It's not that bad, and look at what lovely figures we all have. That's a bonus, isn't it?'

'Most of us have. I swear that Ruth is actually gaining weight. She must have secret food stashes.'

Elizabeth admonished her. 'Ah now, Talia. Poor Ruth. That's not nice.'

'Neither is she!' Talia exclaimed. 'I swear she tries to get me in trouble all the time. It was my turn to do the bloody chickens, and I swapped with one of the kids – I gave him some chocolate that Bud had given me – and she brought it up at the council meeting. That misery Levi backed her too. She talked about how people should not be allowed to bribe others to do their jobs. Honestly, that woman has it in for me. They think because Daniel and I were close that I'm somehow implicated in his wrongdoing. I can't wait to get away from here. Bud says when the war is over, we can go to Biloxi.'

'The way he describes it, it does sound wonderful,' Elizabeth agreed as they passed the children and their friends on the village green.

She resisted the urge to question the young woman further, instead saying, 'I thought Ruth was thinking of going back to Dublin?'

Before she answered, Talia ran playfully into the football game that was going on and stopped a sure score by the refugee team as it blazed to the local's goal area. Shouts of protest in all the languages of Europe erupted amid the cheers of the locals, but Talia just threw her head back and laughed.

'She was, but now she's all calf eyes at Levi, though why is anyone's guess. He looks like an angry hawk with his hooded eyes and long nose. Now that she's got people on her side to gang up on me – well, just Levi really; they are a perfect match, grumpy and grumpier – I wish she'd just go. She went to the dance and scowled at everyone.' Talia rolled her eyes. 'Though you did an amazing job on that dress. She did look much better than she usually does.'

Elizabeth considered rebuking her again. It was so unlike the normally sunny Talia to be so catty, but the young woman and Ruth had never hit it off from the start. And in fairness, Ruth was probably just as bad. It was true that she was always telling tales to the council about Talia; even the children knew it.

'So is there something going on with her and Levi that's keeping her here?' She and Talia went into the house. Elizabeth put the kettle on.

'Oh, who knows? I don't even know what's happening with that. If she and sourpuss Levi have something going on, at least it means nobody else has to put up with either of them. Everyone is just wondering about Daniel, though nobody mentions him, of course.'

'So have you heard any more from him?' Elizabeth asked, glad the conversation had naturally come around to him again.

'No. Nothing since that one letter saying he was so sorry.'

'The rabbi says he is protesting his innocence.' Elizabeth forced her tone to stay conversational.

'Yes, well, I suppose he would. I didn't believe he was a spy, but then, who else could have done those drawings?' Talia sighed. 'I just wish...'

'What?' Elizabeth prompted.

Talia looked pensive. 'I don't know. I suppose I'm just so confused. I'm shocked. They... We all thought Daniel was one of us, you know? But...it's so hard to know.' Talia's wide eyes were innocent. She paused, and then she said, 'I miss him.'

Elizabeth nodded, unsure what to say.

'I love him. I know he doesn't feel like that about me. I...' The young woman's cheeks flushed. 'I tried, ages ago, to see if it would be something else, but he...he never saw me like that.'

'Well, he is much older...' Elizabeth tried to sound impassive.

'That's not why he didn't want me. You know that. I...I can't bear the thought of what they might do to him...' Fat, silent tears slid down her cheeks. Talia was normally so tough that it was very strange to see her so emotional.

Elizabeth put her arms around her, allowing the younger woman to sob, thinking either Talia was the world's best actress or her lies had nothing to do with Daniel's arrest.

* * *

BUD CALLED EARLY the following Saturday morning. He was being relocated to a base near London any day now, and he was devastated. He didn't want to leave Ballycreggan – he'd become so attached to Elizabeth and the children, and he loved Talia. Elizabeth made him tea and listened as he poured his heart out.

She cursed bloody Hitler again in her mind. Such misery he was causing, all over the world. Men, women and children were in despair because of him. She had never hated anyone before, but by God, she hated Adolf Hitler.

'And Talia can't even come with me. Her visa means she must stay here.' Bud was crushed.

'But, Bud, you wouldn't want her over there anyway, would you, with the danger of bombs and fires and everything? At least here, she'll be safe.' Elizabeth tried to reassure the young man. Bud was in his early twenties, but in lots of ways, he seemed younger than that. He was by no means mentally deficient, but he saw with a child's eyes. It was why he got along so well with Erich and Liesl, and in lots of ways, Talia was the same. The pair loved playing and threw themselves into the games with every bit as much gusto as the children did. Her little household had become a home for Bud and Talia. They called without invitation, and she liked having them around. Biloxi and Vienna seemed so far away, and they were both seeking a little normality. Elizabeth was glad to supply it.

'But what if she forgets me, Elizabeth?' He looked like a lost puppy.

'She won't. She's mad about you – everyone can see that.' Elizabeth hoped that what she told him was true. Talia did seem to genuinely like Bud, but her confession that she loved Daniel threw doubt on it.

'Today is my last leave before I'm shipped out. There's a big shipment of stuff coming from the States tomorrow, so it's all hands on deck. But she's not even here,' he said miserably.

Elizabeth wondered if Talia ever told Bud how close she was with Daniel. The attack on the RAF base was considered a close shave, and though there were fatalities and injuries, the authorities deemed it could have been a lot worse. The hangars remained standing, their precious contents still operational. Bud never mentioned Daniel's name, and Daniel never came up in conversation, but everyone knew who was to blame.

Bud only cheered up when Erich arrived with the new model plane Elizabeth had bought him. It needed to be glued together, so Bud and Erich set happily to work, spreading all the pieces out on the kitchen table.

She noticed that Liesl had not yet come down to breakfast, so she went to investigate. She knocked gently on the bedroom door, and when there was no answer, she opened it.

Liesl was in bed, her head barely visible.

'Liesl,' Elizabeth said gently. It was most unlike her not to get up. 'Are you all right? Do you feel sick?'

The girl opened her eyes, and Elizabeth could see she'd been crying.

'Oh, Liesl, what's the matter?' Elizabeth was shocked. Erich was very emotional, often bursting into tears. But she comforted him, and he went off again about his business. Liesl was much deeper, and she didn't open up easily.

'I want my mother,' she said simply.

'Oh, darling.' Elizabeth gathered her in her arms. 'I know you do. You must miss her terribly. I wish I could find her for you, I really do.'

'She's dead, Elizabeth. I won't ever see her again.' Liesl was sure.

'You don't know that, though.' Elizabeth tucked a strand of Liesl's hair behind her ear. 'She could be in hiding, or in a camp. We just don't know.'

'*I* know.' Liesl pointed to her heart. 'In here, I know I won't see my *mutti* or my papa ever again.' The certainty in the child's voice broke Elizabeth's heart.

'Well, you'll see your papa in heaven...' Elizabeth tried to comfort her.

'No.' Liesl wrenched away from her. 'There is no heaven or God or any of it. There is just here, this horrible world where Nazis kill Jews. How could there be a God if this is allowed to happen?'

Elizabeth was at a loss. Liesl always went to Shabbat and observed the laws of Judaism. She'd had her bat mitzvah and learned all the prayers and everything – Elizabeth was sure she was a believer.

'I don't know, Liesl...' she began.

'You see? Even adults can't explain it. If there is a God, then I hate him! I hate what he has allowed to happen...' Liesl was shouting now, something Elizabeth had never heard before.

Bud and Erich came running upstairs at the commotion.

Liesl jumped out of bed, crying and screaming. 'I want to go back! I want them to kill me too! I want to die like *Mutti* and Papa! I don't want to stay here... Let me go back to Berlin! I'm not Irish or British, I'm German... Let me go!'

Before Elizabeth could stop her, she bolted for the door. Luckily,

Bud was there and caught her. He wrapped his arms around her as she flailed and kicked against him.

Erich watched in horror. Liesl was the one who was calm in every situation; she was the one who knew what to do. Liesl out of control frightened him.

Elizabeth moved quickly across the room, kneeling down beside the girl she saw as her daughter, still in Bud's arms.

'My darling, you must stay. It's not safe over there, you know that. And I know you miss your parents, of course you do. I swear to you, when this war is over, we will do everything humanly possible to find your *mutti*, but for now, you and Erich must stay here where it's safe.'

Bud released his grip enough for the girl to turn and face Elizabeth.

'Don't you see, Elizabeth? Nowhere is safe. The Luftwaffe know there's an RAF base just a few miles away, so they will come. They broke your lovely house in Liverpool, and it is only a matter of time before they come here. We are all going to die anyway, and I just want it over with now.' Liesl sobbed.

Elizabeth and Erich were shocked, neither knowing what to say. Despite decades, a faith and a nationality separating them, they were both united in their love of Liesl and their total inability to help her now. Before Elizabeth could think how best to handle the situation, Bud dropped to his knees, his big hands on her thin shoulders, and looked deep into her eyes.

'Liesl, you listen to me now, y'hear?' His eyes burned with intensity. 'The Germans won't win this war because we won't let them. On top of that, America is going to join us soon, and then Hitler is gonna get blasted with a force that will send him to hell where he belongs. Everyone here in Europe is doing their best, but he was allowed to get too strong. So now it's time for the USA to get stuck in, and I know my countrymen – they will.'

Elizabeth stood back; Liesl was transfixed.

'We are sending military equipment and money, we've seized all German assets in the States, we've closed their embassies. FDR and Churchill are on the same page, honey, and so it's just a matter of time until there's American boots on the ground and American weapons in our hands, I promise you. Uncle Sam didn't get into this war easily, but once we do, we ain't goin' home with anything but a total surrender from Hitler and everyone who serves him. You know, they are even makin' grenades the exact shape and weight of a baseball 'cause they know every American boy can throw a baseball? We're ready, all of us – the British, the Europeans who got out, and now we've got Mr Stalin blocking them on the other side. The stupid jerk don't stand a chance, as all of us Allies together got so much fire-power, we can flatten anyone or anything that gets in our way. It's gonna be bad, and bloody, and I'm not lookin' forward to it. I'll lay it on the line for you, I'm scared half to death, but our generals, our officers, and every single man fighting for the good countries on this earth are determined to win. So we *will* win. Right is on our side, Liesl darlin', and America ain't never lost a war, not ever.

'So you and Erich and Elizabeth and Talia and all the people on the farm, y'all just gotta sit tight and let us all get on with it. And when I'm over there, I'll be thinkin' about y'all and fightin' for you, and your mom and your pop, and all the other people those Nazis hurt. And that'll help me. So can you do that, honey? Just wait?'

Liesl's gaze locked with his. Slowly, she nodded.

'Good girl.'

Bud pulled her to his chest and held her tightly. And Elizabeth exhaled with relief.

# CHAPTER 22

*E*lizabeth woke to the sound of her letterbox springing open, then shut. She hurried downstairs. She had received a letter from Rabbi Frank.

*Mrs Klein,*

*I think he will be tried in the coming days, but I cannot be sure. The authorities are not obliged to let us know, and the trial will not be public. Daniel wanted me to let you know.*

*l'shalom*

*David Frank*

Elizabeth folded the short note, a lump in her throat. Familiar feelings of frustration washed over her. Should she go to Detective Inspector Gaughran, tell him what she knew? What *did* she know? That Talia lied about Daniel writing a letter, that she said she didn't sell many paintings and yet the man in the shop said they were all sold and that they had been painted by a man? What would that have to do with Daniel's innocence? She could just see Gaughran's face, her showing up like a lovesick child claiming she had new information when in fact she had nothing. Something wasn't right, but she needed proof for anyone to take her seriously. And what if she was wrong? Talia was her friend, she was just a girl, and she loved Daniel too.

Hadn't she been through enough without someone she saw as a friend accusing her of...well...what? Even if she wanted to confront her, what could she accuse her of? The police had searched the farm from top to bottom and found nothing. They interviewed everyone. What she had was so insignificant. So Talia sold paintings to a gallery. The gallery owner lied, but maybe there was a reason. Perhaps refugees were not allowed to earn money like that and he was protecting her or something? And she lied that Daniel wrote to her, but she'd admitted she loved him. Perhaps it was just wishful thinking on Talia's part? Maybe she wanted people to think Daniel had deeper feelings for her than he had?

Elizabeth toyed with the idea of asking her why she lied. Maybe there was a perfectly logical reason. But something stopped her. What if there was some connection and, by bringing it up, she alerted her? What if somehow Talia did do those drawings? She was artistic surely, but they were different – they were precise, technical. Could Talia have done them?

Round and round the whole situation went in her head. No solutions presented themselves.

Erich's friend called for him to go out to play after breakfast, while Liesl stayed in the sitting room, dressing dolls with Maisie Dornan, one of the local girls.

Unable to settle to anything, she decided on impulse to go to the farm. She told Liesl she was going, and the girl assured her she would keep an eye on Erich, who was now climbing the big cherry tree in the middle of the village green. She had planned to cycle, but as she came out of the house, she spotted Levi in a truck across the road.

'Hello, Levi. Are you going back to the farm?' she asked pleasantly.

He nodded. 'Yes, in five minutes.'

'Can I hitch a lift?'

'Yes,' he replied, taking his toolbox off the seat.

Levi was dark-skinned, with a prominently hooked nose and dark curly hair. He was muscle-bound from all the physical work on the farm, and Elizabeth thought he could be quite pleasant looking if he ever smiled.

She made no effort at conversation, and neither did he. She did not want to have to lie about the purpose of her visit. She wanted to meet the rabbi and talk to him about Daniel. She had more or less decided to confess her worries to him. Perhaps he would not take kindly to her casting doubt over another one of his flock, but she wasn't accusing Talia of anything, just asking his advice.

Once they arrived, Levi immediately went wordlessly back to whatever it was that needed doing. As she strode away, she noticed he glanced in the kitchen window to where Ruth was washing huge pots. He waved and she waved back, a smile on her face.

Being summer holidays, the whole farm swarmed with children, all busily active in farm chores. As she crossed the yard, a loud bell rang to suggest it was time for a break.

The children piled into the dining hall for bread and jam and glasses of milk before going back to work, greeting her as they passed. Elizabeth marvelled at how cheerfully they undertook it all, cleaning chicken coops, peeling potatoes, digging up vegetables or hanging out laundry.

She walked into the main building that housed the administrative centre and the makeshift synagogue. She hoped she would just run into Rabbi Frank rather than having to summon him. He could be very stern and serious, and in truth, he intimidated her a little, but she knew he had a good heart.

Daniel had relayed the story of Rabbi Frank's humiliation as he was taken from his house one night by the Nazis and forced to scrub anti-Nazi slogans off the wall with a sponge before being badly beaten. His hands were raw and bleeding from the scrubbing, and then they set on him, kicking and punching him. Because he was a Chassidic Jew, and Orthodox, he had long peyot that curled in ringlets from his temples, and these were cut as he was forced to kneel, semiconscious, on the street in front of a jeering crowd. When his synagogue was destroyed and set alight, he knew it was time to go. Luckily, he had a brother practising as a rabbi in London who helped get him out. Daniel explained to her how Rabbi Frank didn't feel relief at his survival; rather, he felt profound guilt that he did not stay and defend his people, or at least be with them as they were led away.

Elizabeth pushed the door to the synagogue where she had been with Erich and Liesl on several occasions now for various Jewish events.

As she hoped, Rabbi Frank was there, Torah in hand. But so was Talia. She was speaking to him, their heads close together, and when she looked up, Elizabeth could see that her face was tear-stained. She said something to the rabbi – Elizabeth was too far away to hear what – and then she left, muttering hello to Elizabeth as she passed.

'Ah, Mrs Klein, I was not expecting you. Did we have an appointment?' the rabbi asked. Clearly, she had intruded.

'No, I'm sorry…' she answered, awkward now, knowing her presence was an imposition. 'I…I just wanted to talk to you about Daniel.'

'What about him?' He stood, facing her, shorter at least by five inches. He was dressed in black trousers and a white shirt buttoned to the neck, and had a white beard and grey hair. His peyot had grown back a little, but they now stood out a bit from the sides of his head and curled in ringlets. On his head, he wore a *hoiche*, a high-crowned black hat with a wide brim. His sapphire-blue eyes watched her closely. She knew he was very traditional, and while she was the widow of a Jew, she was gentile, and perhaps that was the reason for his reticence. He was polite and grateful for what she was doing, but he kept her at arm's length. Daniel and the others seemed to hold him in very high regard.

'Just… I don't know, Rabbi. It feels so wrong. I believe him when he says he didn't do those drawings, and I know all the evidence points to him, but I feel like we must do something…' she finished miserably.

The rabbi indicated that she should sit on one of the tubular steel and hardboard chairs that had been acquired somewhere. The entire place was a mishmash of borrowed and leftover furniture. The plan for the new synagogue that Daniel had designed had never materialised.

People had been kind, and the Dublin and Belfast Jewish communities had taken the farm project to their hearts. Daniel had remarked how nice it was for the farm community to feel welcome again, especially after feeling like they had been reduced to the status of vermin in their own countries. The treatment of Jews – not just by Nazis but by their neighbours, people they would have considered friends – had taken a deep psychological toll on everyone. It manifested in the adults and the children in the same way, as stoic determination, but she was sure it masked a hurt so deep, she doubted it would ever heal.

She sat and he sat opposite her. She was glad she'd dressed as appropriately as she could, with a headscarf covering her head and a light summer coat. She had buttoned her coffee-coloured blouse up to the neck, as to show a collarbone was offensive, as was revealing any flesh above the ankles. She smoothed her beige check skirt over her knees. She was wearing thick stockings, her very last pair, which she washed and wore with extreme care, as purchase of a replacement pair was impossible.

'Mrs Klein.' He spoke quietly. 'I, like you, do not believe Daniel is a Nazi, but there is nothing to be done, I am afraid.'

'But, Rabbi, with respect, we can't just sit there and wait for them to hang him.' Her eyes pleaded with his. 'We must do something.'

He smiled, the first time she'd seen it. A slow, sad smile. His English was almost perfect now, though heavily accented.

'I think Daniel will die. And if I may say how ironic it is? Here you are, an Irish woman, so concerned for the life of one Jew, when all over Europe, Jews are dying by the hundreds of thousands. It strikes me, that because Daniel is an individual, and a person who has touched your heart, you care so much. Each of those put on a train east, each person beaten to death on the street or worked to exhaustion in a quarry or a mine, they too are individuals, and their presence on earth touched the heart of another. It is as if we can only process what is happening on this small level – one man, one community. The reality of what is happening in Europe is too hard for one person to understand. The scale is too big.'

He noticed her look of shame. He was right. She was living in relative comfort while those horrors were being enacted on the mainland of Europe. It wasn't that people didn't care – they did – but it was on a scale that seemed impossible to solve.

'Please, Mrs Klein, do not see my words as an admonishment. That is not my intention. It is simply an observation. You have done a very kind thing, taking Liesl and Erich into your home and your heart. The way you care for the children in your class – I see how going to school gives them a break from the endless worry about those people they had to leave behind. You're a good woman, and God will reward you. The Talmud says, "He who saves one life saves the world entire."' He nodded slowly.

'But we can't save Daniel?' she whispered, the anguish she felt draped over every word.

'No. We cannot save Daniel. But he is a good man, he has faith in God, and he will go home.'

She could not raise the subject of Talia. The words died on her lips. Talia was Jewish and a victim and a girl with a broken heart. She wanted to save Daniel too – of course she did.

The rabbi rose and nodded at her before turning and walking away.

For a while, she sat in the room, taking in her surroundings, alone for the first time. There was a reading altar, which they called a bema, and on it was the Torah scroll. Usually it was held in the ark, a special cabinet for that specific purpose. Rabbi Frank had managed to salvage the scroll from his burning synagogue and chose to take it to the farm, though he had only one little suitcase like everyone else. Elizabeth knew how much that Torah meant to the community. It was a link to their past, to their faith, to all they had lost. They saw it as a symbol that they could rise again.

The room and all the furniture faced east towards Jerusalem, as was the tradition. On the wall was an ornately carved Star of David. One of the boys in her class, a twelve-year-old called Jacob, had worked for months on it, and it was a lovely piece of craftsmanship. She felt a pang as she recalled Daniel helping him with it.

A candle burned, similar, she thought, to the sanctuary lamp in a

Catholic church, always burning to remind the faithful of the ever presence of God.

Unlike the Christian churches, there were no statues or paintings depicting the human form, so it felt different to the churches she was used to. But there was a peacefulness that reminded her of St Joseph's parish church in Ballycreggan.

She'd heard others describing the ornate and beautiful synagogues of Europe, the glass and metalwork, the carved and polished wood, but this place was nothing like that. It was just a room, with mismatched chairs and sheets hung as drapes on the windows.

The rabbi and several of the community would have been used to segregated worship, with the women up on the balcony and the men in the main body of the synagogue, but the makeshift nature of the farm allowed for no such rules. Still, there was something lovely about it. She enjoyed the sensation of just being, thinking her thoughts.

She was not much of a churchgoer; she never had been since she left Ireland. Her mother's dogmatic approach to religion had cured her of ever wanting to be involved. Daddy used to go to mass on a Sunday; she remembered him standing at the back with all the other men and smoking his pipe outside the church after, chatting to the neighbours.

Elizabeth could picture her parents in this still, silent place and allowed their images to take form in her mind. Margaret standing upright and severe, her brown skirt and jacket buttoned up, flat brown brogues on her feet and a scowl on her face. Her father, Miah, was softer, physically and emotionally. He was not a tall man, and he had chestnut hair as she had, but his was always kept back with Brylantine. She remembered him as smiling, and she could recall the feel of her little hand in his big one, and how rough his hands were from physical work. She saw him now in her mind's eye, his long leather blacksmith's apron going all the way down to his ankles, his hobnailed boots, his collarless shirt and the rivulets of sweat trickling down his neck as he worked over the fire.

He would look up if she came into the forge on her way home from school, put down his hammers and place his hands in the small of his back to stretch into an upright position. He'd tell her, 'Don't touch me, Lizzie pet. I'm all dirty, and Mammy will murder us if you ruin your dress.'

But he'd smile and give her a farthing to go to Bridie's sweetshop beside the forge for a few lemon sherbets. They were his favourites, and so they were hers too. She'd pop one into his open mouth because his hands were so dirty, and then she'd be on her way.

As an adult, Elizabeth had thought about why her mother was so cold towards them. Margaret seemed to disapprove of both her and her father in equal measure. Perhaps she was jealous of their closeness? Elizabeth loved her daddy with all of her heart, and when he was home, she was happy, but she could have loved her mother too, if only she'd been allowed to. Her father had done everything he could to make Margaret happy, but it was never enough. Then after he died, Elizabeth tried too but it had the same result – a bitter coldness. It was too late to do anything about it now anyway.

She began to whisper. 'Dear God, and Mammy and Daddy and Rudi, I don't know if you can hear me...but if you can, please help Daniel. Or help me to help him. He did nothing wrong, and he's a good man, and, well, I...care...' She paused. 'I love him.' She'd never allowed those words to form in her mind before. Rudi's sweet smiling face swam before her eyes – he was just a boy. She felt no disloyalty, as Rudi was another lifetime ago.

'And look over Ariella, Liesl and Erich's mother. Their father, Peter, is dead, it would seem, but they need their mother now, so please, if you can, keep her safe and bring her home to her children. Amen.'

She blessed herself instinctively and then supposed that wasn't done in a Jewish temple. But she felt sure nobody would mind.

As she walked out, she passed the dining hall where some of the younger children who were too small for chores were sitting. They were colouring while people coming in and out of the kitchen watched them and prepared that evening's meal at the same time. They spotted her and waved.

'I drawed a puppy, Mrs Klein,' Abraham Schultz, an incorrigible yet delightful five-year-old, called. 'Came and see.' His English was good, but like them all, he found the tenses difficult. She didn't correct him; he would learn through conversation, and he was trying so hard, the little pet.

She walked into the room and was greeted with a wave by Ruth, who was boning a chicken on a large table. Levi was leaning against the wall, chatting quietly to her. He seemed much more animated than usual. Elizabeth sat beside the little ones and admired the various puppies, kittens and houses with spiralling smoke they were drawing. She lifted one to look at it more closely and was surprised to see that there seemed to be markings on the other side of the paper. She flipped the page over. There were a series of pencil diagrams, but they had been rubbed out with an eraser; all she could see were the indents of the pencil, but the markings appeared to be very symmetrical.

'Where did you get this paper, children?'

The volunteers were too far away to hear the conversation.

'Talia gave it to us. She had lots of sheets in her art bag. She gave us some, but we ran out, so we took some out of her bag over there,' Rachel Krupp, a chatty little six-year-old, explained quickly in case they were in trouble for taking something they shouldn't.

The child pointed to Talia's bag, which was hanging on the back of the door. It was the brown leather satchel, and Talia was rarely seen without it over her shoulder.

'Oh, is Talia here?' Elizabeth asked.

'She was, but she had to go out again. Rabbi Frank come for her, and she go in the shul with the rabbi.' Abraham said the whole sentence in English and looked very pleased with himself. She smiled at his use of the Yiddish word shul, for the synagogue.

Ruth called them to wash their hands before lunch, so dutifully they trooped off to the sink in the kitchen, leaving Elizabeth alone. Quick as a flash, she went to Talia's bag and took out several sheets of paper, careful to leave many more so as not to alert suspicion. The bag had jars and paintbrushes in the main part as well as in the two outer pockets. Glancing about to make sure nobody could see her, she rolled the sheets of paper and placed them inside her cardigan, under her arm.

She knew if she asked, someone would drive her home in the bus, or she could borrow a bicycle. But she didn't want to draw any attention to herself, so she set off down the rutted lane that led to the main road into Ballycreggan. It was only three miles, and she was thankfully wearing flat shoes. Liesl and Erich would be late getting their lunch, but they would survive. They knew she had gone to the farm, so they wouldn't be worried.

She walked on as several military vehicles passed her by, going to or from the RAF base.

About a quarter of a mile from the farm, she paused. There was a copse of trees where she sometimes took Erich to look for conkers or sticks suitable for making slingshots. She ducked in there, knowing that after a few moments, she would come to a large felled tree. She sat on it, and without allowing herself to think about the invasion of her friend's privacy, she unrolled the papers.

There were several sheaves, some blank, others with watercolours of the local landscape, but nothing with any drawings. The watercolours were really very good. She held one up to the light, and something struck her. She placed the others on the tree stump and secured them with a stone, then moved out of the shade into a clearing where the midday sun poured in and held the painting up again. It was of the azure sea off the coast of Northern Ireland as the sun rose. In the foreground, verdant green fields tumbled steeply to the craggy shore, where dark, treacherous-looking rocks formed small cliffs.

Elizabeth peered at the painting. Frustratingly, the light was just not good enough to confirm what she suspected. The midday sun shining through the canopy of leaves high above her was dappling the paper. She went back, grabbed the remaining pages and made her way back out onto the road. She checked to make sure there was nobody about, and then held the painting up once more, this time in clear sunshine. She wasn't imagining it – once the light shone through the paper, she could make out something, some markings underneath the paint. It was impossible to tell what they were, but the paper definitely had been used before.

What was going on? She put that one down and selected some others. In all cases, there was something written beneath the paint. She tried to make it out, but it was impossible. She cautioned herself that it might be nothing; art paper was scarce – she used newspaper in school for art projects – so perhaps Talia was just recycling paper. It would make sense, but yet something niggled. Were those drawings underneath?

Before setting off again, she folded the sheets and placed them in her coat pocket.

As she put her key in the lock forty-five minutes later, she froze. Coming from the kitchen was the sound of Erich and Talia laughing about something. She tried to act normally as she entered the room.

'Hi, Talia.' She smiled. The young woman had washed her face and looked herself again. 'How are you?' she asked as she sent Erich off to wash up for lunch. Did she imagine the flash of something in the other woman's eyes?

'Oh, fine, thanks. I'm sorry about earlier. I was talking to the rabbi about my family. It... Well, it's hard sometimes.' She shrugged and went on. 'I came into the village because I wanted to try to see Bud, but it's too late. I went to the base, but it seems to be all closed off or something. Anyway, the soldier in charge of the gate wouldn't let me in, or even give Bud a message, and he's being shipped out to England tomorrow, so I won't get to see him.' Talia looked crestfallen, but Elizabeth remembered how she and Erich had been laughing when she came in. Surely if the girl were heartbroken about both her family and Bud, she wouldn't be able to be so cheerful?

'There's a big shipment of stuff coming today,' Erich said as he came back into the room. 'Bud told us. That's why they are all locked up.'

'Erich, remember what I told you? Careless talk costs lives. Bud shouldn't be telling you those things, and you shouldn't be repeating them.' She needed him to understand, as he loved having inside information through Bud.

'But, Elizabeth, it's just Talia,' Erich said innocently. 'It's not like I told Mrs Ashe!' He giggled. The school music teacher was also the biggest gossip in Ballycreggan.

'Erich, don't be rude,' she chided, suppressing a smile. He really was incorrigible.

'It's all right, Erich. I won't tell anyone.' Talia put her finger to her lips theatrically, and Erich chuckled.

'You're welcome to stay for lunch,' Elizabeth said. She wanted to see if she could get something else to take to the police.

'I'd love to, especially as it's my turn to scrub the pots today.' She winked at Erich. 'Let me just pop up to the post office first, as I need to see if there's a telegram. I have a feeling I may have sold a painting. I dropped into the gallery in Belfast yesterday, and a man looked like he wanted to buy one for his wife as a birthday present.'

As the other woman left, Elizabeth's urge was to run to the barracks in the village and alert Gaughran, but she didn't want to alarm the children or alert Talia. So she decided to wait, just in case she could piece another bit of this together. She was very conscious that even with the pictures, she still didn't have much.

# CHAPTER 23

$\mathcal{A}$s Erich and Talia chatted animatedly and Liesl ate quietly over lunch, Elizabeth barely listened. Erich was all talk about the planes he and his friends had seen while they played after school; the aircraft were flying low before coming in to land at the base.

'Well?' Elizabeth asked as she poured some weak tea. The two women were sitting outside in the back garden while the children washed up. Talia loved Elizabeth's garden and often sketched the many shrubs and flowers that grew in profusion, planted years ago by her father. Daniel and the children even tidied up the large shed at the back as a surprise for Elizabeth one day. It had been filled with some of the bigger pieces of heavy furniture and decades of detritus of the Bannon family. At least now she could walk in there, and the walls were lined with shelves full of paint tins and tools. She had donated all of the excess furniture to the farm. It felt good to get rid of her mother's huge dark sideboards and hallstands.

She grimaced at the colour of the tea as she added a drop of milk. It was at the end of the ration, and she had taken, like everyone, to reusing the tea leaves. These were on their third wetting and barely coloured the water.

'Did you sell one?'

Talia sighed. 'No. Well, at least I didn't get a message to say I did anyway. Mr McGuinness, who owns the gallery, is so kind. He wishes he could sell more, and he always explains that because of the war, people have no money for such luxuries as art.' She shrugged and sighed. 'Imagine a world that sees art as a luxury when it is vital to our very existence.'

'And you just approached him one day, and he said he'd stock your paintings?' Elizabeth asked pleasantly.

'Yes. Well, I was in the gallery, and we got to talking about art. I told him I had studied, and he asked to see some of my work. Then he offered to stock it. I don't mind if he doesn't sell any, though. It just feels nice to be painting and behaving like the world is normal.'

Elizabeth deliberately kept her tone light and conversational. 'And did you specialise in landscapes at the art school?' Elizabeth topped up the hot water that passed for tea.

'No, not really. Landscapes never interested me. I liked portraiture, but coming here, well, it's so beautiful and the light is quite incredible. I was enchanted.'

'It must be difficult to get supplies now, though. I know we have awful trouble getting things for the school. We are reduced to painting on old newspaper.'

'Yes, I have to use both sides of the paper. I paint on anything I can find, to be honest, and scrape the very last out of the paints. Mr McGuinness gave me some sketching pads a few weeks ago, so I'm using them very sparingly. It's not as good as oils and canvas, but with watercolours, you can get away with heavy paper.'

Liesl and Erich stuck their heads round the back door to say the kitchen was tidy and they were going back to join their friends outside. Elizabeth allowed the conversation to move away from art. Talia talked about Bud and how much she was going to miss him.

'Do you think you two will get together after the war?' Elizabeth asked.

Talia smiled. 'After the war. We say this all the time – after the war, when the war is over – but what nobody says is when, or who will win. So who knows? Perhaps Hitler will invade next week and slaughter all of us Jews or –'

Elizabeth's face caused Talia to stop. Erich was standing in the doorway, a broken slingshot in his hand. The front door was permanently on the latch when the children played outside. He must have come in to have her repair his toy.

'Will Hitler come, Elizabeth?' The little boy's face raked hers for the truth.

'No, darling. Talia was only joking. Of course he won't. You know what's going to happen – Bud explained. The Americans and the British, together with all the millions of good people in Europe, will defeat Hitler and the Nazis, and all we have to do is wait. It's going to happen, we must just wait.' She drew him into a hug and kissed the top of his head.

Talia looked stricken. 'I'm sorry, Erich. I was being stupid, trying to be funny, I suppose. Of course Elizabeth is right. We are all going to be fine.'

'Daniel isn't going to be fine. He is going to hang,' Erich said. Elizabeth had been dreading this conversation. She knew the whole village was buzzing with gossip, and it was inevitable the children would hear it.

Elizabeth led the child to the table and sat him down. She went out into the hall and called Liesl. Moments later, the girl appeared, her face questioning.

'Sit down, Liesl. I want to talk to you about something.'

They both looked at her with such trust in their eyes, it broke her heart to do this, but she needed to see how Talia reacted.

'I know people in the village have been talking about Daniel and what's going to happen to him, so I wanted you to have the straight story, not gossip.' She never made eye contact with Talia but kept the young woman in her peripheral vision.

'Daniel is facing trial for spying for Germany. The papers that were found at the farm could, the police believe, only have been drawn by him. Daniel says he didn't do those drawings, but whoever did gave information to the Germans. Because when they bombed the

RAF base, they did it with precision, and they knew where everything was.'

'Do you think he did it, Elizabeth? I thought you said you thought he was innocent?' Liesl asked.

Elizabeth glanced at Talia. 'Yes, I know I did, Liesl, but now I just don't know. The police seem sure.'

The younger woman's face registered surprise, but she said nothing. Erich and Liesl were horrified.

'I don't think...' Erich began, his voice cracking from the emotion of it all. 'Daniel wouldn't...'

Erich looked from one to the other, then ran sobbing from the room. Elizabeth started to follow to comfort him, but Liesl stopped her.

'I'll go,' she said, and went after her brother.

As the two women sat alone in the kitchen, Talia finally spoke. 'I don't want to admit it, but I think you're right. I mean, who else could it have been?'

Elizabeth nodded slowly.

'I'm sorry. I know you had feelings for him.' Talia placed her hand on Elizabeth's and patted it.

'Not any more. Anyone who could willingly hurt those children has no place in my life.' Elizabeth held Talia's gaze and smiled sadly.

THE DRONE of the engines woke her, and Elizabeth sat bolt upright. As she struggled to fully wake, she threw back the covers and went to her bedroom window. Directly above the village, planes – ten, possibly even twenty – filled the sky. It was impossible to tell if they were British or German.

She dragged her dressing gown around her shoulders and shoved her feet into her slippers. She, like everyone, had made it a habit to have them at hand immediately in case they needed to evacuate. A small bag was packed downstairs with blankets, crackers and water.

She went to Liesl first, shaking her awake, before going into

Erich's room. She ran to his bed, the noise overhead louder now. He wasn't there. Perhaps he'd gone to the bathroom? She rushed out to the landing – the bathroom door was open.

'Liesl, where's Erich? He's not in his bed!' Elizabeth demanded, but the girl was just as surprised as she was.

'I...I don't know!' Liesl went into her brother's room. 'Elizabeth, his clothes are gone and his boots.'

'Oh, dear God!' Elizabeth grabbed Liesl's hand and half pulled her downstairs.

'Is it the Germans?' the girl asked.

'I don't know, but we need to get you into the shelter – now!'

The first explosion felt like it shook the house to its very foundation; the second, less than a minute later, shattered the glass in the windows. If it were not for the crisscrossed tape to stop flying splinters killing someone, there would be no glass left at all.

Out on the street, neighbours in their nightclothes ran to the village shelter, the basement of St Joseph's Catholic Church.

'They're bombing the base again!' Mrs McElligott yelled as her husband, the second ARP warden for the village after Mr Morris, urged everyone in the direction of the chapel. Babies howled, children, babies and the elderly were half carried, half dragged, and the villagers of Ballycreggan made a motley crew as they ran up the one street in the village to safety.

They scurried into the church, behind the altar into the sacristy and down the narrow spiral staircase to the basement. There was a bottleneck as the stairs were so narrow, but some of the older boys helped the very young and the infirm, passing them like sandbags in a human chain. Father O'Toole and his housekeeper, the indomitable Mrs Forde, had the basement stacked with blankets and pillows and were now in the process of making large pots of hot sweet tea. The dust from the ceiling fell like snow on everyone below with each deafening thud.

Elizabeth settled Liesl with some neighbours and went back to the stairs. She had to wait, as there was a steady stream of people coming down and there was only room for one person at a time on the narrow staircase.

As she waited impatiently, Mr McElligott approached her and asked her to take a seat with Liesl.

'I need to get back up! Erich wasn't at home, Mr McElligott. I don't know where he is! He went to bed as normal, and when we woke to the explosions, he wasn't there!' Elizabeth knew she was screaming – she was borderline hysterical – but panic was taking over.

'What?' Mr McElligott was in his eighties and rather deaf.

Again she screamed the situation.

'Well, Mrs Klein, I'm sorry to say that if he's not down here, and he's not in your house, then I have no idea where the little tyke has got to, but I hope he's got the sense to get down. I don't know what we're facing when we get back up there.' He gestured upwards with his thumb.

'But I need to go back up,' she pleaded.

'Oh, that's quite impossible, Mrs Klein, quite impossible. You'll have to wait until the all clear is sounded.'

'But you don't understand! I need to find –'

'I understand perfectly,' he said, helping a frail old woman down the last few steps. 'But I will not permit you to go back up there, not until the raid is over. Now please, Mrs Klein, take a seat.'

As he spoke, a deafening screeching sound pierced the air, and the entire building shook.

'We've taken a direct hit!' someone yelled.

'Let's get out of here before we're buried alive!' shouted another.

Almost instantaneously, people started screaming, running towards the small stone steps once more, desperate to get out.

Mr McElligott and Father O'Toole stood at the base of the staircase, trying to demand order.

'Ladies, gentlemen, please! We are upsetting the children!' the priest shouted over the din.

They heard a crash – another blast – and large lumps of plaster were knocked off the walls.

The people ignored him, some pushing the burly priest aside to get at the steps once more.

As the crowd surged forward, Mr McElligott took a whistle from his breast pocket and blew it. The shrill sound caused the crowd to pause.

'It is an offence to defy the ARP warden in the event of a raid. I insist that everyone move back and wait. I'll go up and assess the damage and report back.'

The cacophony of horrific noise outside rendered him almost unheard, but because of his statement and the urging of the priest and others, the people who had surged forward did as he asked.

The bombs were dropping constantly now. It was impossible to decipher one blast from another as the village and presumably the RAF station not four miles away were bombarded. Elizabeth found Liesl, and the child clung to her. Together, they stood in the basement, totally helpless to do anything but wait.

After what seemed like ages, the bombs stopped and everyone just stood, rooted to the spot, holding onto their families, waiting.

Unlike in Liverpool, there was no all-clear siren to wait for in Ballycreggan. Mr McElligott, old Dr Parsons, whose son, young Dr Parsons, had been shot down over Germany, and Corny Andrews, the blacksmith, climbed the steps.

'What if they are up there?' Liesl whispered. 'What if they dropped them in parachutes and they are up there waiting for us? What if they've got Erich?' Liesl began to cry, and Elizabeth rubbed her back.

'It was just an air raid, darling. I'm sure of it.'

A thought struck Elizabeth. Did the Luftwaffe come calling this night in particular because they knew the base had been restocked by the US military over the last two days? And if so, how did they know? Daniel couldn't have told them. Perhaps it was a coincidence, but she refused to believe it.

She needed to get out of there, to find Erich. If anything had happened to him... She couldn't even think about it. He was upset because she said she blamed Daniel. In hindsight, it was probably foolish, but she wanted to see Talia's reaction. While she was deeply suspicious of the other woman, she needed something else before going to Gaughran. What if she was wrong? Her reputation with the refugees would be forever damaged, and Liesl and Erich's sense of community with them could be destroyed forever. The stakes were very high, and she wanted to be as positive as she could before she said anything.

Others sat wide-eyed and terrified as they waited to be allowed out, but she just worried constantly about Erich. Where could he be? Would he have gone to the farm? To his friends or Rabbi Frank? A horrible thought struck her – what if he went to the base to try to see Bud?

After what seemed like an eternity, the men came back down and told them it was safe. Wearily, and with deep anxiety about what they might face when they emerged, they began to climb the stairs once more. The sight that greeted them rendered the entire community speechless. The village was in ruins – flames licked the houses that had been hit, and remains of curtains hung in glassless windows. The main street looked like a mouth with several missing teeth. The church spire was gone – all that remained was a pile of rubble – and a large crater had been gouged out of the village green where the children had played earlier that day. The post office was in flames, and beside it, Bridie's sweetshop was but a charred memory.

Elizabeth rushed past all of the carnage, knowing she should probably stop to help, but she needed to find Erich. Thankfully, their end of the street was unharmed apart from broken glass, and she and Liesl let themselves in, calling Erich's name frantically.

He wasn't there. She would try the farm. Pulling on her dress and coat, she told Liesl to stay at home in case he came back. She pushed her bike out the side gate, pedalling furiously for the three miles away from the carnage in the village, until she saw the lights of the farm up ahead. Her dress was wet from perspiration and her hair was hanging down, but she didn't care.

The Jews were all gathered in the dining hall. Though their farm wasn't hit, they could see the flames from the base out on the coast.

'Elizabeth!' Talia ran to her. 'Thank God you are all right. Are Erich and Liesl safe?'

The community gathered around her, anxious for news. It seemed like Liesl, they too feared an invasion.

She ignored their questions, instead telling them about Erich. Nobody had seen him. They asked all of his friends, but nobody had.

'But he went to bed just before I left to come back here. Do you think he snuck out?' Talia seemed distressed.

'I don't know, Talia. I hoped he was here. The only other place he would go is to the base – he might have gone looking for Bud.' Elizabeth allowed those words and what they might mean to sink in. 'Well, if he's not here, then I have to go there,' she decided, getting up to leave.

'They won't let you anywhere near it, not after this,' said Levi. He was sitting with Ruth.

'If my child is there, they will not stop me,' Elizabeth retorted through gritted teeth.

'I'll drive with you. It's safer with two.'

The last thing Elizabeth needed was the monosyllabic Levi, but she had no time to argue and it would be quicker in a car.

'Did anything happen, something to make him run off like that?' Levi asked as they drove.

It was the longest sentence she'd ever heard him say.

'Yes,' she said. There was no point in lying, and if he knew the full story, he might have some ideas about where to find the little boy whom she'd come to think of as her son. 'He asked me if I thought Daniel Lieber would hang, and I said that I thought he would. He was really upset and went off to bed.'

Levi nodded. He took a cigarette from his packet and lit it as he drove. 'Daniel didn't do those drawings, you know.'

'How do you know?'

Levi shrugged. 'I just know he's no German spy. Anyone could have done those. He left his drawings all over the place. We worked together on the boiler for weeks – there was no manual, so he made lots of diagrams of how it worked. We had to take it apart and put it back together again, so he drew the components at each stage so we would be able to rebuild it. On the wall in the barn, where the boiler is, he wrote a legend for what each symbol meant, in case it wasn't him fixing it next time.

'When we were planning the construction of the new shul, he drew the plans for that too. Everyone saw them and could offer suggestions.'

Elizabeth's mind raced. 'Did you tell the police that?' she demanded.

'I did, but they had made their minds up. I think they needed to arrest someone, and Daniel was the obvious choice.'

She was incredulous. Surely the police would have taken that information into account. 'And were you the only one to say it?'

Levi gave her a glance, and she realised she should not take her frustration out on him. He'd done the right thing.

'I brought it up at a meeting, and everyone agreed. Ruth, Talia, the rabbi – everyone knew he left things like that there all the time.'

'But you didn't take it further?'

'No.'

'Why not?' Elizabeth wanted to shake him.

He spoke slowly. 'Because they got the information we had through the interviews they did and later through the rabbi – he's our spokesman.'

'But if you knew...' She was frustrated with his attitude.

'Mrs Klein, we are guests here. We have the legal status of refugees. We told the police what we knew, what we thought, but there wasn't anything else we could do. Daniel is a good man, and I don't believe him to be guilty, but we are not in a position to challenge the authority of the country that is hosting us.'

He turned the car out onto the coast road. 'I don't have any evidence, except that he left his drawings everywhere and my opinion that he didn't do it.'

'I don't think he did it, either, but if not him, who?'

Levi's dark eyes caught hers for a split second.

'Someone who is still here, still passing information, if tonight's raid is anything to go by.' Levi exhaled a long stream of blue smoke.

That was Elizabeth's thought as well. She made a snap decision. 'Can you please go to the base alone? There's no point in two of us going. I'm going back to the village to contact the police. We need help to find Erich.'

It was hard to know who to trust, but she needed to trust this man now.

'I'll come to your house afterwards,' he said as he nodded and pulled the car over. She was less than a mile from the village. The base was still burning in places, the flames visible from the high coast road, despite having fire trucks and pumped water.

That was secondary now. She needed to find Erich. The possibility of anything having happened to him was one she couldn't countenance.

When she ran into Ballycreggan on the main street, she saw the police car outside her house. Her heart lurched, and a cold sweat prickled the skin all over her body. No, please God, no! Please don't let them be there to give her bad news!

Detective Gaughran was in her living room, a uniformed policeman with him. Liesl sat on the couch. She was dry-eyed.

'Ah, Mrs Klein, I understand from this young lady here that her brother is missing?'

'Did you come here... Do you know something?' She was confused.

'No, unfortunately not. I don't know anything about a missing child, but I have my officers on the case now. I came here tonight to ask you a few more questions actually.' He stuck his hands in his pockets. His hat sat far back on his head – it had been a long night. 'Is there somewhere we could talk?'

'Yes, um... Come in the kitchen.' She turned to Liesl. 'Levi is gone to the base. Erich's not at the farm.' She knew she should try to reassure the child, but she was too distraught. What had happened now?

Gaughran followed her into the kitchen and closed the door behind him. The early dawn light was streaking the sky in glorious vermillion and purple. How could the sun rise like it was just another day when the whole world was in chaos?

'Does the name Xavier McGuinness mean anything to you?' His eyes never left her face.

'No.' She frowned. 'I don't know anyone of that name. Should I?'

He extracted a photograph and handed it to her. It was of a very distinguished man in his fifties, longish curly grey hair, perfectly groomed, a luxurious moustache. Unforgettable.

'He runs a gallery in Belfast. I didn't know his name. He sells paintings by Talia Zimmermann there.' She handed the photo back to Gaughran.

'Well, your address was found among his things when he was arrested this evening. It seems he was in possession of a radio transmitter, a wireless set, and had been broadcasting information to Germany. He's known to us as IRA, and we also know he met a person travelling on a German passport in a pub in Belfast in 1938.'

Noting her look of surprise, he explained, 'we make it our business to know what people like him are up to. The IRA have links to Nazi Germany. Hitler's feeding the Irish republicans here and in the South some old guff about getting a United Ireland in return for help to beat the common enemy, Britain. It's no secret that the RAF base was being fairly heavily stocked in the past week or so. We believe he sent a message about the activity in Ballyhalbert over recent days earlier on today, so he's who we have to thank for tonight's attack.'

Gaughran looked exhausted. He took off his hat and ran his hand over his thin hair. 'So, Mrs Klein, do you have any explanation why this man would have your address on a piece of paper in his wallet?'

Elizabeth thought for a moment. She had been putting this off because she wanted to be sure, but now her only concern was finding Erich. On the other hand, the trial could happen any day. She made a decision.

'No, but I do have something to show you.'

She went to her bureau, where she'd hidden the sheets of paper she'd taken from Talia's bag. Returning to the kitchen, she said, 'You might need to come outside. I think the light may not be good enough in here.'

She opened the back door, and he followed her out into the early morning light. She held the paintings up, showing him what she saw, and he peered.

'Where did you get these?' he asked.

She explained everything as quickly and as efficiently as she could – the visit to the gallery, the alleged letter, and then finding the paper in Talia's bag.

'And you only thought you would mention this now?' Gaughran's voice was a mix of frustration and incredulity.

'I didn't know anything concrete until yesterday when I found the painting. I was going to come to you today. Talia was here yesterday evening. I wanted to be sure – they have all been through so much, and if I were accusing someone in the wrong, just because I wanted to clear Daniel's name...' She paused, willing him to understand. 'But then the raid, and Erich going missing...'

'All right, Mrs Klein. I'm going to need you to make an official statement –'

She interrupted him. 'Look, my little boy is missing, and I need to find him. Perhaps later I can –' She got up to go, but Gaughran stood in front of her.

'I'll ensure the officers assigned to looking for Erich spare no effort, Mrs Klein, but for now, I'm going to have to ask you to come to Belfast with me for questioning.'

His words crashed over her like an icy shower. Was he serious? Was she under arrest? She'd told him everything she knew.

'I can't go now! I have to find Erich!'

'I don't want to arrest you, Mrs Klein, but I will if I need to.' Suddenly all friendliness was gone; the detective's voice was cold.

'You can't seriously think I had anything to do with –' she began.

'I don't know, Mrs Klein.' He opened the door, gesturing that she go ahead of him. 'All I know is the man we have in custody as a spy was a close personal friend of yours, and now another man who is sending messages to Nazi Germany has your address in his wallet. I'd say that warrants a few questions, wouldn't you?'

Elizabeth was dumbstruck. 'I must speak to Liesl. Please! She's upset enough... Let me just...'

Gaughran nodded, and Elizabeth went into the sitting room. Liesl was describing Erich's blue jersey and grey flannel short trousers.

'Liesl, darling, I need to go with Detective Gaughran for a little while, so can you go to the farm? Find Levi or Rabbi Frank or Ruth' – she deliberately didn't mention Talia – 'and ask them to take care of you until I get back. I won't be long.'

Liesl looked stricken. 'But what about Erich? We must look for him!'

Detective Gaughran spoke. 'Liesl, I'm going to put Officer Wilson here in charge of finding Erich. We'll make contact with the RAF base officially, and they can let us know if he's there. In the meantime, we'll search everywhere we can think of.'

The detective didn't make any false promises that Erich would be found safe and well, Elizabeth noticed. Liesl ran into her arms, and she held the girl tightly, kissing the top of her head. 'Be a brave girl now, and I'll be home soon.' Elizabeth gave her what she hoped was a reassuring smile and followed Gaughran out to the police car.

# CHAPTER 24

*O*nce at the station, she was escorted into an interview room. It was almost identical to the one where she had met with Daniel.

'Now, Mrs Klein, you understand you are not under arrest? You are here giving a statement of your own free will?'

Elizabeth nodded.

'So you don't know Xavier McGuinness?' he asked again.

'Apart from meeting him in his gallery, no. I didn't know his name.'

She repeated everything she'd told Gaughran in her kitchen, and apart from one or two questions for clarity, he let her speak. A uniformed officer took copious notes. Gaughran already had the paintings in his possession.

Then she went on to explain how Levi said that Daniel drew all sorts of things and they were to be found all over the farm. Diagrams of the boiler, plans for various structures – anyone could have had access to them, could have copied his drawing style. She even explained about the legend on the wall beside the boiler, denoting the meaning of different symbols.

'And do you think this Talia Zimmermann would have known the details of the shipments coming into the RAF base this week?' he asked, his eyes giving nothing away.

'Yes,' Elizabeth confirmed, feeling treacherous. 'Talia was going out with an RAF serviceman, an American with a British mother.'

'And his name?' Gaughran was writing in his notebook now.

'Corporal Thomas Johnson, but everyone calls him Bud.' She thought of Bud's enthusiastic innocence and how he comforted Liesl. She prayed she wasn't getting him into trouble.

'So let me get this straight. This painting, and others you attest were done by Miss Zimmermann – underneath the paint are markings of some kind?'

She nodded.

'And you found this piece of paper in her bag earlier, and you think it is reused paper, that something else is underneath the paint?'

Elizabeth flushed. It sounded so silly when he said it out loud. People reused everything these days. With each passing minute, she felt like she'd made a terrible mistake. 'Look, I don't know, but whoever is passing on information is still at large and free to do so. Daniel couldn't be –'

'So tell me again from the beginning, in as much detail as you can,' Gaughran interrupted.

Over and over the same ground they went: the visit to Daniel confirming that he'd never written to Talia, seeing Talia go into the gallery, Elizabeth's subsequent encounter with McGuinness, going to see Rabbi Frank, Talia crying in the synagogue, the incident with the younger children and the bag, then having a late lunch with Talia and the children.

'And she stayed in your house all afternoon?' He interrupted again.

'Yes... Well, actually, not all the time. Erich was talking about all the planes and everything landing on the base and the tanks going by on flatbed trucks. He's an expert in all that stuff, and he can name all the different types of military vehicles. And Talia didn't know that these new deliveries were why Bud couldn't see her. Apparently, she'd gone to the base earlier that morning to try to see him before he was shipped out.'

'So she left your house?'

'Yes, she said she wanted to run up to the post office to see if the gallery owner had left her a message. Apparently, he would telegram if he sold one of her paintings, and there had been someone browsing that day that she thought might buy one, which I knew was a lie. She was only gone a few minutes. Then she came back and we had lunch. We chatted afterwards for a while in the garden, and then she left for the farm.'

'And did anything else happen?' he asked.

'Well, I know you find this hard to believe, Inspector, but I was coming to see you. I just wanted to be sure I was doing the right thing. My foster children are very connected to the farm, and Talia is one of the refugees. It would have done irreparable damage to their relationships and to my professional career as their teacher if I went about accusing Jews of being spies without any evidence. I knew that she'd lied about the letter and this McGuinness lied about who had done the paintings, but that did not make Talia a spy. I couldn't see a link between those facts and Daniel's arrest, not until I found the paintings in her bag. And...' – she felt her face flush – 'Daniel Lieber and I are close, so I knew that anything I said would be seen as an effort on my part to blame someone other than him.'

'But you told me there was no relationship between you?'

'There isn't, not as such.' She felt so foolish but wanted to be totally honest. 'But we do care for each other, and if things were different, then perhaps we would have a relationship.'

'I see.' The detective was grim. 'We are going to need to search your house, Mrs Klein.'

'Fine,' Elizabeth said with a sigh. 'I've nothing to hide.'

Gaughran left the room and returned a few moments later with a lukewarm cup of weak tea.

Over and over, he asked the same questions: Daniel and his relationship with Talia, had Daniel ever been to the gallery, had she ever collected post for anyone at her house, what was it about Talia's behaviour that was suspicious, what exactly had Bud revealed about the shipments of supplies, when did Talia know about it, when did

Elizabeth know about it? Round and round the questions went, and Elizabeth fought the urge to panic. They already had one man facing trial for something he didn't do – did they seriously think that she might have had anything to do with betraying national security?

Gaughran then changed tack; he started asking about Rudi and then about her uncle and his German wife.

'And you claim to have never met Peter Bannon or his wife?'

'I'm not *claiming* I have never met Peter or Ariella, I am *telling* you I have never met them. Ask Liesl, she'll tell you.'

'And you have never been to Germany?'

'No, of course I haven't,' she snapped exasperatedly. 'I've told you. I lived in Ballycreggan, then I lived in Liverpool, and now I'm back here.' Elizabeth was trying and failing not to lose her temper. She was worried sick about Erich, but every time she raised the issue, Gaughran just said the police were doing all they could.

'*Sprechen Sie Deutsch?*' He slipped the question smoothly into the middle of the conversation.

'What?' she asked, confused.

'*Deutsch?*' he repeated.

'German? Are you asking me if I can speak German? No, I learned a few phrases before the children came in case they had no English, but it turns out their mother spoke several languages and she conversed with them in not just English and German but French and Italian as well.'

Suddenly, she was very tired. Bone-crushingly weary. The last twenty-four hours had been hell, and the stress was not over yet.

'I haven't done anything wrong, Detective Gaughran. I swear to you on Liesl and Erich's lives. Neither did Daniel. Surely you can see that now? Someone else is feeding information to the Germans, but it's not him and it's not me. Now, can I go?'

Her eyes searched his face for a trace of empathy, or any sense that he knew she was telling the truth, but there was none. Eventually, he nodded at the uniformed officer, who packed up his notebook and pen and left the room.

'Of course. Thank you for your help.' He nodded again and stood.

Elizabeth walked past him as he held the interview room door open for her. She glanced at him, noting again the inscrutable face, but she was past caring.

'Can you check to see if they have found Erich?' she asked Gaughran as he went to say something quietly to a passing officer.

'Officer Wilson will keep you updated, Mrs Klein,' he said, and she thought she heard a note of comfort in his voice. He stood in front of her, looking almost as weary as she felt. 'Please be assured, I will personally make sure everything that can be done to find the boy is done.'

'Thank you.' She buttoned up her coat and tried to fix her hair so she wouldn't be the talk of the parish.

'See Mrs Klein is driven home,' Gaughran instructed the young policeman on the desk as they passed the public area of the station. He escorted her outside, and she longed for some fresh air; she felt dirty.

Elizabeth sat in the back of the police car, visibly shaken. They drove in silence past the Crumlin Road prison, where Daniel awaited his fate, oblivious to everything. She longed to see him, to talk this whole thing through with him, but they would never allow it, and besides, she needed to get home.

'Have you heard anything from Officer Wilson?' she asked the policeman driving her.

'No, ma'am,' he replied.

She sat back and thought they would never get to Ballycreggan. The roads were clogged with military vehicles trying to manage the carnage. The main street was closed off, but she got out at the top of the village by the decimated Catholic church and ran to her house, ignoring the despair on the faces of her neighbours at the sight of their village in ruins.

The key was in the front door, and she turned it. Liesl greeted her with a squeal of delight. 'Elizabeth! He's all right! Erich is back!'

The little boy ran to her and launched himself into her arms, nearly knocking her over.

'Oh, Erich, oh my love, where were you? We nearly went out of our minds!' Only then did she spot Levi and Ruth standing in the kitchen beside Officer Wilson. She noticed two other officers out in the shed. She wasn't surprised; Gaughran was nothing if not thorough.

'He was on the road to Belfast,' Levi said quietly.

'What? What were you doing there?' Elizabeth bent down to be eye level with the child, and her eyes raked his face, searching for an explanation.

'I wanted to see Daniel. I thought if I went to the prison, they might let me see him, or even he could look out the window at me.' Erich's brown eyes filled with tears. 'I don't want them to hang Daniel, Elizabeth. He didn't do anything wrong.'

She pulled him close and held his little body close to hers. 'I know he didn't,' she whispered into his ear.

'We'll let you to it, ma'am. I'm glad the lad is home safe. The house has been searched thoroughly as per Inspector Gaughran's orders, so it's just the garden to do now.' The policeman excused himself and left to join his colleagues outside, but Levi and Ruth hung back. Elizabeth wished they'd go too. Ruth and Levi had done their best to clean up the mess after the raid, the windows were broken but they'd swept up the shards of glass and stuck card over the biggest of the holes. She would have to see to getting the glass replaced, though how she would achieve that she had no idea. Glass, just like everything else was in very short supply. She longed for a bath and a change of clothes, and she then wanted to go up to the school to see what damage had been done there.

'Liesl, can you take Erich upstairs and give him a wash and get him some clean clothes? He looks a bit the worse for wear – we both do.' She smiled and ruffled his hair.

As the children went upstairs, Levi spoke. 'Talia has gone missing now.'

'Really?' Elizabeth asked, wondering how much they suspected.

'Do you think it was her?' Ruth asked.

Elizabeth raked the Irish woman's face for signs of malice. Could Ruth have set Talia up? They didn't like each other… Was she the spy?

She mentally shook herself – she was becoming paranoid. Ruth looked worried and tired, just like everyone.

Elizabeth shrugged. 'I don't know, but it looks strange.' She decided to trust them. 'According to the police, the man she was dealing with is IRA, and apparently, they have been in cahoots with the Nazis for ages, the Germans promising them guns and a United Ireland and all sorts if they helped the Nazi cause. Maybe her association with him is innocent, but I found some paintings of hers, and there looked to be other drawings underneath the watercolours. I handed them over to the police, so it's up to them now.'

The Czech man looked at her, and she thought she saw something there – a flash of mistrust?

'Do you want us to stay or...?' Ruth was uncertain.

'No, thanks, I'll be fine. I'll let you know.' Elizabeth walked with them to the door. 'Thank you for helping so much to find Erich,' she said, locking eyes with Levi.

'He's one of us,' the man replied. He nodded and left with Ruth.

Her eyes fell on the photograph of her parents on the side table in the large square hallway, an old sepia one of her mother sitting on a hardbacked chair looking austere and her daddy behind her, a smile threatening around his eyes. Margaret Bannon would have a stroke if she'd been around to see the house crawling with police and Jews and Americans and all sorts. That was the thing about her mother – she hated almost everyone equally, but Elizabeth most of all. Now that she had Liesl and Erich in her life, she could not understand how her mother could have just cut her off like she did. No matter what either of the children did, she would always forgive them.

Wearily, she climbed the stairs to the bathroom. She filled the bath with the regulation five inches of water and allowed herself the luxury of adding some of her mother's rosewater. When she'd arrived from Liverpool, the bathroom was full of all sorts of bubble bath and bath salts and soaps, but she and the children had almost worked their way through it all.

She sat in the bath, longing for the prewar days when she could fill the bath with warm water, drop in bath salts and luxuriate, topping it up with her toe when it got cold.

Washing, like everything else these days, was reduced to its most utilitarian basics. She scrubbed her hair and rinsed it in cold water and emerged feeling a bit better. She dressed in a clean dress and cardigan and pinned her hair back. At least now she looked like the capable schoolteacher she was, even if inside she was in turmoil.

When she went back downstairs, Erich and Liesl were sitting on the sofa, the girl's arm around her little brother. His hair was damp and brushed, and he was dressed in clean clothes. Liesl was reading to him as he leaned against her, his eyes heavy with tiredness.

As Elizabeth was about to go into the kitchen to make something for them to eat, there was a knock on the door. She sighed. *What now?* It was Gaughran again.

'Inspector,' she said, without enthusiasm.

'Mrs Klein, may I come in?'

'Of course.' She stood back to allow him to pass, and gestured that he should proceed down the hall to the kitchen.

She shut the kitchen door behind her, as she didn't want the children to hear whatever he had to say now – they'd had more than enough upset for the time being. She was also anxious to get to the point. She was tired and hungry, and the children needed her.

'Talia Zimmermann is not at the farm, nor has anyone seen her in the village. Based on your evidence, we are very keen to speak to her.' He paused. 'I believe you, Mrs Klein.' His voice was unusually kind. 'This has been very hard for you and the children, and I apologise for dragging you through it all, but it is a matter of the utmost importance, as you can appreciate. Can I ask you something, off the record?'

She turned to face him. 'Yes.'

'Who do you think is feeding the information? Someone is, that's for sure. Do you think this Talia Zimmermann is capable?'

Elizabeth thought about the question before answering. Did she think Talia could do that? The young woman was always sunny and cheerful, and all of the children apart from Liesl loved her. Bud loved her, and everyone on the farm seemed charmed by her – except Ruth, but that could have been born out of jealousy. But there was something about her, something Elizabeth couldn't put her finger on.

'I don't know, and that's the truth. It seems implausible, as she is such a nice person. Maybe she made some drawings of the base. I have met her out on that headland painting landscapes – maybe she painted over the drawings? Perhaps watercolour would be easy to remove? The colours were very pale, and she didn't go into a lot of detail or dark colours, but I really don't know. And if this man, this Xavier McGuinness, is IRA as you say, and they have links to the Nazis, it would be a way of her transferring back the information.'

Gaughran said nothing, but she could tell he was absorbing every word.

'The fact that the latest bombing was just after the base was heavily restocked, and while Daniel was in jail, it must mean he is innocent even if Talia isn't guilty?'

'Not necessarily. There are too many ifs, buts and maybes for me, Mrs Klein. Thank you for your time and your cooperation. I realise it has been gruelling. I'll be in touch.' He tipped his hat and let himself out through the garden gate.

Elizabeth could feel the net around Talia tighten. Where was she?

# CHAPTER 25

*T*hat night, Elizabeth couldn't sleep, and she sat up when Erich pushed her bedroom door open.

'Can I come in, Elizabeth?' he whispered.

'Of course, darling.' She pulled the covers back for him. He got in beside her and snuggled up to her.

'Do you think the Germans knew we were here? Is that why they sent the bombers?' he asked quietly.

She held his little body close to hers and kissed the top of his head. 'No, I don't. I think they were aiming for the base and they dropped their bombs on the village as well by accident.'

'But do you think if they knew there were lots of Jews here, they'd try to kill us?'

Elizabeth's heart ached. Why any little child should believe that a group of people were trying to kill him was so hard to comprehend.

'I don't. They don't want Jews in Germany for some stupid reason that we can't understand, but they wouldn't have let so many go if they wanted to go after them in other countries, would they?'

'I suppose not,' he said, and she felt him relax.

'So you're safe, my love.'

'I wish Daniel was too,' he whispered.

'So do I, Erich. Believe me, so do I,' she said into his dark silky hair.

After a few moments, she felt his rhythmic breathing and knew he was sleeping. Still, she couldn't drop off; everything was just going round and round in her head.

She wondered what the consequences would be. The people of Ballycreggan were as welcoming as she could have hoped for, but beneath a friendly façade, she knew they were still very suspicious of the Jews. Would they interpret the decimation of the village as an attempt to hit the farm as much as the base?

Morning came eventually, and she got up and dressed early, hoping to go out and offer whatever support she could to her neighbours. Erich and Liesl were still asleep, so she left them a note on the kitchen table saying where she was.

The relief effort was being coordinated from the village hall, and as she entered, she overheard Jenny Foster's mother saying, 'The sooner we're shot of those Jews or Germans or whatever they are, the better. Drawing Hitler on us, they are, and some of them are helping him into the bargain. I don't know – send them packing, I say...'

Mrs Bridges, the butcher's wife, caught Elizabeth's eye as she entered the hall and immediately blushed pink, knowing Elizabeth had overheard the remark.

Elizabeth took a deep breath and walked over to the gathered women. 'Those *refugees*, Mrs Foster, are children who have lost everything – their homes, their schools, their families – all at the hands of Hitler, and what is the point of winning this war if we can't take the moral high ground?'

The three other women in the hall studiously examined their shoes.

'What we as a village are doing is offering sanctuary to those in dire need. Please don't let the Nazis divide us, I'm asking you, as a mother yourself. If it were reversed and it was our country that was behaving despicably, would you not pray that someone would care for Jenny and Kitty?'

The silence hung heavily in the air as Elizabeth waited for an answer.

These were good people, and it was natural they should become mistrustful after everything they had was destroyed in one night, but she needed them to find their compassion again. If she could win back the mothers, the fathers and children would follow.

She looked at Madeline Taylor, the chairperson of the local women's institute and the boss of the village.

Madeline sighed. 'It's not the children's fault, I suppose.'

There seemed to be general agreement, and Elizabeth took that as a positive step. The next hour or so, they made lists of who needed what and decided to put notices up so that anyone who had anything to spare could drop it off. A kitchen was set up as well, providing soup and freshly baked soda bread to anyone in need. Over the next hour, everyone from the village appeared, bringing what they could, making lists of what was most needed. The entire community, Protestant and Catholic, united in unprecedented cooperation.

Amid all the activity and a little after ten a.m., the door opened and Rabbi Frank entered and approached her. The level of conversation in the hall dropped to a murmur.

'Hello, Rabbi,' Elizabeth said, conscious that several people thought as the women she'd spoken to did.

'Good morning, Mrs Klein. I wonder if I could have a word?'

'Of course. Would you like to stay here or...'

'Actually, I wanted to speak to everyone, if that is all right?'

'Um...yes. Yes, of course.' Elizabeth looked around; all eyes were on her.

'Rabbi Frank would like to say something,' she announced in a loud, clear voice, the one Erich called her teacher voice, the one he said he wished she would leave at school.

The gathered people of Ballycreggan turned expectantly to the rabbi. They'd seen him, of course – he was distinctive with his dark suit, hat and peyot – but he rarely interacted.

He waited until everyone was gathered around, silent and waiting for him to speak.

'*Shalom aleichem*. Good morning. I apologise for interrupting your work, but I wanted to come to say something to you all.'

Elizabeth was used to him calling into the school – he visited once a term, and she knew how much the children loved to see him coming – but this was a different crowd.

At school, the children beamed at his praise as he took in all the artwork on the walls. He strolled around the room, examining each piece in detail and asking the child whose masterpiece it was all about it. They answered him enthusiastically, and while she knew back in their home countries, a rabbi was someone to be admired and respected, they were often at a distance. Necessity had brought this Orthodox rabbi much closer to his flock, and Elizabeth observed how both he and his people benefitted. She watched as he spoke to each child in turn, looking at their exercise books, praising their neat handwriting, their pages of mathematical sums.

Today, however, there was suspicion and animosity; it could almost be felt in the air.

'I have brought with me some food and furniture and clothing from our farm. I hope it will be of use. We are at your disposal for whatever you need. Our people are outside, and they want to help you rebuild your village. I hope you will accept our help.'

The people of Ballycreggan looked surprised, and one or two shared a glance. The rabbi went on. 'You all know why we are here?'

A few people nodded.

'We are here because we have had to leave our homes on account of Hitler's policies to rid Europe of Jews. We are the lucky ones, and we will survive, we will go on, we will keep our faith alive. Not just for ourselves but for all of our families and friends. Some of our community will not survive this war, some of us have lost loved ones already, and I fear the same fate awaits many more of us. It is through your kindness and your generosity that we are alive. We will never be able to thank you, but I can assure you of one thing – your hospitality has not gone unnoticed, either by us or by God.'

'Every time we pray, I say to the community, especially the little ones, in the face of all of this evil, we must remember those who help us. We remember them, and more importantly, God sees their self-lessness. And when the time comes, they will be rewarded for their labours, often against terrible dangers. The people who organised to bring us here, the people who continue to help Jews to escape secretly out of Europe, the people of Ballycreggan who have shown such goodness, we remember you in our prayers.'

The entire group was transfixed.

'And while it is hard, we must trust in God. It may seem like the world is against us all, but this is not true. All around us are good, kind people who have opened their hearts and their homes and their schools to us, and we must remember that. Even back in Germany, Austria, Czechoslovakia, Poland, wherever we come from, there are good people fighting to stop this terrible regime.

'And so I came to your broken village today to bring you what we have, to offer our help in every way we can and to tell you that for Shabbat tomorrow night, we will pray for you a very special prayer. This is a prayer of thanks. Usually this prayer, *Birkat HaGomel*, is said after a journey or an ordeal, but we want to say it to thank God for all of you here. I know your children are the friends of ours, and that makes us all a community. This miraculous integration happened because of one very special person. That special person is the teacher, Mrs Klein. I know how much she does to take care of our children and help them feel not alone, so today, we will pray for the people of Ballycreggan and for Mrs Klein.'

Elizabeth swallowed the lump in her throat.

'Mrs Klein is an example of what I am talking about. She is love.'

Movement at the back of the crowd caused everyone to turn around. Father O'Toole and Reverend Parkes made their way to where the rabbi stood. The priest in his soutane and the Protestant vicar in his dark suit with pink shirt and clerical collar stood beside the rabbi, the whole village watching to see what would happen next. Reverend Parkes and Father O'Toole had ministered to their respective congregations for many years without a cross word, but neither had been seen with the rabbi before this.

'Thank you, Rabbi Frank, we appreciate it,' Father O'Toole began. 'And I know I speak for the community here in Ballycreggan when I say you are all welcome here. We have been through a terrible ordeal, and so have all of you, so we must not let this divide us. We must make sure it cements us.' The two men shook hands, and there was almost a collective exhale of relief.

'Maybe we could say your prayer together?' Reverend Parkes suggested.

The rabbi smiled and nodded. 'We say the prayer in Hebrew, but can someone here explain to everyone what it means?' The rabbi addressed all of the Jewish children who'd come in from outside. He scanned the room. Liesl's friend Viola raised her hand.

'Yes, Viola, can you translate the prayer for us?'

Viola stood and turned to Elizabeth, her blue eyes locked with her teacher's. 'It means blessed are you, oh Lord, who rewards the undeserving with goodness, and who has rewarded me with goodness.' She paused. 'And then we reply, "May he who has rewarded you with all goodness, reward us with all goodness forever."'

'Very good, Viola, excellent in fact.' The rabbi smiled. 'This beautiful prayer can be recited for many reasons, such as when one survives a great ordeal or makes a long journey, and it also can be used for women when they become mothers.' His eyes rested on Elizabeth. 'Today we will recite the prayer for all of you who have taken us to your hearts.'

The rabbi began to chant the prayer in the singsong way Elizabeth had become used to on her visits to celebrate Shabbat on the farm.

'*Baruch ata Adonai, Eloheinu melech ha-olam, ha-gomel l'chayavim tovot sh-g'malani kol tuv.*'

The Jews, from the youngest to the oldest responded enthusiastically. '*Mi she-g'malcha kol tuv, hu yi-g'malcha kol tuv selah.*'

Elizabeth stood and absorbed their love. Each child turned towards her, and she realised that never in her life had she received a gift so precious.

'Thank you. *Todah,*' Reverend Parkes said. 'We face a challenge – to rebuild our village. Though our communities have been divided along sectarian lines for a long time, Ballycreggan has been spared the worst of that hatred and mistrust. Let us offer the hand of friendship now as we try to rebuild, not just to our Catholic or Protestant neighbours, but also to our Jewish ones. Together we are stronger than anything Hitler can throw at us.'

'We are happy having you all here, and thank you for your prayer,' Father O'Toole added.

The group relaxed and moved off in various directions to begin the process of providing for those in need. The Jews carried in boxes of farm produce, as well as clothing and blankets, and Elizabeth found herself directing operations. All of the men, locals and refugees alike, divided into work details, and each group took on a house to assess the damage and decide what was needed. The women organised food, temporary accommodation and clothing.

She overheard Levi talking to Pat Gordon, the local publican. 'There are others, some of the older children, working on some basic furniture back at the farm – tables, chairs, beds. But if you let us know what is most in need, we will try to produce it quickly.'

'That's great, thanks very much.' Pat instructed some local children to help bring in the generous contributions from the farm.

The three clerics stood by, surveying their congregations working together.

Elizabeth explained to the children how to man the various stalls, and how to arrange donated shoes by size. She sent Viola for Erich and Liesl with instructions to bring all the spare hangers from her house. David, one of the older boys from the farm, set up rudimentary rails on which to hang clothes.

The rabbi approached her and gently led her away from the noise and activity. 'You know the police came looking for Talia? I spoke to Inspector Gaughran. They need to interview her, but she is not here. When he left, I had some people I know check up on her – I know some Viennese Jews who are taking refuge in England. Nobody in the Jewish community or in the political world of resistance to the Anschluss in Vienna has heard of anybody by her name. She told us her mother was Jewish and her father a gentile and that both were actively resisting the annexation. We took her on face value, but it seems that may have been a mistake. Perhaps Talia is not what she seems. But then, everything is so chaotic, it is hard to know.'

'You seem surprised?' she remarked, wanting to draw him further.

'Yes, well, she came to me often, like the others. She spoke of her family, the loss of them, her grief. I tried to console her, but...' he shrugged, his palms open, 'words do not help I usually find. She was truthfully, very sad. It is hard to believe it was all an act, but then...' he shrugged again.

Elizabeth nodded. 'What does this mean for Daniel, do you think, Rabbi? Surely they cannot think he is still guilty now?'

The rabbi shrugged. 'Who knows?'

Elizabeth tried to hide her frustration. It was as if the rabbi had resigned himself to Daniel's execution, and because he was a man of such faith, he believed completely that Daniel was going to heaven, so there was no problem. Elizabeth had no such serenity.

'So if the police don't find and convict Talia and exonerate Daniel in the process, he could still hang.'

The rabbi nodded. 'That is true. And even convicting Talia, if they do, will not mean that Daniel is automatically free.' He gave a slow, sad smile. 'You love him.' It was a statement, not a question.

Elizabeth didn't know what to say.

The rabbi went on. 'He feels the same about you. He told me.'

This news shook Elizabeth, and while the revelation filled her heart with joy and relief, the situation seemed hopeless. 'I do,' she said.

'He is a good man, and he is worthy of your love.' Rabbi Frank's air of resignation made Elizabeth want to shake him. In any other circumstances, she would have been pleased at his endorsement. She knew he admired her, but supporting the relationship between a Jewish man and a gentile woman was new for him.

'Will you tell him?' she asked.

'If you want me to, then of course I will,' he replied.

'Yes. Please tell him.' She wanted to say more, to have him convey to Daniel all he meant to her and the children, but she couldn't.

'Of course. Goodbye, Mrs Klein.'

'And thank you for coming today, for the prayer and the food and everything... It meant a lot,' Elizabeth added.

'The Lord will watch over you, Mrs Klein, and over Daniel. You are in safe hands.'

She watched his black-clothed back move off in the direction of some boys who were manoeuvring a makeshift bed, and he helped them carry it.

Daniel loved her. She loved him. It was wonderful news, but her heart was breaking.

# CHAPTER 26

*E*lizabeth tried to contact Inspector Gaughran in the days that followed, but he seemed to be unavailable. Erich and Liesl were agitated and bickering much more than usual, and she knew it was all the upheaval: Daniel's fate, the sudden disappearance of Talia, Bud being moved overseas, the devastation that greeted them every time they went outside the front door. The village green where they played had become a huge crater, their beloved cherry trees cut down to use for timber. All of this made them feel lost, and whatever stability she had managed to achieve for them was being eroded on a daily basis.

She wondered if the rabbi had told Daniel how she felt. She'd written to him, telling him herself, but she had no idea if he received her letters. He didn't or couldn't reply. She'd requested a visit from the governor, but again, got no response. The lack of information was so frustrating.

She went through the motions of life, cooking and cleaning, helping the neighbours who'd lost everything in the raid to get their lives back together. The people of Ballycreggan, with the help of the men and women from the farm and those either too young or too old to be in uniform, worked tirelessly to rebuild. Everyone worked on every property until each was some version of habitable again. At least it was summertime, with long evenings and warm days. What was lost were only things, and everyone went about with the same mantra on their lips – 'Thank God nobody was killed. Things can be replaced.' But she knew what it was like to lose everything.

She tried to stay busy, though all she did was think about Daniel. It was in the hands of the magistrate now; there was nothing more she or anyone else could do. The rabbi had said all he was willing to say on the subject, and so it was just a matter of waiting for news.

The whole village was a hive of activity. Poor Bridie had been devastated to see her beloved sweetshop gone, but three of the older Jewish boys were working from dawn to well after dark trying to rebuild it. Sugar and sweets were so rationed now that at least she'd not lost much stock. They'd even asked Elizabeth if they could look in her shed for paint. They found some red gloss and a large tin of white, which they mixed together to make a lovely lurid pink colour. They painted the timber hoarding that served as the front wall of the building, so Bridie's shop was the beacon in the village for children it had always been.

Elizabeth donated anything they had that wasn't vital. Most of her mother's extra furniture had been given to the farm in the early days, and they in turn gave it back to those with nothing.

She decided to go into the attic. She'd not been up there since coming home, but there was a chance her mother stored some things that might be useful to the neighbours. They needed blankets, pots and pans, cutlery, crockery...everything really.

She got Liesl to hold the ladder as she climbed up to the trapdoor at the top of the stairs. Erich was in his element with his school friends, painting and hammering and helping in every way he could on the reconstruction of the village.

'Hold it steady, Liesl. I'm not a huge fan of heights, and let's just pray there are no furry friends up here,' Elizabeth said as she shoved the trapdoor upwards. She expected it to be stiff or strung with cobwebs or dust, but it opened easily with no debris to be seen. The dark attic smelled dry and musty. She listened for any ominous scurrying and was relieved to hear none. She had a torch tucked into the waistband of her skirt. Teetering up the last few rungs, she managed to get herself into the attic.

To her relief, it was floored – she couldn't remember if it had been – and she was able to crawl through the trapdoor. In the apex of the roof, it was tall enough for her to stand.

On one side was a small window with a wooden shutter on it. Using the torch, she opened the latch holding the wooden shutter closed. It opened easily, a shower of dust and dead spiders hitting the wooden floor. Immediately, the dark attic was transformed as light flooded in the window, and she could see clearly. As she suspected, there were wooden tea chests stacked neatly, and as she opened them, she discovered all sorts of household things: odd cups and saucers, basins and buckets, and several pairs of wellington boots in varying sizes. Her father's old work clothes were laundered and neatly folded in another, and she held a sweater to her face to see if it smelled like him. It didn't. There were boxes of books – all her old schoolbooks – everything neatly packed away. It would be nice to be able to offer the things to those in the village who needed them.

She opened box after box. A small one, the size of a shoebox, was on a shelf. In it were Christmas cards. It was only when she opened them that she realised they were the annual Christmas cards she'd sent to her mother every single year since she left, each one ignored. But to Elizabeth's astonishment, Margaret Bannon had kept every card, opened and read but still in their envelopes.

Behind the neatly stacked cards was an envelope, buff in colour and bigger than the cards. She opened it and found a whole bundle of other Christmas cards.

They were luxurious, not the thin flimsy ones she'd sent. These were on heavy card, some of them embossed with gold leaf. She opened one.

*Dear Elizabeth,*

*Thank you for your lovely card. I hope you and Rudi are well and enjoying the Christmas season. Ballycreggan is as it always is. I'd love to see you, Elizabeth, and I'm sorry for the way I acted. Your father would have been better if he'd been spared. I miss you and send you all my love.*

*Mammy*

She swallowed, a wave of emotion crashing over her. She stared at her mother's copperplate writing. Such love and affection written here, things that she was never able to say. Why had her mother written those words of conciliation but never sent the card? All those years, she could have had a mother, and Margaret could have had a daughter. She wasn't the warmest of women, there was no doubt about it, but Elizabeth had sent the cards every Christmas in the hope that her mother would soften. Only when she saw a tear drop onto the card did she realise she was crying.

All the other cards were in a similar vein, each to her, each wishing her a happy Christmas, an odd one with news of who died or who got married in Ballycreggan, sometimes a reminiscence of her father. And in those words, again she felt a softness that she'd never experienced with her mother in real life.

There was a mass card. 'The Holy Sacrifice of the Mass has been offered for the repose of the soul of Rudi Klein.' On it, her mother had written,

*Dear Elizabeth,*

*I am so sorry to hear of Rudi's death. He was just a young lad with his whole life ahead of him. I'm sorry for the way I behaved. I wish I'd met him. Take care, my love.*

*Mammy*

In each card, she said how she missed her. She even signed some of them, 'all my love, Mammy'.

'Elizabeth? Are you all right up there?' Liesl's voice cut through her reverie.

'Yes, yes, pet, I'm fine,' she replied, her voice hoarse with emotion. She wiped her face with the sleeve of her cardigan. Such a waste.

She put the cards back in the box and placed it on top of her old schoolbooks, taking a few steadying breaths. She could not deal with this now on top of everything else.

She heaved a few boxes of kitchen utensils over to the trapdoor. 'If

I lower these down, can you take them?' she asked Liesl. 'They're not too heavy, and some of this stuff will be useful.'

'Of course.' Liesl was delighted to help.

For the next twenty minutes, Elizabeth lowered boxes of things. She didn't open them all, as she could go through the stuff downstairs and donate what might be useful and either dump or repack anything that wasn't. Her back ached from bending down to reach the boxes stacked against the wall. She slid box after box towards the trapdoor and lowered them down to Liesl's waiting arms. Lastly, she handed the girl the box of cards.

Eventually, the attic cleared, she lowered herself down the ladder once more, closing the trapdoor behind her.

'That wasn't as bad as I thought. I don't think anyone has been up there for decades – anything could have been up there.' Elizabeth tried to smile brightly, ignoring the shock and deep sadness she felt at her discovery. She brushed dust from her blouse and skirt and a cobweb from her hair.

'There's a lot of stuff,' Liesl remarked as she counted the boxes.

'Yes, my mother was a hoarder, threw nothing out. But she insisted on putting everything away neatly, so this stuff should be usable for someone. Let's pull it into the spare bedroom there and go through each box. I couldn't do it up there – my back was killing me.'

They took each box in turn. It really was incredible the things her mother kept. Several boxes of coats, hats and shoes, all of her father's old clothes, men's overcoats and working boots. Elizabeth gasped at the boxes of her own childhood clothes – dresses she remembered wearing, shoes, coats, pullovers handknitted by her mother, cardigans, even the hand-embroidered handkerchiefs – all stored lovingly in tissue paper and layered with mothballs. Everything was perfect.

They opened boxes of toys, jigsaws and books, and Liesl was enchanted by a beautiful doll with a china face. She wore a blood-red gown and had a red matching bonnet and long curly blonde hair.

'Oh, that's Rosie. I got her from Santa Claus when I was about six.' Elizabeth examined the little doll's face, her voice cracking with emotion. 'My mother made her a whole wardrobe of clothes, even a playsuit for when I took her out to the garden digging with my father.'

Elizabeth caught Liesl's eye, seeing the question there. 'I know I've told you my mother wasn't very nice, but you must be thinking that that was a kind thing to do for a little girl, so maybe she wasn't all bad?'

Liesl thought for a moment. 'Well, it was nice of her, and she kept all of your things so beautifully. Maybe she missed you and couldn't tell you?'

Elizabeth nodded slowly. 'You know, Liesl? You're right. I would never have believed it but...' She sat on the spare bed and patted the space beside her for Liesl to sit down. She then picked up the box of cards.

'I found these.' She showed them to the girl. 'Every year, I wrote my mother a Christmas card, and she never once replied. I even wrote to say Rudi had been killed, and still nothing. It hurt so much. I was all alone over in England. Rudi's family were nice, but I wasn't Jewish, and anyway, I hardly knew them, so I was really lonely. I needed my mother, even if she was a bit of a dragon.' Elizabeth gave a small smile and Liesl giggled.

'When I got a letter from her solicitor to say she had died – I didn't even know she was sick – I was devastated. I was really surprised with how I reacted because I hadn't seen her for over two decades, but I suppose a part of me thought that we would patch it up at some stage. Then she died, and I had to face the fact that we never would.'

A tear leaked from the side of her eye, and Liesl handed over a handkerchief. Elizabeth accepted it and wiped her eyes.

'I just found these, replies to all my cards, a mass card for Rudi, and in each of them, she says she was sorry for throwing me out and that she loved me. But she never posted them. It's so sad, isn't it?'

Liesl opened one or two of the cards, reading the inscriptions inside. 'It really is. For her and for you. She died here, alone, and if only she could have sent the letters, you would have come back, wouldn't you?'

'Of course. I don't know why she didn't post them, I really don't.' Elizabeth opened a few more, showing them to Liesl.

'Maybe she was afraid that you would not want to see her,' the girl suggested, her dark eyes innocent.

Elizabeth felt a rush of love for the child she saw as her daughter. 'Probably. Promise me, Liesl, that no matter what happens, when you are grown up and I'm an old lady, that we won't ever lose touch?'

'I promise.' Liesl rested her head on Elizabeth's shoulder. 'You are our mum now. We have lost our lovely *mutti*. You would have loved her, Elizabeth. She was so funny and always wanted to play. I loved it when she brushed my hair, and she would sing to us, all kinds of songs in all different languages. Silly songs about goats and dogs and boys and girls, and Erich and I would sing along. And then if Papa came home when we were singing, he would join in too. And she let us help her when she was cooking or baking bread. We would climb onto two stools at the kitchen table, and she would give us our own piece of dough. She was beautiful, my *mutti*. She had beautiful dark-red curly hair and brown eyes. Everybody noticed her. When we would go to the synagogue, she was the only one with hair like copper. Everybody admired her. I wish I looked like her. Papa said she was like a magical mermaid, and she was…'

It struck her that the child used the past tense. Liesl was convinced her mother was dead.

'You have her eyes, and you will grow to be a beautiful woman, Liesl, just like your *mutti*. I think she would be so proud of you and Erich.'

The girl nodded sadly. 'Yes, I think she would. And she would be so grateful to you for caring for us. She loved us so much.'

They sat together in companionable silence for a long moment, the warm summer sun shining through the window.

# CHAPTER 27

*I*n the week after the attack, Reverend Parkes and Father O'Toole continually made appeals to their respective congregations, as well as to neighbouring parishes, to bring anything they could spare to the hall and allow those who'd lost everything to try to rebuild their lives. It struck Elizabeth how heartening it was to see people be so generous when they had so little themselves. The entire perimeter of the hall was lined with tables borrowed from the school, and people were laying out their wares for their neighbours to take. Everyone from the farm also was there as often as possible to help out.

Levi and a few others were in a corner where he'd set up a repair station to mend things that were salvageable.

The whole hall was a hive of activity. The ladies of the parish had set up a tea-and-bun stall, and each child who worked hard was promised a sticky bun at the end of the day.

Elizabeth unpacked a box of her childhood clothes, not seen in daylight for over thirty years, and placed them on the table. They were old-fashioned undoubtedly but good quality, and she could see several mothers eyeing her covetously.

She had enlisted the help of some of the older children to bring the boxes from the attic to the hall. She had labelled each box, and Liesl was busy unpacking a men's clothes and tools stand while Erich was making one of kitchen utensils, crockery, cutlery and lots of curtains and tablecloths. Elizabeth set about filling two tables, one with her mother's old clothes and another with her own.

As she unpacked, Elizabeth was surprised to find a satchel at the bottom of one of the boxes. It was canvas and had metal buckles. It looked to be army issue.

She opened the satchel and extracted the contents. There was a large brown envelope, inside of which was a passport, or at least papers of some kind – the writing was in German, so she didn't understand it. Inside was a photograph of Talia but with the name Sophia Becker. Elizabeth could feel her heart thumping in her chest. What on earth was this, and what was it doing in a box in her attic?

There were clothes, a map and a compass, and then another set of papers, again with Talia's picture but this time in English with the name Josephine Turner. At the bottom of the satchel, wrapped in a piece of brown cloth, was a pistol.

In an outside pocket was a smaller envelope, and in it was another set of papers, identical to the German ones, with the name Hans Hoffman. The photograph made her gasp.

It was of Daniel.

Her heart pounded in her chest. What was this? Who had put these things in her house, in her attic? She didn't know what to do. She needed to tell someone, but who? Whom could she trust? Was Daniel a spy after all? Were he and Talia working together? Why would he need other identification papers if he wasn't? She hastily shoved everything back in the bag. She needed to think.

'I forgot something at home. You two man the tables, and I'll be back shortly, all right?' she called to Liesl and Erich as she almost ran out of the hall, clutching the satchel.

'Elizabeth, I think we can fix this if I could use the bench vice in your shed...' Levi tried to stop her, but she just barrelled past him.

She kept her head down and walked the length of the village.

Thankfully, everyone was in the hall, so she was able to get home uninterrupted.

She fumbled with the key, as her hands were trembling, but eventually she managed to open the front door.

She stopped dead in the hall as she heard a thump from upstairs. Someone was in her house. She heard footsteps. Her blood ran cold, and prickles of sweat rose on her neck and back.

Her instinct was to turn, to run and leave, but she was rooted to the spot. A young man appeared from the kitchen. She didn't recognise him, but he was pointing a gun right at her head. He was wearing dark clothing and had short brown hair and a moustache.

'It's most unfortunate that you came back, Mrs Klein,' he said softly. He was local; his accent was County Down. 'But you seem to have something of ours, so drop the bag and take one step back, please.' He padded towards her, his feet making no sound on the carpet.

She did as he told her, terrified he'd shoot. As she dropped the bag, she looked up the stairs. Talia was there, dressed in dark clothing, and she looked wretched.

'Elizabeth, do what he says. You won't get hurt – just do as he says.' The younger woman's voice sounded as terrified as Elizabeth felt.

'Get out of my house this minute, both of you,' she said through gritted teeth.

'We'll be happy to, Mrs Klein, but I'll be needing that back.' He came towards her and picked up the satchel, checking inside.

Elizabeth turned to Talia, the woman she'd seen as a friend. 'How could you? Erich and Liesl, all the children loved you. How could you betray them like this?'

'It's more complicated than you think.' Talia shrugged. 'I had a job to do. I'm not Jewish, but I don't care about that. The only future for my country is National Socialism and the Fuhrer – without him, there is no Germany. Without him, we are just like everyone else, weak and pathetic.'

'How can you support him? I don't understand...' Elizabeth had almost forgotten the man pointing the gun at her, so horrified was she to hear Talia's opinion.

'You don't know, you don't understand! The Jews, they are like parasites, like cockroaches. They breed and colonise, and ordinary hardworking Germans, we can't get anywhere. They control everything. We need them out. I like you, Elizabeth, and you mean well. We're friends, and I don't want any harm to come to you. You gave me a sense of home in these long lonely months. But those Jews, they can't be allowed to survive. If you could only understand that! You can't see what a parasite they are on decent people like us...'

'But –' Elizabeth began, but the man stopped her.

'This wee cosy chat is all very well and fine, ladies, but I've a job to do, so if you don't mind. Now then.' He smiled. 'I could shoot you, and that would be the end of it, but I know you're the local schoolteacher, so I'd rather not. And you've those two wee bairns to take care of too, and unlike my German friend here, I couldn't give a monkey's what religion they are. We're on the same side, you and me, Mrs Klein, and when all of this is over and Germany wins the war, us Catholics will be united with our countrymen in the South and all will be well.'

He smiled and she shivered.

'I am nothing like you,' she spat, fury at having her home invaded like this overtaking her terror. How dare this man enter her house, endanger Liesl and Erich and claim they had anything in common. 'Nothing at all. This cannot be about Irish nationalism. What Hitler is doing is wrong, so horrible, and if you can help him, then you're all as bad as he is... And as for you' – she turned to Talia, who was now beside her in the hall – 'you traitorous bitch! You pretended to love those children, *my* children, when all along you were every bit as bad as those Nazis that strut about in their uniforms. You're both pathetic. Get out of my house!'

She snapped her head back to face the man at the sound of the pistol being cocked.

'No, don't shoot!' Talia screamed, charging at him. The shot fired and Elizabeth dropped to the floor. She could see feet and hear shouting – Talia and the man were struggling. Then blood. It wasn't hers, she was almost sure. She got up on her hands and knees and tried to help Talia, who was pinned under the weight of the man now, blood spurting from her shoulder. His gun was still in his hand as he punched Talia in the face. The young woman stilled.

Elizabeth launched herself on him, trying to pull him off Talia, but as he swung around, his fist connected with her mouth. She sprawled onto her back. Blood spurted from her lip, and her head was throbbing. She must have banged it on the corner of the hallstand as she fell.

There was a ringing in her ears. She tried to get up, but then the man bent down and dragged her roughly to her feet, his fist clasping a bunch of her hair. He jerked her head painfully, and whispered slowly in her ear, 'I'm not interested in what you think of me, but let me tell you this. The German lass won't ever speak to anyone again, but if you do – and I mean if you tell anyone about this – know that something very bad will happen to those wains of yours. Do you hear me?'

He shook her and repeated, 'Do you hear me?'

She refused to answer, her face inches from his, his sour breath assaulting her nostrils.

'Now, I know some unsavoury characters who'd love nothing better than some time alone with that wee lass of yours. The wee lad too, if you know what I mean? And if you say a word to anyone, then that's exactly what will happen, and they'll be praying they'd gone to the camps with their mammy and daddy. Do we have an agreement, Mrs Klein?'

Elizabeth nodded. She could feel that her front tooth was loose, her mouth was filling with blood, and she thought she might vomit.

He shoved her, and she fell back down on the floor, forward this time, landing painfully on her knee. Her head was beside Talia's foot. He then stood on her ankle, putting his whole weight on it. She screamed and felt she might pass out.

# CHAPTER 28

he door slammed and he was gone. Elizabeth forced herself to focus, to not pass out, though the pain was excruciating. She dragged herself level with Talia, and realised the younger woman was breathing. It was shallow, and her shoulder was soaked in blood, but she was alive.

'Talia, wake up! You're all right, wake up...' Elizabeth pleaded.

The younger woman's eyes fluttered for a moment, 'Elizabeth,' she whispered. 'Daniel...' She couldn't say more.

'Daniel what?' Elizabeth gasped, spitting blood.

But Talia's eyes were closed again.

Elizabeth dragged herself, inch by painful inch, to the door. There was no way she could gather the strength to reach the latch, but she managed to take her mother's cast iron boot cleaner, a heavy thing, and bang the inside of the door, hoping someone passing by would hear.

'Help...' She knew her voice wasn't strong enough. A few thumps on the door were all she could manage. The room was spinning, and a wave of nausea made her vomit. It was a mixture of blood and the contents of her stomach, and she retched until there was nothing left.

Her ankle was so painful, and she could see it was at a very odd angle; it was certainly broken. She wiped her eye on her sleeve – more blood.

She would have to try something else. As she attempted to drag herself into the sitting room where there was a window onto the street, she heard voices outside.

The people outdoors knocked, and she tried to speak, to call out, but she couldn't.

'I wonder if the side is open. I only need the tools in the shed.'

She heard Levi's voice as he moved away from the front door. Then the sound of the garden gate being opened. *Please let them look in.* They might see Talia, as the door between the kitchen and the hall was open. She tried once more to drag herself back, and to her relief, heard raised voices, followed by the sound of glass breaking.

'Mrs Klein!' Bridie's brother-in-law John ran to her. Levi bent down beside Talia.

'Call the police!' Levi shouted at two of the boys, standing terrified on the doorstep, who were helping to lift a broken bedframe. He tried to find a pulse in Talia's neck.

John Mac lifted Elizabeth to the couch, having made sure her neck and back were all right. Despite his efforts to be gentle, she whimpered in agony.

The alarm was raised by the boys, and within moments, crowds surged from the hall. The police were on constant alert in the village after everything that had happened, so the local constables arrived within moments.

Constable Wilson asked her questions, but she couldn't focus on them, his face swimming in and out of her line of vision.

'Liesl... Erich...' she managed.

'Liesl and Erich are outside, but Mrs Morris is keeping them in the kitchen until we clean you up,' Dr Parsons said as he shooed everyone else out except Eli, the Polish dentist from the farm.

Dr Parsons did a preliminary examination. He shone a light in her eyes and determined that her ankle was indeed broken, her knee possibly dislocated and her head and lip would need stitches. He filled his syringe with something that he then administered to her through her arm.

'We'd better get you to hospital as soon as possible,' he said, putting his stethoscope back in the bag. 'I'm calling the ambulance, so just stay here until it comes.' His tone brooked no argument.

'Eli, could you have a look? There's one loose anyway, but you'd have a better idea of the damage.' The doctor stood back and allowed Eli to examine her mouth. The two men had become friends in the past few months and were often seen enjoying a game of chess in the pub.

Eli prodded her teeth gently with his fingers and then smiled. 'Just one loose. The others are fine. You have some abrasions to your inner cheek and lip, but they can patch that up. Don't eat anything hard, and you might not lose it.'

'But I…' She tried to get up, but a searing pain in her head stopped her. She winced and lay back down. 'Can you ask Constable Wilson to come in here?' she said.

'Can't it wait?' the old doctor asked, his huge hairy eyebrows furrowed in disapproval.

'No…it really can't.'

'Very well, but you need to rest, Elizabeth. I won't have you doing anything until you get the all clear from the hospital, do you understand?'

She nodded and smiled weakly. He had been their family doctor until she left for England, and beneath his gruff manner, he was a very kind man.

She remembered him setting her nose when she had been hit by a football in the schoolyard when she was nine, and he'd taken very good care of the people of Ballycreggan for over fifty years. Losing his son in 1940 had almost killed him; his wife died of TB in the thirties sometime, and he and his boy were very close. Mr Morris had told her how proud he was when young Douglas Parsons was accepted to study medicine in Queens University, Belfast. That boy should now be running the practice and old Dr Parsons spending his days fly fishing, but the war meant there was no such thing as retirement. Douglas was younger than Elizabeth; she remembered him being born just before she left for England. To Dr Parsons, Douglas was a loss from which he would never recover, but in the great scheme of things, he was just one more in an ever-increasing death toll. Dr Parsons' friendship with Eli had brought him out of his depression, and everyone was relieved for him, and for themselves.

'I do, Dr Parsons, I promise. But I have to speak to the police as fast as possible – it's really important.' Whatever injection he'd given her was working, and while the pain was still very much present, it wasn't all-consuming. 'I feel better.'

'That will be the morphine. It will get you over the worst until we can get you to hospital.' He placed his hand on her forehead, checking her temperature. 'Very well.' He sighed as he packed up his things in the bag that was as old as he was.

'Oh, Dr Parsons, is Talia dead?' she asked as he left.

'No, she's gone in the first ambulance. They arrived a few minutes after I did.' He nodded, saying no more, and left.

Within a minute, the young constable arrived in the sitting room. 'I'm glad you feel up to talking now, Mrs Klein. Now if I could just ask you a few –'

She cut him off. 'I need you to bring Gaughran here immediately.' Even talking hurt.

'Well, I'm sure Inspector Gaughran will be happy to speak to you in due course, but in the meantime, I am the police officer in –'

She held up her hand to stop him. He was in his late twenties and full of his own importance. She had no patience for him. 'Just get Gaughran, please. I'll only speak to him.'

Her insistence must have worked because as she was lifted by the paramedics to the waiting ambulance, she heard him say, 'I'll have the inspector meet you at the hospital, Mrs Klein.'

She managed to nod. She felt peculiar, like she was not in her body.

Erich and Liesl broke away from Mrs Morris to see her being carried out on a stretcher.

'I'm all right, my darlings, just a little cut...' she managed to rasp. They were snow-white and looked terrified.

'Don't worry,' a kind paramedic said as he carried the end of the stretcher. 'Your mum will be right as rain in a few days. She just needs patching up.'

The journey to the hospital was a blur, and she assumed they must have given her something to make her sleep because when she woke, she was in a private room with a view over Dunville Park.

She was parched and twisted her head painfully to see if someone was around to get her a drink. Sitting on a chair reading the paper beside her was Detective Gaughran.

'Ah, Mrs Klein, you're back to us.' He smiled.

She couldn't talk as her mouth was so dry, so she gestured to the jug of water on the nightstand. He understood and poured her a glass, which she drank in one gulp. He refilled it.

'Are Liesl and Erich all right?' She remembered the IRA man's threat.

'They are with Mrs Morris and her husband. They said they'd take care of them until you were home. Don't worry – they're fine.'

'I need to tell you...' She felt a bit woolly in the head. It must have been the drugs, but she hoped she was making sense, as she needed Gaughran to understand everything. Her leg was in traction; her ankle must have been set while she was unconscious. The pain was manageable, dull and definitely there, but she needed to think clearly.

She told him everything that had happened since she uncovered the satchel, breaking frequently for sips of water.

She told him about the papers, the two sets for Talia and the one in the name of Hans Hoffman but with Daniel's photograph. She explained as best she could what Talia had said, how she seemed enslaved to Hitler's ideology, but how – as far as she remembered it anyway – Talia jumped on the IRA man to stop him shooting Elizabeth.

He allowed her to speak, never interrupting her, and when she concluded, he simply nodded. 'Thank you, Mrs Klein. You've been more than helpful. Miss Zimmermann is now in custody, and her chances of survival are good though she's lost a lot of blood. We are hoping that she will help us with our investigation once she's fit enough. My officers have arrested a man we are sure was the one who attacked you. He had those documents on his person, so we have that evidence now, and both he and McGuinness will also be helping us with our enquiries before facing trial for treason.'

'Is Daniel a spy?' she whispered, hardly able to face the answer.

'I'm afraid I can't comment, as it is an active investigation, but thank you for your cooperation.'

He stood to go.

'But you can't just go and not tell me... What about the threat against Liesl and Erich? He...he said he knew people who would hurt them. I won't be able to let them out of my sight.'

Gaughran turned, his face showing compassion, a rare emotion. 'That was a terrible threat, I know. And you must be worried, but I can tell you this. I have been dealing with the IRA all of my career, and in this case, we know McGuinness and his accomplice were operating outside of them. McGuinness was IRA at one stage, no doubt, but he doesn't take direction well, so the top brass had more or less cut him loose. I can't go into any detail on the case we are investigating at the moment, but I can assure you that the man he sent was just trying to scare you. I have it on the best authority from those he threatened you with that neither you nor the children are in any danger from them. The IRA have no gripe with you, Mrs Klein, and both McGuinness and his accomplice are in custody and will be remaining so for a very long time, I would imagine, so you need not worry. Even so, I will ensure an extra policeman is stationed in Ballycreggan until this whole situation is resolved.'

She believed him. There was something about Gaughran. He wasn't friendly or comforting, but there was an integrity to the man she appreciated.

'I'll be in touch if I have any further questions. Get well soon, Mrs Klein.' And he was gone.

For the rest of the day, apart from visits from various doctors and nurses checking her ankle and knee as well as the stitches to her lip, inside and outside her mouth, and the twelve to the gash over her eye, she just stared at the ceiling, mulling over everything. Had Daniel ever been in the attic? Had Talia? She remembered thinking how it was strange that the trapdoor opened so easily and that there were few cobwebs or little dust considering that, as far as she was concerned, nobody had been up there for decades. She was wrong, clearly.

She racked her brain to try to think of opportunities either one of them might have had. Daniel was never alone in her house as far as she knew, but then he could have let himself in during the day when she was at school. The back door was always open. Would he do that? What was Talia trying to tell her at the end? She just said 'Daniel'. What did she want her to know? That Daniel was innocent? Daniel was guilty?

She thought back to the day she visited him when she asked him outright if he was a spy. He had locked eyes with her and totally denied it. Was he lying? Surely she'd have seen it there, as it takes a very accomplished liar to lie straight to someone's face and give nothing away. But then, that's how they trained spies, wasn't it?

Talia had ample opportunity. She babysat, so she could have gone up when the children were asleep, though it was hard to visualise. Liesl was a very light sleeper, so someone clattering about on the landing with a ladder would surely have woken her. Was she a spy? It seemed the most likely option, but then was she acting alone? Were she and Daniel a team?

Later that day, she was thrilled to see her door open and Liesl and Erich's faces appear. Mrs Morris was with them; Mr Morris was waiting in the car.

'Elizabeth!' They rushed to her. 'Are you all right?'

Erich's eyes were like saucers when he saw the big cast on her leg and the bandages on her face. The nurse said the gash over her eye was deep and the area around it was very bruised. She knew she must look terrifying.

'I'm fine. Honestly, I look worse than I am.' She tried to sit up but failed.

'Mrs Morris, thank you so much for taking care of them. I don't know when I'm going to be allowed out, but –'

'Don't worry, my dear. They are fine at our house, aren't you, children?' She smiled and Erich piped up.

'Mrs Morris is making us pancakes for breakfast tomorrow.'

'Well, the way to this one's heart is definitely through his stomach.' Elizabeth started to smile but stopped, the action hurting her face.

'Do the police know who did this to you?' Liesl asked, her face full of concern.

'Oh, just a burglar. He knew the houses in Ballycreggan would be empty with the thing in the hall, so he thought he'd pop in and help himself. I turned up at the wrong time is all. Don't worry – the police got there, so we are quite safe, and he'll be going to jail for a long time, so all's well that ends well.' She tried to infuse her voice with optimism and reassurance.

'Was it anything to do with Talia? She was hurt too, wasn't she?' Liesl whispered.

'Oh no, nothing like that. She just called in, wanting to help with the cleanup.'

Elizabeth hated lying, but the truth was far too much for them to endure. She changed the subject. 'Now, what have we here?' she asked, looking in the brown paper bag the children had brought. 'An apple and a sticky bun!' she exclaimed with delight, though with her loose tooth, she wasn't going to take any chances. 'Yummy! I was worried I'd missed out.'

They seemed relieved that she wasn't too badly injured, and they spent the rest of the visit talking about how successful the event was in the hall and how every single thing she'd found in the attic was now being used by a needy family.

Mrs Morris explained how the school had avoided a direct hit, so that was something.

'Levi and Ruth said we could stay up at the farm if we wanted to, but the food is nicer at Mrs Morris's,' Erich whispered to her as they prepared to leave.

The principal and his wife had no children, much to their sadness. They loved their pupils, and so Elizabeth knew her two were in good hands.

'Thank you again, Mrs Morris. I really appreciate it,' Elizabeth said as she kissed the children goodbye. Erich was a little teary, but Liesl put her arm around him.

'Oh, it's lovely having them,' Mrs Morris said kindly. 'Honestly, it's no bother at all. Please now, just rest and take it easy. Edmund and I are perfectly well able to care for this pair. It's summer holidays anyway, so we are always at a bit of a loose end. Though with all the activity in the village trying to patch everything up, we're very busy.'

Elizabeth thanked her again, glad that the presence of the Bannon children was bringing her joy. Elizabeth knew Mrs Morris in particular hated the long holidays. She'd once confided that the long summer seemed endless.

As they gathered their things to go, Erich decided he needed the toilet, so Mrs Morris accompanied him, and Elizabeth called Liesl back. She didn't want to alarm the girl further, but she needed to figure this out.

'Darling, do you think Talia was ever alone in our house?'

Something in the child's face made her realise there was some secret there.

'What? You can tell me,' Elizabeth said.

'She asked me not to say, but I suppose now it doesn't matter...' Liesl looked mortified.

'Go on, sweetheart, it's fine. Whatever it is, tell me.'

'Well, one day you were going up to the farm after school and we were to go with you – a few weeks ago, remember?'

Elizabeth nodded.

'Well, I forgot my rubber boots, and the farm is so muddy, so when the bell rang, I ran home to get them, and I went in the back door. I went up to my room, but I heard someone in the spare room, and I opened it...' The child's cheeks were flaming.

'Go on, Liesl…' Elizabeth encouraged her.

'Well, Bud and Talia were there, in…in the bed…and they were not wearing anything…' She managed to blurt out the last bit.

Elizabeth had had the conversation with Liesl about boys and girls and babies and all of that, so clearly the child knew exactly what was going on.

'They begged me not to say anything. They said you would be really cross, and they had nowhere else to go…'

'Oh, that's all right, my love.' She held Liesl's hand. 'I don't mind, not really.'

'Are you sure?' Liesl asked. 'I felt awful not telling you, but I promised.'

'Of course I am. We talked about that, and you know when people are in love, they like to be alone together. Bud and Talia love each other, and so…' She smiled again though it hurt.

Liesl seemed relieved, and at that moment, Mrs Morris and Erich reappeared.

They said their goodbyes again, and she was alone with her thoughts once more. So Bud and Talia were using her house, were they? If Talia would do that, use her spare bed without permission, then she was surely capable of letting herself in alone. But Daniel, was he guilty too? That was the crux of it. She feared what she told Gaughran would be the final nail in Daniel's coffin. Nobody had need of second identity papers unless they were up to no good. His face swam before her as she closed her eyes and lay back on the pillows. A nurse came and gave her some pills, and soon she was drifting off to sleep again.

The following days were a blur of pills and sleep and waking after nightmares of the children being abducted. She was agitated and had a vague recollection of a doctor saying something about infection. She woke and slept, and felt hot then freezing cold. Some people came and went – she couldn't be sure who – and it was difficult to tell reality from dreams.

On one occasion when she woke, Levi and Ruth were by her bed.

'Are the children all right?' she managed to say, her voice raspy.

'Yes, they're fine. Everything is fine, Elizabeth,' Ruth soothed.

'Daniel?' she asked. She had trouble focusing on the other woman's face.

'No news yet.'

Later, it was dark outside, and a doctor came. She struggled to focus on what he was saying. He was tall and had a condescending tone.

'Elizabeth, you've been very ill for the last week. I'm afraid you've got rather a bad infection. It's called streptococcal septicaemia. There is a new drug – it is only out of clinical trial, but it has been used to treat your type of infection in America rather successfully. It's called penicillin, and I would like to try it. How do you feel about that?'

She tried hard to concentrate on his words, but it sounded like he was very far away or down a well. She needed to get better; Liesl and Erich needed her. She nodded.

'Jolly good. I'm afraid I can't allow any more visitors, so from now on, you'll be in isolation, but I'm very hopeful about this drug, and I plan to have you up and about in no time.'

She hated his patronising tone – he was younger than she was for God's sake – but if he held the key to getting her life back, then she'd do whatever he said.

Sometime later, she was again drifting in and out of sleep when she heard the birds singing outside. She opened her eyes, and while every part of her body ached, she felt quite clear mentally. She heaved a sigh of relief. The feeling of being disoriented and in a fog was horrible.

She managed to pull herself into a semi-reclining position and rang the bell. Moments later, a nurse appeared.

'Ah, Mrs Klein, how are ya? Back in the land of the livin'?' Her smiling, broad, freckled face was a welcome sight. 'You've lost a few days, but you're lookin' much better, so y'are!'

'Thirsty,' she said, her voice sounding strange to her own ears.

The nurse poured her some water and held the glass to her lips. Elizabeth drank, spilling some down her chin and chest in her haste to rehydrate.

The nurse then helped her into a sitting position and propped her up with pillows. She checked the bandages on her head, examining the wound, and took her temperature and pulse.

'Dr Emerson will be with you shortly. He'll be delighted to see you lookin' so perky.'

Elizabeth would have laughed if she could. Perky was the total opposite of how she felt.

The news that she'd come round and was fine after the miracle drug seemed to create quite a stir in the Royal Victoria. Penicillin was being used fairly routinely in London and the United States, but the novelty had not worn off. The self-satisfied Dr Emerson appeared and explained that she was the first of his patients to make a complete recovery from infection using penicillin. She wondered if he thought she should congratulate him.

With each passing hour, she felt stronger.

'Can I see my children?' she asked as yet another doctor was brought in to see the wonderous effects of this new drug. She was tired of being on display.

'I don't see why not,' Dr Emerson announced. His strong cologne was nauseating. 'Thanks to this drug, all that remains is the physical recovery from the fractures and lesions.'

'How long more will I be here?' she asked.

He absentmindedly looked up from her chart. 'Hmm? Oh, I would say a few weeks. We'll get you mobile again and make sure those cuts are well and truly healing, and you'll be right as rain.'

He swept out, his white coat swinging behind him.

A few weeks. She didn't even know what day it was or how long she'd been there. She didn't like to call the nurse just to ask her that – she'd feel silly – so she just waited.

A while later, the same freckled, red-haired nurse reappeared with a tray. 'Could you manage a cup of tea and a slice of toast?'

Elizabeth's mouth watered at the prospect. 'That would be lovely.'

'Aye, well, I'd like to tell you there's butter on the toast, but it's just a scrape of marg, and the tea is as weak as water. Matron says you'd need to bless it before drinking it, but what can we do? Only carry on, eh?' She prattled away, straightening bedsheets and opening the window.

'I know it's brass monkeys out there, but I'll just air the place up for a few minutes, shall I?' The cold wind gushed through the window, and Elizabeth shuddered.

'What day is it?' Elizabeth asked, feeling foolish.

'It's Friday, all day long.' The nurse smiled at her own joke. 'I'll tell ya what, everyone will be dead happy to see you up and about, so they will. You're a popular lady, so y'are. There's a huge card outside that all the children in your class made for you. I'll tell you somethin' for nothin', I didn't have a teacher I'd make a card for, I can tell you. Dragons, the whole lot of them. But they must be mad about you altogether, and you've had that many visitors, we had to keep them away. Your man Emerson would have a wee stroke if he thought his prize patient was being disturbed. He'd give you the dry bokes, he would, and he thinks he's God's gift, y'know. The state of him.' She whispered conspiratorially in Elizabeth's ear as she straightened the bedclothes.

'But aye, loads of visitors. In fact, I think one of them is outside now. Will I bring 'em in, a wee bit of company for you?'

Elizabeth wondered who she meant. She was pure Belfast, rapid talking. 'I'd like that.'

'Aye, well, we better tidy you up a wee bit first then, you look a fright.' She laughed. 'I shouldn't probably say that, but you'd not thank me after if I let people see you with your hair all wild, would ya? Here now, let me see if I can fix you up...'

She took off the huge bandage from Elizabeth's head and replaced it with a smaller one. She removed the dressing from her lip altogether. She found Elizabeth's hairbrush in the sponge bag that someone had brought in for her, and she brushed her hair and tied it back with a small green ribbon.

'Will we get you into a clean nightie?' she asked. 'You've that one on for days!'

Elizabeth was mortified; she must stink of old sweat.

'I'm Angie, by the way. Now, let me get a basin. We'll give you a wee wash, and there's some nice cologne in that bag of yours there, and you'll be like a field of flowers in no time.'

Angie removed the old nightie and her brassiere and found fresh ones. The nurse washed her, and though the sponge felt cold on her skin, it was refreshing. Someone must have packed a bag for her from home. The new nightgown was a nice pink silk one, a rare extravagence that she'd allowed herself to after the bombing. To her embarrassment, she wasn't wearing any knickers. She flushed at the thought of how many strangers had seen her naked over the last week.

She was mortified as she put her arms around Angie's neck to lift herself enough to pull the nightie down over her hips, but at least she felt like herself again.

There was a bed jacket in the bag as well, a rose-pink one with ribbon threaded through the collar. Angie located some underwear in the bag and helped her to pull them up over her huge plaster cast. Every movement was excruciating, and once they were finished, Elizabeth lay back on the pillows, relieved.

'Sure it's no worse than having the babies, is it? They'd have the whole of Belfast looking at you then, as you know from your two...' Angie went on as she shoved Elizabeth's old nightdress and underwear into her bag.

Elizabeth could have enlightened her, but she didn't want to. Angie thought Liesl and Erich were Elizabeth's daughter and son, and she was happy to play that role.

'Thanks, Angie, I really appreciate it,' she said, spraying a little cologne on her wrists.

'No bother. We can't have you receivin' guests looking like the wreck of the Hesperus now, can we?' She patted Elizabeth's hand. 'I'll be back in a bit with the coloured water and toast.' She gave a guffaw and left.

Elizabeth relaxed and allowed her body to settle again after all the movement. Her thickly plastered leg ached, but at least it was down on the bed and not up in traction like she'd been last week. She wished she had a mirror, though perhaps she was better off not knowing.

She wondered who was outside. She hoped it was not Levi or Rabbi Frank. She'd feel so awkward lying in a bed in her nightclothes. Perhaps it was Ruth or someone from the village.

There was a gentle knock on the door, and she waited for it to open. She couldn't believe who was there.

'Daniel! What on earth... How...' She remembered the identity cards for Hans Hoffman – maybe this wasn't Daniel at all... She didn't know what to think.

'Hello, Elizabeth. I am so happy you are well again. We were all so worried.' He looked anxious. 'May I come in?'

She nodded, unable to speak. 'What...' she began again.

'I was released last Wednesday, fully exonerated. I did not know that English word before.' He smiled. He looked like his old self, not the pinched, stressed man she'd met in the Crumlin Road prison.

'They found you not guilty...' A maelstrom of emotions churned about inside her. She didn't understand.

'May I?' He gestured at the chair beside the bed.

She nodded.

'Yes. Not guilty. Thanks to you. Talia is the spy. She's not a Jew, she's a perfect Aryan, and she infiltrated the Kindertransport. Her real name is Gretta Werner. But anyway, she stole my drawings of boilers, buildings, all of that. I left them around, and she learned the codes and used them so that if she were caught, I would look guilty. She made accurate plans of the RAF base and then painted light watercolours over them. The police told me it was you who suspected her first, and it was you who gave the art to them. That man in the art gallery was her contact.' He shrugged. 'He sent some paintings back to Germany, and they washed off the watercolour somehow, perhaps they gave her special paint or something, I don't know. But they had perfect drawings of the base, also information on troop movements and things like this. She was watching everything – that's how they knew where to bomb so precisely.'

'And the documents I found in my attic?' she asked, praying he had a reasonable explanation.

'Yes, those were hers, in case she needed to get out quickly. She made or had made papers for me too. She took my German identity card – it was thrown careless in the workshop as I think I do not need it any more, so she take it and made papers. She was going to plant them so I would look more guilty, take the light off her. Also, someone, like Talia, a young blonde woman travelling on German papers met this man McGuinness in a pub in Belfast in 1938. Even then, they were watching him.'

'And how do you know all of this?' Elizabeth asked.

'In court, Detective Gaughran testified, he tells it all to the judge, and he also said that he is sure I had nothing to do with it. Talia, or Gretta, confessed everything to him in the hospital, including that I was totally innocent.'

'So what happens to her now?' Elizabeth was struggling to take it all in.

'Nothing – she's dead. Took the potassium cyanide pill the Germans give her in case she was captured. She didn't need to confess – she could have taken the pill first – but then there would have been a question over me still, so she did a good thing in the end. I think she was just brainwashed. She believed all of Hitler's lies, like so many more. She was not a completely evil person. She saved me when she didn't have to, and she tried to save you, I think. And she loved that American boy, I believe that, but in the end, she chose her fate.'

Elizabeth felt the tears course down her cheeks. She didn't know why exactly, except that she was sad and relieved and sore.

Daniel took his handkerchief out of his pocket and gently dabbed her battered face.

'It's all right. It's over now... Everything is all right.' His voice soothed her.

'Oh, Daniel, I'm sorry I doubted you...'

'You didn't doubt me, not really. I know it looked bad. Anyone else would have felt the same...'

She whispered, his face close to hers now, 'I knew in my heart you were innocent.'

'I know you did.'

He smiled and she smiled back at him. Maybe things were going to be all right after everything.

'So everybody knows you didn't do anything?' she asked.

'Yes. Rabbi Frank was called to the trial, though it was a private case. Gaughran knew I would be set free, so he needed someone to come for me, I think. Levi drive him, so they brought me back, and we told everyone on the farm that night. Then Rabbi Frank went to the priest and the vicar and Mr Morris in the school and everyone he could find in Ballycreggan – he even made a point of telling Liesl and Erich.'

'Have you seen them?' she asked.

'Yes, they are still with Mr and Mrs Morris, but we've had a long talk about everything, and they are fine.' He held her hand. 'I could go and get them now if you like? I have the car outside.'

'I'd love to see them.' She sighed and Daniel squeezed her hand gently.

'I must look a fright,' she said ruefully.

'You look beautiful, like always.' He paused. 'I have a confession to make.'

'What?' She panicked again – what now?

'When they brought that man who hurt you into prison, he was bragging about what he had done, all of that. He don't know who I am. One day, he was working in the laundry, same as me, and I accidentally dropped the huge hot metal press on his hands. He has a bad burn there. Very painful, I think.'

Daniel looked down at his own hands. 'That was the only thing I ever did to hurt another person, I swear to you, Elizabeth. But the governor say yes, he is sure it was accident, and nothing happens to me. I am not a violent man, I'm not made like that, but when I heard that he hurt you, I...I wanted to kill him.'

She squeezed his hand. 'Thanks for sticking up for me.' She grinned and winced immediately. 'Ow!'

'Don't smile, not until your beautiful face is healed.' He gazed at her, as if planning what to say next.

'I'm so happy to see you, Daniel. I was so worried...' she said, turning her face towards him. He looked the same as he always had. His olive skin was a few shades paler after being indoors for so long, but his brown eyes, his dark hair now streaked with grey, remained the same.

Instinctively, she reached up and placed her hand on his cheek. His eyes never left hers as he turned his face to kiss her palm.

'I love you,' he whispered.

'I love you too,' she replied.

# CHAPTER 29

*ovember, 1941*
Liesl fixed the veil on Elizabeth's head as Elizabeth got out of the car at the farm and smoothed her long-sleeved, fitted dress of ivory lace and silk. It wasn't her style really – she would have chosen something much plainer – but she knew it was what her mother wore when she married her father back in 1900. She had seen it in the photograph on the mantelpiece.

In the weeks during her convalescence, she read and reread the cards her mother had written, many of them mentioning her late husband in tones of affection. Elizabeth knew she would never understand her mother, but there was more to the woman than she first thought. She would have loved just five minutes more with her – she had so many questions, so much to say. She was happy to wear her mother's wedding dress; it made her parents feel a bit closer.

The courtyard had been swept and the ramshackle collection of outbuildings was transformed. Everything had been painted white, and the lawns around the main buildings were lushly green, the sky was blue but there was a biting cold breeze. Levi actually had a smile on his face for once as he helped her out of the car.

Elizabeth turned to her young bridesmaid. 'Well? Shall we do this?'

Liesl looked beautiful in a dark-green satin dress Elizabeth had made for her out of an old one of Margaret's they'd found upstairs. She was blossoming into a young woman now, and for the millionth time, Elizabeth wished her mother and father could see what a wonderful girl she had become.

Liesl had even helped Daniel stage his proposal. The day Elizabeth came home from the hospital, using a cane as her ankle and knee were still weak, he collected her. She felt Dr Emerson was keeping her longer than was necessary, so proud was he of what he'd managed to do, and she finally had to demand to be released. He looked quite crestfallen as she departed.

Erich and Liesl were at home, and Liesl remembered how her mother would make lebkuchen, traditional German frosted gingerbread, for special occasions. Daniel managed to source the ingredients, or close variations anyway, and they'd made a batch of cookies together. He'd even found a bottle of wine. They'd also made a chicken casserole, and it all smelled marvellous.

She was delighted to be home. The children led her to the sofa, took her coat and gave her a glass of wine and a cookie. Erich put a footstool under her feet and a cushion behind her back. Miraculously, the glass had even been fixed in her windows.

'The whole house looks and smells amazing. Oh, I've missed you so much.'

Daniel had disappeared, and the children chatted happily with her as she sipped her wine and ate her cookie. Though Daniel had brought them to visit her every second day, it wasn't the same as being home with them.

She was laughing at some story Erich had about Mr Morris trying to get his budgie, Firebolt, to sing, but stopped in her tracks as Daniel came into the room. His bulk filled the doorway, and he had changed his clothes.

He took her breath away. In a pale-blue shirt and dark trousers, his hair brushed back off his face, he was the most handsome man she'd ever seen.

Before she could say anything, Daniel crossed the room, got down on one knee and produced a small box.

He opened it, and there on the black velvet was the most exquisite ring. Not a traditional diamond, but lots of different coloured metals wound around each other, and in the centre was a piece of black marble, polished till it shone. It was the most incredible thing she'd ever seen.

'My beautiful Elizabeth, and Liesl and Erich – I want to ask all of you, since you are already a family – will you marry me?'

She looked first to Liesl, whose eyes were bright with tears. The girl gave a small nod. And then to Erich, who pleaded, 'Please say yes, Elizabeth! Then we'll be like a proper family.'

She turned back to Daniel. 'I would love to marry you, Daniel.'

'You will?' he asked, almost afraid to believe it. 'I don't have anything, as you know, and I'll buy you a proper ring after the war. But I had to make you this one for now... I hope it's enough...'

She slipped the incredible piece of jewellery on her ring finger. 'I will never want another ring to the day I die. It is beautiful, thank you.'

Gently, so as not to hurt her healing leg, he helped her stand. He drew Liesl and Erich into the embrace as well, and then, to Erich's loud disgust, he kissed Elizabeth deeply.

They decided to ask Rabbi Frank to marry them. She wasn't a practising Catholic, and the Jewish faith meant a lot to Daniel and the children.

The whole village and everyone at the farm had been invited to the wedding, and as she straightened her dress, she could see that the new building, which served as a meeting house and a synagogue, where everyone had worked tirelessly for weeks to have it ready for the wedding, was full to capacity.

The Jewish women on the farm explained what she would do. Her marriage to Rudi all those years ago had been in the registry office, so this was her first Jewish wedding.

Daniel would stand beneath the chuppah, or canopy, and she was to circle him three times. According to tradition, this symbolised the three virtues of marriage, but Ruth joked it was to make sure you knew what you were getting.

She had found her mother's wedding band and had it sized up for Daniel, though men wearing wedding rings wasn't exactly traditional, he said he would like one. They would then exchange their rings with the vow, 'I am my beloved's and my beloved is mine.'

Then, to legalise the wedding Daniel would say, in Hebrew, 'Behold you are sanctified to me with this ring, according to the law of Moses and Israel.'

Finally, once the rabbi blessed the marriage, Daniel would smash a glass with his right foot to shouts of mazel tov, and then they were married. She couldn't wait.

To see the entire population of Ballycreggan gathered to wish them well delighted her. These people opened their hearts and their homes, and in return, they were offered friendship and support by the refugees.

The community on the farm worked day and night to rebuild the village after the raid. In this world of chaos and hatred and violence, it felt like a little oasis of peace and love.

The ceremony went by in a blink, and soon they were pronounced man and wife.

'And now it is time for *yichud*,' the rabbi announced, and Elizabeth saw some of the younger adults in the Jewish community give a smirk. Ruth had warned her that this was also part of the marriage ceremony, but she thought the other woman was only joking. Apparently, it was the done thing for the couple to be left alone for a little while, before the feasting and celebrating began, to consummate their marriage. Elizabeth was mortified, but Daniel just chuckled.

The rabbi led them away to a room off the main room, which had been decorated with drapes of different colours and a chaise longue she recognised as having once inhabited the waiting room of Dr Parsons.

The rabbi withdrew, and Elizabeth wanted the ground to open and swallow her. She said as much to her new husband.

'Don't worry – it is just part of the ceremony. We don't need to do anything.' He put his arms around her. 'I have arranged for Liesl and Erich to stay here tonight. They are excited to stay with their friends, and you and I are going to go back to your house –'

'Our house,' she corrected him.

'All right.' He smiled. 'Our house, and we will make love all night with nobody watching or listening. How does that sound?' He nuzzled her neck, and she felt her body instantly respond to him.

'We could do that,' she whispered in his ear, 'and we should, but now that we're here and the door is locked...'

He chuckled again, that gorgeous deep-throated sound that came from low in his chest. 'Mrs Lieber, are you suggesting that we do what is expected of *yichud*, with everyone waiting outside?'

'I think I am.' And she met his eager lips with hers.

# EPILOGUE

he woman waited until she was sure the entire household was asleep. She had promised Frau Braun that she would not stir during the day, not even a muscle, in case she was heard. The frau's son was home from the front on leave and two lodgers were constantly coming and going. She lay on the sacking and recited poems, alternating languages in her head. Sometimes, she thought she was going mad, but then she would focus on two little faces, a boy and a girl, and she knew that no matter what it took, she would do it to see them again.

She didn't even dare open the precious bundle of letters and cards she kept under the cushion she used as a pillow. She had to wait until night-time to open them, and by then it was hard to see, but she didn't care. They were torn on the creases, so often had she read them. Every two weeks, she got a new one.

She and Frau Braun had a code. She could see the light going off on the landing through the crack in the attic floor. That meant it was safe. Everyone was sleeping. If Herr Braun knew she was up there, he would turn her in for sure, but so far, so good. She had no idea how long it had been now – years definitely, but how many she didn't know as she'd lost count. She never moved all day, not even to go to the toilet, and at night she crept to where Frau Braun left her a little bread, sometimes a bit of vegetable soup and some water. And every two weeks, a letter. When she'd eaten and gone to the toilet in the bucket, she would sit under the tiny window with her letters and look up at the moon and the stars, knowing her children were safe, loved and happy.

The End.

# AFTERWORD

I sincerely hope you enjoyed this book. I certainly loved writing it, though the research was harrowing. It gave me a new appreciation for the bravery and sacrifice of those parents who handed their children to strangers in the desperate hope of them being safe.

I was inspired to write it one day as I waited for a friend in Liverpool Street Station in London beside the commemorative statue of the Kindertransport. As a parent I cannot imagine the wrench of handing your little ones over, and it is a testament to the all-powerful love a parent has for their child as well as the goodness of ordinary people in extraordinary times, that so many lives were saved.

The sequel to this book, *The Emerald Horizon*, is due for publication on January 3rd 2020. You can download it here as a preorder and it will appear on your device on launch day.

http://mybook.to/theemeraldhorizon

If you would like to know more about my books, hear about special offers or to download a free full-length novel, pop along to my website www.jeangrainger.com where you can join my readers club. It is free and always will be, and you can unsubscribe any time.

If you did enjoy this book I would really appreciate it if you would consider leaving a review on Amazon, Goodreads or Bookbub. I read every single one.

Le grá,
  Jean Grainger
  Cork 2019

# ABOUT THE AUTHOR

Jean Grainger is a USA Today bestselling author of contemporary and historical Irish fiction. She lives in County Cork with her husband, the youngest two of her four children, and two micro-dogs called Scrappy and Scoobie. Her older two children come home with laundry and to raid the fridge.

*The Star and the Shamrock* is her fourteenth novel.

## ALSO BY JEAN GRAINGER

The Tour

Safe at the Edge of the World

The Story of Grenville King

The Homecoming of Bubbles O'Leary

What Once Was True

Return to Robinswood

So Much Owed

Shadow of a Century

Under Heaven's Shining Stars

Letters of Freedom

The Future's Not Ours To See

What Will Be

Catriona's War

Made in the USA
San Bernardino, CA
07 May 2020